A DAFFODIL FOR ANGIE

Connie Lacy

Wild Falls Publishing

~ ~ ~

Atlanta, GA

ISBN-13: 978-0-9996084-1-8

Published by Wild Falls Publishing
PO Box 29452
Atlanta, GA 30359

For my father who served in Vietnam

~

Other books by Connie Lacy

~1~

"I've said it before and I'll say it again. The road to popularity is paved with pompoms."

My mother's exact words as she dropped me off for my first day of high school. She didn't hear me groan under my breath as I slammed the car door.

Mom said I was sure to be picked for the jayvee cheerleading squad. My sister Deedee said I'd finally be able to get a boyfriend. But there was a little voice inside my head that kept whispering: *This is 1966. A woman is prime minister of India.* Which made me wonder – was it still cool to be a cheerleading beauty queen?

My life was full of "buts." I was dying to frost my hair, but now that I had those blonde highlights I felt self-conscious. I don't know why exactly. Over the summer I got my first pair of contacts. But now I felt naked without my glasses, like a part of me had been surgically removed. Still, when I looked in the mirror that morning, nervous as a five-year-old starting kindergarten, I had to admit I didn't look bad.

Still, the "buts" clogged my brain and pinched my forehead, spoiling my new look.

"Remember," Mom called through the open window, "find out when cheerleading tryouts are. Deedee says being her

1

younger sister means you're a shoo-in."

That was a scary thought – being compared to Miss Sexpot. My sister was head cheerleader, homecoming queen *and* Miss LHS of 1964. Now she was majoring in Cheerleading and Husband Hunting at NC State.

I smoothed my baby blue A-line and fluffed my hair, trying to repair the damage from the drive to school. Oh, for a new car with air conditioning so we didn't have to drive with the windows down.

"One more thing," Mom shouted. "The boys aren't gonna give you a second look if you keep that scowl on your face!"

How embarrassing. Did other mothers nag their daughters to flirt?

She peeled a wheel as she sped off like she was driving a Ferrari instead of that big beige aircraft carrier. Like the boys might be impressed with a middle-aged Clairol redhead tearing out of the parking lot. I closed my eyes for a moment and took a deep breath.

Lafayette Senior High was an old school – two-story brick, with white columns along the front and a cupola on top that looked almost like a church steeple. Two giant spruce trees stood on either side of the wide steps leading up to the door. That's where the kids hung out. The white kids, that is. A small group of Negro kids stood at the other end under the branches of a couple of big maples. My sister said she was glad she graduated before integration. But the only thing that bothered me about it was the chill it caused, even on a hot, muggy day like today.

I scanned the crowd looking for someone I knew. It was definitely uncool to stand by yourself.

"Angie! Angie!"

Janet and Dottie trotted up. What a relief. Janet had been my best friend since we moved to North Carolina when I was in fifth grade. But lately she'd been spending a lot of time with Dottie.

"Wow, your hair! It looks amazing with all those blonde streaks," Dottie called out.

"Her mom let her frost it, can you believe it?" Janet said. "My mom won't..."

"And you got contacts!" Dottie gushed. "Your eyes look so green without your glasses! You look *tres fabulous!*"

"*Merci*," I said, then turned to Janet whose smile had turned into a pout. "Blimey, you look like an English model!"

That helped. She didn't look so irritated. See, it dawned on me that Janet was competing with me. It was another "but" in my life. I liked my new image but I hated that it was making my best friend jealous. It was obvious she'd gone into overdrive trying for the Mod Look.

"Where'd you get those go-go boots?" I asked.

"I flew to London over the weekend and went shopping at Harrods," she said, smirking first at Dottie and then at me. "Had tea with Prince Charles, who, by the way, is cuter in person than he is in the magazines."

We joined together for a first-day-of-high-school giggle.

Janet's shiny brunette hair was styled in a short, angular, Sassoon cut. She even had on fake eyelashes and reeked of Estee Lauder. And her green long-sleeved baby doll dress really did have an English flair. She was too short and curvy, though, to be a model like the willowy Jean Shrimpton. Which, unfortunately, was her fondest dream.

3

Dottie towered over her. But unlike Janet, she was always two steps behind, fashion-wise. Her sleeveless pink shirtwaist dress was cut a tad too low so you could see her Grand Canyon Cleavage. And although it was a sweltering day, it just wasn't cool to wear summer clothes to school in the fall, even if the temperature was hovering in the nineties. She had long, honey blonde hair and thick cat-eye glasses that made her eyes look enormous. Her ambition was to be a Playboy bunny. And it wasn't hard to imagine her with a fluffy cotton tail, spike heels and silk bunny ears – once she lost the glasses, that is.

"Oh my God," Dottie said, her hand shading her eyes from the bright morning sun. "Craig Anderson's coming this way. His sister – she's a friend of mine – she told me he was asking about you." She looked meaningfully into my eyes. "She said he saw you last week and didn't recognize you at first."

She drew a lock of hair over her shoulder, twirling it around her finger.

"The very definition of handsome," Janet whispered, forcing her chest out and her stomach in.

"Angie! Is that you?" Craig called.

I looked over my shoulder, casual as you please. Janet was right. Tall, muscular, with blonde hair covering his forehead and a sparkle in his Carolina blue eyes. Better looking than Ryan O'Neal on *Peyton Place,* I swear. Pretending to be indifferent wasn't easy. Not with a swarm of butterflies dive-bombing my stomach.

"Boy, you sure look different than the last time I saw you in junior high," he said.

I started to say thank you, but just as I opened my mouth I realized it wasn't exactly a compliment.

4

"I like the new you," he said, ignoring Janet and Dottie.

Now, you'd think any girl would be thrilled to hear a gorgeous guy say that. But now that I'd gotten what I'd been dreaming of – some attention from the opposite sex – I found myself taking offense. It was kind of like telling a girl she was beautiful as long as she wore heavy makeup and a girdle.

Of course, I admit the makeover was my idea. I think. My mom always promised I could get contacts when I was fifteen and she and Deedee both said I'd look great with frosted hair. But did I really look that bad all those years with my brown hair and glasses?

"Hi, Craig. You remember me – Janet Foley?" Janet said.

Her words were innocent but her tone was not.

The bell rang as if signaling the start of a horse race.

"Sure, yeah," he said, flashing his Hollywood smile, his eyes still fixed on me.

And the look in those eyes. How could I feel the least bit insulted? Was I crazy? It was all I could do not to let out a big fat sigh. I needed to say something witty, something encouraging, without sounding like I was throwing myself at him.

"Guess we'll run into you around school," I said, heading for the steps, pulling Janet and Dottie with me.

"That's a pleasant thought," he called after us.

"Great choice of words," Dottie whispered.

Janet smiled as she looked over her shoulder.

"He drives a brand new GTO convertible," Dottie said. "It's so tough looking. Bright red. And... he's a quarterback on the football team."

"Second string," Janet said. "He's only a junior."

5

"First string next year," Dottie said, pumping her eyebrows.

We followed the herd toward the building as I pictured myself sitting next to the Good Looking Hombre in his GTO, top down, in the Homecoming parade.

You might say it was the perfect start to my high school career. The best-looking guy in Fayetteville, North Carolina said hello – a very warm hello – before the first bell. I imagined myself walking hand in hand with Craig Anderson, him leaning in for a kiss.

But my romantic reverie was interrupted when something sailed over my head as we headed up the front steps. I looked to my left and saw a guy catch a blue and green plaid book satchel – like something I used to carry in third grade. It was Billy Wyler, the only boy I knew who bragged about how many times he was paddled by the principal in elementary school. Thirty-seven times. And I had no reason to doubt him. He laughed as he twirled the satchel around and tossed it to another boy.

"Come on, Angie!" Janet said.

But I paused to scan the crowd for the owner of the book bag.

One of the creeps lobbed it over my head again and Billy the Butthead caught it again. He waved it around, holding his nose with his other hand.

"P.U! Smells like…" and he sniffed it a couple of times, "smells like jigaboo."

He and his friends hooted.

I needed to escape. This shouldn't be happening on my first day of high school. This was not a day for ugliness.

Janet and Dottie squeezed through the horde of students and made it inside. I tried to follow but got caught in the human traffic jam. Lots of people laughed at the nasty keep-away game but the Negro kids stood silently under the maples, watching. I would've been crying my eyes out if those boys did that to me. Either that, or screaming at them to give it back.

Billy passed the satchel above my head once more. It was so close, if I reached up I could grab it. My right hand jerked. I had a fleeting mental image of a black student thanking me as I returned the bag. But what would Craig think? It wasn't a very feminine thing to do, interfering in a situation like this. Where was a Boy Scout when you needed one? Surely, there was a guy in the crowd who had enough nerve to put a stop to this obnoxiousness. But what if the game went on and on? Maybe I could at least knock the satchel out of the air so someone else could pick it up. But did I really want that kind of attention on my first day at Lafayette High? Just as my hand came even with my face, I pulled it back, and instead of grabbing the satchel, I tucked my hair behind my ear. I couldn't bring myself to get involved. I watched in disgust as it sailed over my head.

Then I heard a guy behind me shout: "Jesus, get that thing away from me!" And the bag went flying through the air again. Before I could turn around to see who threw it, a boy with shaggy brown hair made an interception. He stuffed it under his arm like he was running for yardage and jumped down from the steps to the ground.

"Throw it!" Billy shouted.

"Come on, man," someone yelled.

The guy ignored them and jogged over to the group of Negro kids. I was so relieved.

But just as I entered the building I heard a boy behind me shout "nigger lover!" I cringed, staring at the floor to keep from looking anyone in the eye. To say I was embarrassed would be an understatement of the highest magnitude. I was mortified.

That hateful scene played over and over in my mind. It was like something on a newsreel from Alabama or Mississippi. Stuff like that wasn't supposed to happen where *I* lived. And why would anyone want to spoil the first day of school? I tried to shift gears as I inched along the stifling hallway, students packed so tightly together, I was momentarily overwhelmed by a wave of claustrophobia compounded by nausea.

The heat, together with all the unpleasantness, made my hair go limp. I wiped beads of perspiration from my upper lip with the back of my hand just before walking into my home-room.

The walls were institutional green and it was like stepping into a giant Easy-Bake Oven. Not what you'd call inviting. Standing at the front was a slender woman about my height, five-seven. "Dr. Anne Kelley" was written in white on the black chalkboard. Which was strange. How many PhDs teach high school?

"Angie!"

It was Linda Young, excitable as ever.

"Your hair!" she cried. "And you look so different without glasses! Your nose..."

"What about my nose?" I said, automatically touching it.

"It looks smaller without your glasses. Like a model's

nose."

"Well, it's the same nose," I said, hoping there was enough chatter in the room to drown out her silly comment. "Looks like you've lost some weight."

"Oh, thanks," she said, playing with her necklace. "You trying out for cheerleader Thursday? I know you'll get picked. I saw your sister when…"

"You trying out?" I asked.

"Me?"

Linda was a little plump but cheerleading would take that off.

"I'd love to be a cheerleader," she said. "I saw your sister when…"

But the bell sent her scurrying to her seat, which was a relief. I didn't want to hear how great my sister was. I chose a seat in front so I'd get a breeze from the giant floor fan next to the teacher's desk.

In addition to being my homeroom, this was the top track history class. Only the smart kids were in here, supposedly. I knew about half of them. I looked around to see who else I recognized and noticed something I'd never seen before in any of my classes. A Negro student.

She paused at the door and looked at a piece of paper in her hand. Dr. Kelley smiled and gestured for her to take a seat. But the geniuses sitting all around me stared like she'd mistaken our classroom for the janitor's closet.

Her drab Navy blue skirt fell just below the knee, topped by a white blouse as though she were in Catholic school. Her black hair was pulled into a small bun on the back of her head, not a single strand out of place. Her cheeks were like scoops of chocolate ice cream glistening in the sun. And clutched in her left hand – a scuffed blue and green plaid book satchel. The keep-away victim.

~2~

"This is room one thirty-five," the teacher said, her voice a cross between a drill sergeant and a Hollywood leading lady. "Check your schedules to make sure you're in the right place."

I swear everyone's eyes zeroed in on the Negro girl as she made her way to an empty desk. She looked older than a tenth grader. But I suspected it was a mask she hid behind.

"My name is Dr. Anne Kelley," the teacher said, drawing our attention to the front again. "I'm your homeroom teacher and your history teacher. I'm also the adviser for the school newspaper."

She was younger than my mother and her short, dark hair was blunt cut and modern looking. Not at all like the teased, hairspray helmets other women wore. Her op-art dress – black and white circles floating on a sea of black and white squares – made it clear she didn't shop at Sears and Roebuck, that's for sure.

She clapped her hands and rubbed her palms together as if we were hot biscuits waiting to be buttered.

"Like you, this is my first year at Lafayette Senior High. I've been teaching at East Carolina University for the past ten years but decided I wanted to teach high school."

Which made me wonder if she'd been fired.

The first thing she did was re-seat us alphabetically. Which put me, Angie Finley, in the second row, fourth from the front, the sweaty bodies in front of me now blocking the breeze from the fan. Right behind me was the Negro girl – Valerie Franklin.

I was doubly, triply, quadruply, even quintuply glad I was white. Who'd want a roomful of strangers giving you the evil eye on the first day of school after being humiliated on the front lawn by a bunch of brainless bullies? Of course, who'd be dumb enough to bring a dopey book satchel to high school in the first place? I wouldn't be caught dead with one. Not since elementary school. Everyone carried their books in their arms – girls in front with both arms, boys one-handed on the side.

To my left was Donna Jenkins, whose opinion of herself was as vaulted as her teased, bleached blonde flip. She nearly knocked the boys out of their seats swinging her hips on the way to her desk. She had said maybe two dozen words to me in ninth grade even though we were both on the junior high cheerleading team. I was a girl, therefore I was her rival.

On my right, just my luck, the boy who caught the book satchel and returned it. He was dressed in jeans and faded green canvas sneakers, no socks. None of the guys I knew wore jeans to school. Or sneakers. And socks were required by the dress code. Obviously a rule breaker.

I didn't want to be reminded of the keep-away game. But it was like a rerun of a god-awful show you hated watching the first time, and now there was nothing else on TV and you were sitting there watching reruns like a dimwit. I should've reached up and grabbed that dumb book satchel myself. I could've intercepted it before Mr. Long-haired Hero got it. Why had I automatically thought a boy should step forward? I could've given it back. But now I had to sit next to the guy who caught it and in front of the girl he returned it to.

As if the seating arrangement wasn't bad enough, sitting right in front of me was Junior Boring as a Head of Lettuce Duncan. I hate alphabetical.

The second thing Dr. Kelley did was ask for a show of hands if we had someone in our family stationed in Vietnam. What a peculiar thing to ask. My arm wasn't stuck now, I noticed. Me and seven others raised our hands, including Uppity Donna, who made a show of looking as pitiful as possible. Actually, I was surprised there weren't more, Fayetteville being an Army town.

Which reminded me – I needed to write my dad.

"Hey, Angie," Junior whispered, swiveling around in his seat when the teacher turned her back.

Oh God. He was smiling at me. Junior wasn't ugly. But he was a little heavy and a little pimply and he reminded me of a big goofy dog who wagged his tail and tried to lick your face when he saw you coming.

"I didn't recognize you without your glasses at first," he whispered.

I gave him a sort of friendly but not overly friendly smile. I didn't want to encourage him. At lunch one day in seventh grade he handed me an old Hank Williams record after hearing me tell Janet I liked *Hey, Good Lookin*. I gave it back the very next day and thanked him for loaning it to me even though I knew it was supposed to be a gift.

Then Sockless Boy Hero on my right whispered something to me.

"Excuse me," he said. "Since we'll be sitting next to each other, could you please not wear perfume to school?"

Junior snickered.

I couldn't believe anyone would say that to me, even if he did save the book satchel.

"Class, may I have your attention?" Dr. Kelley said.

I glared at Mr. Satchel Saver Perfume Hater. His brown hair covered his eyebrows and nearly covered his ears, longer than any of the other boys and sure to be sent home from school for a haircut. He didn't look like an athlete and wasn't what you'd call handsome.

Facing front again, I watched out of the corner of my eye as he scribbled something on a piece of notebook paper, carefully tearing it off and laying it on my desk. It said: "No offense. It's just that perfume makes me sick. PS – my name is Stan Bukowski."

All normal boys liked perfume, didn't they? That was the gospel according to Deedee. "Just don't take a bath in it," she always said. And I never did. I only wore a tiny dab of White Shoulders behind each ear. I refused to look at him again, even when he cracked his knuckles, giving my full attention to Dr. Kelley.

"I always ask my students to help teach my classes," she said, smiling like she'd made a witty remark. "So each of you will be required to do a report on an activist in American history."

She held up a piece of paper.

"This is the sign-up sheet. Please write your name next to

the person you choose. These are people who are either not included in our history book or who are given short shrift. You'll do an oral report, at least five minutes in length. And you have to turn in a written report as well, at least fifteen hundred words."

Cue the communal groan.

"Typed, if possible. If not, all I can say is, if I can't read it, you didn't write it," she continued. "Staggered due dates are listed beside each name."

A boy next to the window whispered "Jesus Christ!"

It was Billy Wyler, ringleader of the keep-away game. Not fair that everyone involved in the morning's stomach-turning spectacle seemed to be in my class.

"Jesus Christ *was* an extremely important activist," Dr. Kelley deadpanned, "but he was not an *American* activist. And this is, after all, US history."

Which triggered a wave of appreciative chuckling as she continued.

"Without activists, often labeled radicals during their day, rather like Jesus was," she said, glancing at Billy, "we might still be part of Great Britain, slavery would not have been abolished, poor children would still work twelve-hour days, there would be no such thing as the weekend, and women wouldn't have the right to vote or own property. So, you see, activists *are* our history."

Billy the Butthead looked at Donna who studied her pink fingernails.

~

"Who'd you choose?" I asked Valerie, steeling myself for the onslaught of hostile stares as we filed out of class after the bell.

I may not have had the nerve to stop the keep-away game but I could do something Mr. Satchel Saver probably couldn't do. Be friendly.

"Mother Jones," she said, her voice so soft, I had to strain to hear her. "And you?"

"Susan B. Anthony."

"Oh, you'll enjoy reading about her," she said, glancing over her shoulder.

We stepped into the hallway, jammed with students squeezing past each other in both directions, reeking of body odor and cheap cologne. And it wasn't even 9:30 yet.

"Well, guess we better get going. Second period beckons," I said, turning away to find my geometry class, relieved I'd done my duty by speaking to the black girl.

But before I'd taken two steps, I heard a small shriek behind me. Whirling around, I saw Valerie, her mouth open in surprise, water dripping from her face and hair. Two boys were hightailing it down the hallway – Billy the Butthead and another guy.

Maybe I could ask for a transfer to a different class. I thought back to the flutter in my stomach that morning when I looked into Craig's eyes. I wanted that exhilaration back. My life had seemed so full of exciting possibilities at 8:25. Now it was like I'd bitten into a fresh peach only to find a worm inside.

"I'll get Dr. Kelley," Stan said, stepping forward.

"No!" Valerie blurted, then lowered her voice as she wiped

her face with her hand. "It's all right, really. I needed cooling off anyway." She forced a little smile. "I'm sure it was just an accident."

But we all knew better.

"We should..." he said.

"I don't want to be late for second period," she cut in. "Thank you, Stan."

She knew his name. Of course. They'd already met when he returned her satchel.

She hurried off while Stan glared at everyone, then bounded past me like he thought he was Batman or something.

I took a step but Junior Duncan blocked my path.

"Angie, I need to tell you something."

Oh God, I didn't want Mr. Fascinating as Field Peas talking to me. A) I wasn't interested in anything he had to say; B) I didn't want to be seen with him; and C) he always sounded like he needed to clear his throat, which got on my nerves.

"Don't get me wrong," he said. "I'm telling you this as a friend. Not because, you know, not because I feel this way. But it doesn't look good for you to talk with that colored girl."

"Excuse me. I've gotta get an angle on a geometry teacher."

"Angie, you'll get a reputation."

"A reputation?"

"As a nigger lover," he whispered, wrinkling his nose.

"Shut up, Junior!"

I looked around, afraid a black student might've heard.

"That's not what I think," he said, shrugging his shoulders. "It's what other people will think, if you know what I mean."

I turned on my heel and hurried along the corridor,

gritting my teeth. Even if he was quoting someone else, I hated that word. Besides, who did he think he was, telling me who I should talk to?

"I'm just trying to help," he called after me, "because... because I..."

I floored it before he could spit it out, zooming through the crowd like I was on the homestretch at Daytona.

~3~

Dreaded Thursday arrived too soon.

"See you at tryouts," Janet said as we parted ways in the front hallway that morning.

"Maybe."

"Maybe? You did it last year. You've certainly got the hair for it!"

Surly sarcasm had become as much a part of Janet's style lately as the thick black eyeliner she painted so meticulously around her eyes.

"We all know you'll get picked," she snapped.

She parked her hand on her hip like she always did when she was irritated. But the hallway was such a sardine can, a tall boy bumped her protruding elbow, nearly knocking her over.

"Don't tell me," she called out, allowing herself to be swept away by the crush of bodies, "too much homework in all your exclusive classes!"

Honestly, I didn't know what to say. The closeness we'd shared in elementary school had evaporated in junior high, like morning dew burned off by the hot summer sun. It boiled down to competition in her eyes – her against me, especially when it came to boys.

The day was long. My classes dragged like a slow-moving,

hundred car train holding up shoppers on Hay Street on a busy Saturday. I found myself counting black students. One in my history class – Valerie. Zero in geometry. None in English or biology. One in my French class. And three in P.E. Then it was time for tryouts.

I knew if I didn't go, my mother and sister would hound me for eternity. Mom would tell me my life would be ruined if I wasn't a cheerleader. Like Deedee, my mother was a cheerleader when she was in high school too. She always said cheerleading was a girl's ticket to success. To which Deedee would nod her head like it was an axiom for the ages. This stuff was vitally important to them. The last thing I wanted was to confess I'd skipped tryouts. I could just imagine the explosion.

More importantly, there was Craig to consider. He'd be a lot more likely to ask me out if I was on the squad. He probably assumed I would be since I'd done it in junior high. Of course, I had seen his GTO. And it was positively divine. So I went.

Even though I'd changed into shorts and a sleeveless top, my armpits were wet with sweat just walking to the girls' baseball diamond, which was basically a dusty depression way out by the back fence where no breezes were allowed to blow. The temperature hovered in the mid-nineties as the sun blazed above us.

Janet was there. Dottie too. Linda Young came, although she was about as comfortable as if she'd accidentally walked into the boys' bathroom. She wore a long shirt to hide her body and probably regretted listening to me about trying out. Donna, the Snob Queen, bounced on the balls of her feet, dressed in her red and white pleated cheering skirt and matching top from junior high. The thought of another year listening to her holier-than-thou chatter caused me to heave a cavernous sigh.

There must've been forty girls trying out for ten spots. All white girls, I noticed.

"Okay, ladies, let's get to work!" Miss Murphy shouted.

Just looking at her, you'd never guess she was the cheer-leading sponsor. Miss Murphy was the P.E. teacher. No makeup. Permanent frown. Curly brown hair almost as short as a man's. She had a whistle around her neck and knee-length blue walking shorts that looked like they came from the men's department at Woolworth's.

What a contrast with the three peppy varsity cheerleaders beside her.

"Many of you were cheerleaders in junior high, but that does not guarantee you'll make the jayvee squad here," Miss Murphy bellowed. "You have to prove you've got what it takes. We want to see precision and rhythm. We also want to see that cheerleader spunk. And if you don't know what I'm talking about, you might as well skedaddle right now."

She looked at us for a moment like she was waiting for some of us to clear out.

"Now, Vicky's going to teach you a basic cheer."

The short, bow-legged girl with the long, blonde ponytail stepped forward. She worked with us for a few minutes and then we took turns showing our stuff. Miss Murphy and her judges marked on their clipboards. They wasted no time, call-ing girls by name and letting them get one cheer out before shutting them up and moving to the next. I had to wait until most of the girls were through.

"Angie Finley," she finally called.

"Here!"

"Deedee's sister?"

"Yes ma'am."

"Go ahead."

All eyes were on me. I hated it.

I planted myself and began clapping, knowing I was being compared to my sister.

"Fight! Fight! Defense, hold tight!" But my voice didn't come out with its usual strength. I sounded timid. "Fight! Fight…" I started again.

Miss Murphy raised her hand like she was stopping traffic.

I realized then I hadn't practiced even once. That I'd only thought about tryouts in the abstract. From there it only got worse. Vicky showed us a couple of moves and Miss Murphy called our names again and asked each of us to do a side hurdler jump with a kick.

Donna, her blonde hair pulled into a water fountain on top of her head, had obviously been practicing every single day of the summer.

When my turn came, I leaped into the air, only to realize I was doing the wrong jump. So I immediately jumped again, doing a side hurdler. But when I started to do my kick, I was rushing and nearly fell down.

"Oops, sorry," I said, like I was auditioning for a job as a circus clown.

Miss Murphy called out the next girl's name and scribbled something on her clipboard as she turned away.

I was relieved when the ordeal was over. That little voice

in my brain was speaking to me again, telling me that cheerleading was kind of silly. Girls with long hair wearing short skirts, screaming their heads off, bouncing up and down to help people watch a game? It was like the girls were decorations on the sideline while the real action was on the field. The guys were actually doing something – trying to vanquish the enemy. Well, the pretend enemy.

"I'll post the list on my office door Monday morning," Miss Murphy said, bringing the sweaty competition to a close.

~

It was Miss America pageant weekend, something I used to love when I was little. We'd gather in front of the TV and pull for our favorites. But, somehow, watching young women try to out-pretty each other didn't seem romantic anymore. And I wasn't sure I wanted to take part when it came time for our school pageant either. Although I knew my mother would be jazzed up about it, just like she was when Deedee was in high school. Of course, beauty was Mom's business. She started out as a beautician and now owned her own salon.

Ever since the divorce, she held a Miss America Hen Party, complete with beer, chips and dip, deviled eggs and a roomful of jabbering, smoking women. All of them were former beauty pageant contestants who matured into plump, middle-aged, self-appointed beauty experts. They ranted and raved about each and every contestant's legs, hair, teeth, makeup, evening gown, bathing suit, choice of shoes and breast size.

I sat on the front porch, trying to keep my distance as the ladies passed judgment, turning our house into the Beer Hall for Catty Women.

The two yellow maples in the front yard were still green,

but their leaves were getting ready to morph into that brilliant golden color that made our house look kind of charming in the fall. It was thanks to Dad that Mom didn't have them chopped down when we moved in. She argued they killed the grass with their shade. He convinced her they'd increase the resale value someday.

It was a modest house – three bedrooms and one bath – but Dad also planted pink azaleas and blue hydrangea bushes in the front yard, which made me get my camera out every spring to take pictures. And he set out a big patch of daffodils by the mailbox that poked their pretty yellow heads up every January, like beacons of hope reminding me, even in the dead of winter, that spring really was just around the corner. Mom had to concede Dad's gardening did actually "enhance our home's curb appeal."

A huge guffaw wafted through the door.

The porch was my refuge after failing to come up with a better alternative. I'd called Janet, but she said Dottie and Craig's sister, Sherry, were coming over to watch the pageant with her. She said I could come too, but you know how it is when someone only invites you last minute like that. And, besides, I wanted something better to do. Like have a date with a boy? Like Craig, maybe?

Unfortunately, a squadron of mosquitoes used me as their evening field rations, forcing me to retreat to my room much sooner than I'd hoped. I slipped inside by the carport door, snagging a Coke as I tiptoed through the kitchen.

The clucking from the living room got louder and louder.

"Lord-a-mercy! That one's way too busty."

"She just needs a better bra!"

"Judges don't want giant, bouncing boobs."

"But men do!"

"Har har har!"

They didn't notice me at all, glued as they were to our new TV.

You see, this year, for the very first time, the show was in color. Which meant my mother had driven downtown to Sears the week before to buy our first color TV – on credit, of course. So she and her friends now had to critique not just the style of each contestant's evening gown and bathing suit, but also the color.

Closing my bedroom door to muffle the noise, I listened to WFNC while I wrote my dad a letter. They did requests on Saturday night from Steve's Tower in the Sky. It sounded so old-fashioned. "Next up – *You're My Soul and Inspiration* by the Righteous Brothers, to Marsha from Don, with love and passionate, wet kisses." That's what I wanted – passionate, wet kisses.

~

There was a knot of girls by Miss Murphy's door first thing Monday morning. Shrieks of joy echoed through the gym, drowning out the hidden tears of those whose names were not on the list.

"Jump up and roar! My name's on the door!" Donna crowed.

She held her arms up in a V formation as she skipped along the basketball court, showing a lot of leg and nearly knocking poor Linda over where she'd stopped to blow her nose.

I was in no hurry, myself. I was afraid my name wasn't on the list. Then again, I was afraid it *was* on the list. My history book slipped from my arms and slammed onto the floor, echoing around the gym. As I stooped to pick it up, two other books fell.

Dottie and Janet burst through the door as Donna bounded out.

"Ever notice falsies don't bounce?" Janet sniped as they hurried past, causing Dottie to giggle and turn red.

Then they broke into a run toward Miss Murphy's office. I watched them as I took my time restacking my books. Dottie was so tall she read the list over Janet's head.

Then they squealed and hugged each other. It was like watching a movie. After a moment, they turned my way. And just like in a movie, the smiles disappeared and they both studied the list again.

I felt like I'd been tackled from behind. But where was the ref with the clipping call? I was humiliated. And yet I was also relieved. I hadn't made the squad. No more practices. No more jumping up and down while boys – and their dads – ogled my body. No more having to watch football and basketball week after week, keeping up with first downs, minutes remaining and who had how many fouls. But I was embarrassed too, you know? If I hadn't tried out at all, I wouldn't look like a failure. What would Craig think?

"There must be some mistake," Janet called out as she and Dottie crossed the gym toward me.

But it was as obvious as the odor of cigarettes clinging to her dark hair that she was downright ecstatic she made the team and I didn't.

"Yeah," Dottie said, giving me a sympathetic look. "I think you need to talk with Miss Murphy."

"Congratulations," I said, making sure my books were stacked properly.

I was going to say something else but couldn't decide what, so I hurried off to first period. Although history wasn't the escape I was looking for. Not with Donna holding court in the middle row. I paused in the doorway, wishing I could disappear.

"We have our first practice tomorrow," she boasted, lowering her eyelids so we could all see her heavy blue eyeshadow and black eyeliner.

"Who's on the squad?" Stan asked.

She looked at him like he was from Lower Slobovia.

"What's it to ya?"

"We're doing a story for the school paper."

When Donna saw me watching, she tilted her head and grinned.

"Well, I don't have a complete list," she said, "but I do know I'm the only one in this class who made the roster."

It was hard to swallow. And so was Donna's attitude, which she wore like a fancy fur coat on a shopping trip to buy a loaf of bread at Piggly Wiggly.

Then the bell rang and Dr. Kelley gave me a nudge as she swept into the room.

"Good morning, class," she boomed.

I took my seat, but I was in no mood to listen to her enthusiastic lecture on the fathers of our country. Who cared about George Washington, Thomas Jefferson and John Adams? I had more important things on my mind, like why I flopped so miserably at tryouts. Why I felt so confused about how I felt! When I was younger I knew what I wanted. I knew when to be disappointed and when to be excited. Like, I knew I wanted the Lennon Sisters paper dolls when I was eight. And when I found them under the Christmas tree I was on cloud nine. And I knew I wanted the Beatles' *Rubber Soul* album for my last birthday and I was crushed when Dad gave me a Beach Boys album instead. But I couldn't bear to hurt his feelings so I acted like it was perfect.

Now I was relieved and depressed at the same time. Maybe cheerleading *was* shallow. But I'd done a cheering belly flop and I was afraid Craig might not give me another look. And, oh boy, did I want him to give me another look.

A note appeared on my desk.

"Want to help me write a story for the newspaper on how dumb cheerleading is?" It was signed "Stan."

I stared at the words. Did he really not understand he was inviting me to commit social suicide? Criticize cheerleading? Right.

"Too busy," I wrote.

I folded the note and handed it back as Dr. Kelley turned to write "France" on the board.

In the back of my mind there was still this tiny nugget of hope that my mom would rumble into Miss Murphy's office like a steamroller on hot asphalt and smooth everything out.

The next thing I knew everyone was getting up to leave, but I hadn't heard the bell. I looked behind me at Valerie for some kind of clue. As usual, she was dressed like she was trying to be invisible, in grey and white. Quite a contrast with my short, gold A-line dress and matching Mary Janes.

"Library," she whispered. "Activist reports."

I picked up my books and followed her. Stan was waiting

for us, leaning against the wall just outside the door.

"We could use some more help on the school paper," he said, slipping in beside us.

Valerie smiled when I rolled my eyes at her.

"Hey, it's important work," he said. "And we need some girls."

"To write a cooking page?" I asked.

"Nigger-loving Polack!"

It was Billy the Bigot spewing his venom, sauntering by with Jack Thompson. They both flipped Stan the bird as they did their impression of sneering villains on a TV western, their beady eyes too close together to play the hero.

"Oh, Valerie," I whispered, feeling ill. "I'm so sorry."

"Not your fault," she said.

That revolting word had been officially banned at my house when my dad explained to me and Deedee he learned an important lesson during the Korean War. He said two guys in his unit were patched up after being wounded, one white, the other Negro. But he said they both had the same color blood.

I couldn't help wondering now as I stood there between Valerie and Stan: was the whole school year going to be like this? Would it always be like this?

Mom said the real estate guy she was dating told her some parents were organizing a group to start a private school so their kids wouldn't have to go to school with Negroes. Funny, it was people like Billy Wyler I didn't want to go to school with.

Then Valerie touched Stan's arm and I noticed his hands had turned into fists.

"They're not worth it," she said in a low voice.

"Don't worry," he said, cracking the knuckles first on one hand, then the other. "I don't pick on pea brains."

Which helped defuse the tension a bit.

She nodded her head toward the library, like we should put the shameful scene behind us.

"Think about it," Stan said, as we split up to find our books. I must've had a blank look on my face because he added, "the school paper."

Fans were scattered here and there inside the library, which kept the air moving. And there were fewer windows to let warm sunshine in. Which was a relief. Carpeting muffled what little noise there was – the occasional whispers and the low voices of librarians checking out books.

"Angie!"

It was Craig, waving for me to join him in the 700's. He looked awfully good in a blue and white striped, button down shirt. Holding a book on Johnny Unitas, he had a small earplug in his ear with a wire that disappeared into his shirt pocket. All I can say is: he had some nerve listening to a transistor radio in the school library.

I almost reached up to fluff my hair but managed, at the last second, to keep my hands at my sides.

"Did you see our first scrimmage?" he whispered, pulling the ear plug out and dropping it in his pocket so I could hear what sounded like munchkin Motown music.

"Well..."

"Is that up-and-coming quarterback Craig Anderson?"

It was Donna the Sexpot Jenkins cooing behind him.

He spun around.

"I saw you complete that pass to Buddy Thompson before the defenders reached you," she said, keeping her voice low. "Nice pass under pressure. You may be moving into the starting quarterback slot sooner than you think."

Wow. His pass couldn't have been half as smooth as hers.

"I know you, don't I?" he said.

"Of course, you do. I'm Donna Jenkins. Head cheerleader of the jayvee cheerleading squad."

And right there in the stacks she went down on one knee, holding her arms straight out in a cheerleader pose.

"Cool," he said, chuckling, then turned to me again. "So you two..."

"Unfortunately, Angie didn't make the team," Donna said, jumping to her feet. "It's too bad, really."

Craig looked from me to Donna and then at me again. I could see it in his eyes – his brain chugging, that is. Like he was working a math equation. If 10 over "x" equals the jayvee cheerleading squad and 50 over "y" equals the varsity football team, then how can "y" date "z," who looks like a cheerleader, but isn't?

A librarian in glasses and a long, straight skirt suddenly appeared behind Donna, giving us a professional shush.

"I've gotta go," I whispered, heading back the way I came.

"She's actually a good cheerleader," Donna said in her loudest stage whisper. "She looked like she was sick at tryouts."

What an actress!

I found my biography and got in line at the circulation desk just as Craig walked by with Donna still bending his ear.

He nodded at me as they passed. The agony! I could just see her sitting next to him in his red GTO.

~

As if I wasn't already feeling bad enough, Mom served me an extra helping of guilt at supper that night. Although I knew, for sure, it would've been much worse if Deedee were home from college.

"You didn't practice, did you?" she said. "I reminded you at least once a week this summer, didn't I?"

I took another bite of my sandwich.

"Well? What the hell happened?"

I shrugged and continued chewing.

"Not good," she said. "Not good at all! I wonder if maybe I should talk to Miss Murphy. She and I got along when Deedee..."

"That would just make her hate me," I said, even though I had briefly considered the same idea.

"You never know. She might listen."

"Mom, if by some miracle she agreed to let me cheer, whoever she booted would spread the word and everyone in the school would know."

She rose from her chair and got a can of Schlitz from the fridge.

"Lord, you're gonna have to work like hell before next fall's tryouts for any chance to make the varsity squad," she said, pulling the tab off the can as she sat down again. "Maybe Deedee might have some advice. I'll ask her when she calls this weekend. I can't believe you fluffed it."

~4~

We got a lesson in counterattack strategy the next day, although it wasn't something in Dr. Kelley's lesson plan. Just as we were getting settled, Donna walked in with her father in tow. It was like Aphrodite arriving with Zeus. She looked that haughty and he looked that domineering.

Mr. Jenkins was about six feet tall and looked like a high school football player whose muscle had mushroomed into a big pot belly. He wore a brown suit and narrow tie. It was amazing how much Donna looked like him, although his middle-aged face was jowly and his nose was red. Made me wonder what she'd look like in thirty years.

"Mrs. Kelley?" he thundered, drawing all eyes to the front and silencing even the bad seeds on the far side of the room.

"Good morning," Dr. Kelley replied, giving him a polite smile. "Mr. Jenkins?"

"I'll get right to the point," he said, looking down his nose at her. "I've got a problem with one of your assignments."

Donna glanced at the class as if to say "watch this," patting her mile-high yellow hair and swaying from side to side as her father continued.

"I don't approve of my daughter being forced to do a report on a rabble-rouser. A rabble-rouser who wrote a sacrilegious *woman's* Bible, for Christ's sake! I won't tolerate it. This is supposed to be an American history class."

I thought Dr. Kelley might take them into the hall, but I was wrong.

"If you object to her reading about Elizabeth Cady Stanton, we have others to choose from," she said, as pleasant as ever. "I'll be happy to…"

"You don't seem to take my meaning," he said. "I don't approve of you telling these kids they have to study radicals at all!"

It's a safe bet that most of us wished we didn't have to do those reports. But I was pulling for Dr. Kelley.

"Well, Mr. Jenkins," she said, turning to her green file cabinet, "my curriculum was approved by Mr. Lancaster and the school superintendent. It teaches the students a lot about the history of our country. I've found it works very well." She retrieved a folder and let the drawer close with a loud clang.

"Well, I think maybe you're forgetting, Mrs. Kelley, this is high school – not some liberal college."

"And my requirements for this class are in line with what's expected in tenth grade. Now, Donna," and she turned her gaze to Aphrodite, who suddenly looked a little less sure of herself, "you can choose a different activist if you'd prefer, although that might put you a little behind."

Dr. Kelley opened the folder and pulled a piece of paper out.

"As you can see, there are still a few left over. There's Harriet Tubman. Now she's very interesting. And there's…"

At that point, Mr. Jenkins drew himself up to his full height and folded his arms across his barrel chest.

"Mrs. Kelley, I don't think you completely under..."

"Oh, but I do, Mr. Jenkins." Her eyes locked on his like John Wayne about to draw his six-gun on the bad guy, her voice as sharp as the toes of her black stilettos.

"Well, looks like I need to have a sit-down with Mr. Lancaster," he finally snarled. "And maybe the school board, too!"

"By all means," Dr. Kelley said.

It was so quiet, we could hear Zeus's nose whistling.

She waited a moment, then nodded at him like he was dismissed, returning the folder to the filing cabinet.

He stormed out of the room and down the hall, cussing under his breath.

Donna stared after him, a dazed expression on her face. Her hips didn't have their usual locomotion on the way to her desk.

Her big blowhard dad was obviously used to intimidating people. He'd probably expected to leave his daughter's history teacher in tears with her students as his audience. It was hard for me to imagine having the kind of strength Dr. Kelley had to stand up to him without even the tiniest quiver in her voice. I wondered if I'd ever be able to do something like that.

I have to admit I'd been dreading that report. But now I couldn't wait to get home and open my biography of Susan B. What's-her-name. If the pompous, brown-suited father of the Falsified Prima Donna opposed this assignment, I felt duty-bound to throw myself into it.

"Did you know that one of the reasons the British army wore those bright red uniforms was so deserters could be spotted trying to sneak away?" Dr. Kelley asked suddenly, like she was gossiping with us. "And... so the blood wouldn't show on their uniforms if they were wounded, since that might scare the other soldiers."

After class, Stan grabbed me on my way out. Literally. He put his hand on my right arm and guided me down the hallway.

"I think Dr. Kelley's really a spy," he said.

"What?"

"Why else would someone intelligent and strong like that be teaching at LHS?"

I laughed.

"Wasn't she great in there? I mean, she went three rounds with Godzilla and sent him packing," he said.

"Yeah, it was kind of fun watching Donna wilt too, like a fresh-cut gladiola drooping in a dusty vase."

"Very poetic. I bet you're a good writer."

I shook my head.

"Which reminds me," he said, "why don't you come to the newspaper meeting this afternoon?"

I scrunched up my face.

"Come on," he said. "It's fun."

He didn't blink, just stared. He had long eyelashes for a guy, I noticed, but his nose was a little big.

"Whaddya say?" he said, releasing my arm.

I tried to visualize myself writing a front-page article with a prominent byline. One thing was certain – I'd have more free time this year than last year since I didn't have cheerleading practices or games to go to.

"Okay, okay," I said.

He walked backwards down the hall, a mischievous expression on his face.

"Dr. Kelley's room, three forty-five," he said.

Maybe I'd be like Lois Lane chasing news stories. And maybe Superman would take notice. Needless to say, Superman didn't hold a candle to Craig in the looks department.

I wondered who else wrote for *The Wildcat*. You know, what kind of people I'd be working with. I wasn't a hundred percent sure I wanted people to see me with Stan and others of his species. He had, I don't know, an odd look. And he didn't wear the right clothes exactly. Other boys wore button down shirts and slacks. Stan wore jeans or chinos and faded polo shirts, like his clothes were hand-me-downs. And I don't think he even owned a pair of loafers. I'd just have to make it clear I was only interested in reporting for the school paper and I wasn't there because of him. As long as it was clear from the get-go.

~

When I walked into Dr. Kelley's classroom after school, I felt like I'd stumbled into a war zone. The green walls were the jungle foliage. Dr. Kelley's desk was her bunker. To her right were two guys I recognized as seniors. To her left was Stan, waving his arms and spouting off about the Vietnam War. In the middle, two girls watched the verbal grenades as they were lobbed back and forth. I wasn't sure I wanted to be there so I stayed in the demilitarized zone of the doorway.

"You don't know what you're talking about," a guy with horn-rimmed glasses shouted.

"We've got to stop the bombing first," Stan yelled. "They've already said they'll talk peace if we just quit bombing the hell out of them!"

"And you trust those Communists?"

"At least as much as I trust LBJ!"

"Okay, guys, that's enough," Dr. Kelley said. "Let's not scare off any new journalists."

She waved me toward one of the empty desks. I sat beside Stan who raised an eyebrow in welcome.

"This is Angie Finley," Dr. Kelley announced. "Angie, this is the editor, Mike Andrews," she said, gesturing at the boy in glasses, "and Rick Peterson, Yvonne Williams and Patsy Carlucci."

Patsy, who had thick, straight brown hair and an easy smile, fanned herself energetically with a spiral notebook. Yvonne clutched a church fan in one hand while holding her long dishwater blonde hair off her neck with the other. The only concession the boys made to the heat was untucking their shirttails.

I fastened a fake smile on my face like I was perfectly comfortable walking into the overheated skirmish.

"We were talking about stories for the next issue," Dr. Kelley explained, raising her voice to be heard over the monster floor fan that only succeeded in pushing the hot air around, not cooling it. "Though somehow..." and she looked at Stan and Mike, "we got off track. But we decided to do a story about the new public high school opening up next year and how that will affect LHS. Mike, who's going to work on that?"

Mike glanced at some notes.

"I think Rick and I can handle it."

"And what other stories do you have in mind?" Dr. Kelley asked.

"A story about who's on the cheerleading squads," he said. "You know, short profiles with photos. I figured Patsy and Yvonne could take care of that."

"But I'll take the pictures," Rick said, doing a Groucho impression.

He even looked a bit like Groucho Marx. Dark hair, thick eyebrows. But no mustache.

Rick and Mike laughed and the girls rolled their eyes.

"Stan, you can do a piece on the football teams," Mike said. "Who's playing what position on the varsity and jayvee squads, what kind of season the coaches are expecting."

"I have something else in mind," said Stan. "Something a little more meaningful – interviewing seniors to find out how many will register for the draft on their birthday, whether any guys might refuse."

"You mean like Cassius Clay?" Mike said. "Who claims to be a conscientious objector, but who's just fine beating another man to a pulp as long as he's getting paid millions of dollars to do it in a boxing ring!"

He glared at Stan, looking, for a moment like he might leap from his seat and punch him in the nose.

"Ali has a valid point," Stan said.

"You mean Clay?" Mike said.

"He changed his name to Muhammad Ali."

"Right," Mike said.

"I think he's funny," said Patsy, giggling softly. "He floats like a butterfly and he's the cutest boxer I've ever seen."

But her giggle died when she noticed the others staring at her like she'd lost her mind.

"Well, you know," she added, "for a Negro."

Yvonne gave her a horrified look, causing Patsy to lower her eyes and fidget with her pen.

"She's right," I said, glancing from Yvonne to Mike to Rick. "He's a handsome guy."

Patsy kept her head down but sneaked a furtive look in my direction.

"All right," Dr. Kelley said. "Let's get back to your story idea, Stan."

"Yeah, so I wanna ask how many guys are planning on joining the Army when they graduate. You know, how many seniors are headed straight to Nam."

"We need a story on the football teams," Mike snapped.

"Find someone else to do it," Stan shot back. "I'm not a sports reporter. I don't even go to stupid football games."

Dr. Kelley looked up from the doodles she was making on a legal pad.

"I think it's a good story idea. You've got college men around the country burning their draft cards," she said.

Mike heaved a sigh of defeat and looked at the ceiling.

"I'll need some help," Stan said, glancing at me.

I fixed my eyes on Dr. Kelley, hoping for a sign, but she went back to her doodling.

"Maybe I could do the article on the football teams," I suggested.

Although it wasn't the kind of story I had in mind, it might be just the ticket. I could interview Craig. No doubt, he'd be impressed.

"Yeah, right," Rick said.

The girls laughed in a friendly way like I'd made a good joke. Even Stan snickered. Dr. Kelley raised one eyebrow and continued drawing.

"Why don't you help the radical reporter here?" Mike said, lowering his head and looking at me over the top of his glasses.

I chewed my lower lip, wishing I'd had the foresight to come up with my own story idea.

When the meeting was over, Stan walked me out.

"Let's go to Horne's and have a Coke," he said. "We can talk logistics."

"Logistics?"

"For the story. Won't take long."

I should've said no. But he looked so hopeful. So we sat in one of those high-backed wooden booths at Horne's Drug Store and ordered Cokes and lime sherbets. It took ten minutes to talk about the questions we'd ask and twenty minutes for Stan to tell me how stupid the war was as customers shopping for Alka Seltzer and corn pads gave us disapproving glances.

"God," he said, "with President Johnson sending more and more troops over there, the death toll's gonna go through the roof."

I didn't want to talk about the death toll. Despite my dad's reassurances that he was just a supply sergeant and nowhere near the front line, I didn't want to hear about soldiers being killed or wounded or Vietnamese villages being burned. That's why I didn't like watching the evening news. We definitely needed to change the subject.

"By the way, where'd you go to school last year?" I asked.

"We moved here from Fort Campbell. My stepfather was reassigned to Fort Bragg when he came back from Vietnam."

"Any brothers or sisters?"

"One brother. At the University of California, Berkeley. He's active in SDS."

"SDS?"

"Students for a Democratic Society. Antiwar group. They've got branches at colleges around the country."

So much for changing the subject.

"How's your stepdad feel about that?" I asked.

"Nick doesn't give a shit what our stepfather thinks."

"Which must mean your stepdad doesn't like it."

"Yeah, he thinks we should be good little soldiers like he is. Do our part to keep Communism from taking over the world. He swallows Johnson's lies, hook, line and sinker."

"What about your real dad?" I asked, taking a sip of my Coke.

"He's dead," he said, popping one of his knuckles.

"I'm so sorry," I whispered, unsure whether I should say anything else.

He finished his Coke, wiped his mouth and immediately guided the conversation back to politics and the war.

"Nick says it's obvious Johnson is either a liar or a fool. Of course, the way he's going, he won't be president much longer. The latest polls show Bobby Kennedy whipping his ass." He bobbed his head in approval. "We oughta put 'em in the wrestling ring. Johnson could wear a black mask."

"And call himself the Long-eared Texan," I said, playing along.

"Maybe the Masked War Monger."

We chuckled at our wittiness.

We were still joking around when he lit a Marlboro as we walked along the busy sidewalk.

"Let's see, are you the same guy who sent me a note saying – and I changed my voice to a whiny baby voice – 'please don't wear perfume because it makes me sicky wicky?'"

He looked at me, then at his cigarette, and gave me a sheepish grin.

I shook my head.

So he dropped the cigarette on the sidewalk and made a big show of crushing it with his sneaker. Then he pulled a nearly empty pack of Marlboros from his pocket and walked a few feet to a trash can and waved it around like he was doing a magic trick before letting it drop.

"I wouldn't want to make you sicky wicky," he said.

"Well, turnabout *is* fair play."

He held his hands up in surrender.

"So what about *your* dad?" he said. "When does he come home?"

"Not until next July."

"Bummer. Where's he stationed?"

"An Khê."

"What unit?"

"82nd Airborne, First Air Cav Division."

"My stepfather's a paratrooper too," he said.

Crap. We suddenly had a lot in common. I needed to change the subject again.

"Oh, God," I said as we passed the store I loved to make fun of. "Have you heard the commercial on the radio?" I imitated the most annoying nasal chant: "Shop Quality Shop! Shop Quality Shop!"

I must've been pretty good because he nearly died laughing.

"You sound just like the commercial!" he said.

I took a bow.

When we got back to school I turned to say good-bye near the bus stop where several Negro women in shirtwaist dresses were standing, their faces dotted with perspiration in the late afternoon sun.

"I'll start interviewing right away," he said. "Can you type?"

"Type?"

"You *can* type, can't you?"

I took a deep breath.

"No, can you?" I said, oozing politeness.

"Me? Of course not. I just thought..."

"You just thought since I'm a girl?"

He opened his mouth to speak, but I didn't give him a chance.

"So that's why you wanted me to help you," I said, squinting at him in disbelief. "Well, I don't intend to become a secretary."

Only girls who didn't plan on going to college took typing and Home Ec. And I wasn't one of them.

The brakes on the green city bus squealed as it pulled to the curb. Stan called my name but I ignored him and climbed the steps, dropped my fifteen cents in the fare box and took a seat on the other side so he couldn't see me through the window. The black ladies had waited for me to board first. As they made their way to the back, one of them nodded her head slightly in my direction in what I could only interpret as a gesture of approval. Which surprised me.

As the bus roared down the street, I realized I was grumbling under my breath. I couldn't type worth a doodle but I was convinced I'd be a good interviewer and a good writer. And I planned to start right away.

~5~

I had a notebook and pen ready when Mom dropped me at school the next morning. Wearing my figure-flattering burgundy dress with the bell sleeves, I was ready to interview every senior boy I ran into. But the first guy I saw wasn't a senior – he was a junior. A very good-looking junior. And if I'm not mistaken, he was waiting for me.

"Just the girl I wanna see," Craig said, his eyes focused on the bodice of my dress. Or, more precisely, what was inside the bodice of my dress.

I could hear music coming from his ear jack as he dropped it in his shirt pocket.

But then Janet hurried over, all out of breath, sweating in the heat, wearing a Donovan cap that matched her olive green mini-skirt. If I were paranoid, I'd say she wanted to make sure I didn't have a minute alone with Craig. *If* I were paranoid, which I'm not.

"Hi Craig!" she sang out.

"Hi, Jeannie," he said.

I cringed.

"Janet," she said.

"Right. Sorry, Janet."

There was an awkward silence.

"Yeah, Janet, no offense or anything, but I need to talk with Angie in private."

"No problem," she said. "See ya later."

She bounded off, looking as happy as if he'd told her she looked like Twiggy on the cover of *Seventeen* magazine. But, Janet being Janet, I knew otherwise.

"Angie, I wanted to..." he said.

"Angie!"

It was Dottie.

"You've got too many friends," he whispered.

"Janet's looking for you," I said. "She just went thataway."

I pointed in Janet's direction.

"Thanks," she said, taking my not-so-subtle hint.

Craig laughed and looked at his watch.

"The bell's gonna ring any minute so I'll make this quick. Would you go to Homecoming with me?"

A giddy smile was all I could manage in reply.

"Does that mean yes?" he asked.

The bell sounded and everyone headed toward the front door. Everyone but me and Craig. I must've looked like I was in a trance. Which I was.

"Yes, it means yes."

I looked up into his movie star eyes. He was better looking than Clint Eastwood in *Rawhide*. He could've starred in his *own* TV series. He rocked his head back and forth real quick like there was music playing in his head.

"Cool," he said.

To say I was high would be an understatement. I could see myself sitting next to him in his convertible, top down, wind blowing through my hair. And Dottie was right. Next year he'd be the starting quarterback on the varsity squad. I'd practically be school royalty, regardless of whether I was a cheerleader or not.

We started up the steps.

"What do they do for Homecoming?" I asked, pretending I didn't already know.

"Well, there's the parade, of course. I'm driving my GTO. You'll ride shotgun up front," he said, giving me a cocky smile. "My buddy Dave and his girlfriend can sit in back. Then we go to the bonfire."

He put his hand on my back as we reached the top step and I forced myself not to shiver.

"The next night there's the game, of course." He stopped walking and turned toward me when we reached the front hall. "And there's the dance after the game. You like to dance?"

"Does a baby pee in the woods?"

Which is not what I meant, you know, but he laughed so hard, you'd have thought I was Phyllis Diller cracking up Johnny Carson on *The Tonight Show*.

"This is so great," he said.

Then he leaned in and gave me the softest kiss, ignoring the crush of people swarming by us. When he pulled his lips from mine, he didn't back away. Neither did I. He smelled so good. I had this overwhelming urge to wrap my arms around him.

The final bell made me jump. I forced myself to turn away and hurry down the hallway. I didn't dare look back.

I was almost hyperventilating as I dashed into history class where everyone else was already seated. Dr. Kelley raised one eyebrow but said nothing. I slipped into my desk and set my books down as quietly as possible.

Morning announcements filled the room. A girl's voice droned on and on but my ears weren't plugged in. My head was filled with a pounding like blood was surging through my veins. I knew people were staring at me but I didn't care. I didn't care if they wondered why my face was flushed, why my eyes were closed, why I smelled of English Leather.

Then Dr. Kelley began talking but I didn't hear the words, leaving my books stacked in front of me. I was still tingling.

"Angie."

What if we'd just walked back out of the school and down the street when the bell rang? What if we'd walked to the park.

"Angie?"

What if we'd sat by the stream? What if he'd put his arm around my waist? What if we'd lain down together on that big rock and gazed into each other's eyes with the sound of the water splashing behind us. What if he'd pulled me close and...

"Angie!"

I opened my eyes. Dr. Kelley was standing right in front of me.

"Angie, are you all right?"

I nodded.

"If you need to see the school nurse, I'll give you a note."

I shook my head.

She studied me for a moment, then returned to the front of the room.

"Many of our country's early leaders opposed the creation

of political parties, but their wishes were ignored," she said, scrawling "Federalists" and "Democratic-Republicans" on the chalk board.

Concentrating on her words was impossible. But I opened my notebook, holding a pen in my hand, and pretended to listen.

I kept feeling his warm breath on my face. His voice saying my name. I liked his voice. Deep, but not too deep. His laugh was so real and full. I wondered what his hair felt like. It was thick and shiny, the color of the fresh straw they scattered on our newly planted grass so it wouldn't wash away – grass that would help sell our house so Mom could move us from the ho-hum suburbs to a more fashionable address in the city.

I drew circles on my paper which turned into Craig's eyes. Then a hand appeared in front of me, leaving a scrap of paper on my notebook.

"I did three interviews this morning. Meet me at lunch," it said.

Oh yeah, Mister Girls Are Only Good for Typing Bukowski.

I slipped the note under several sheets of paper and kept doodling. I wished I could talk with a friend. I had this urge to brag about the kiss. But there was no way I'd confide in Janet anymore. She'd just sulk and act jealous. Craig said I had too many friends. He had no idea how wrong he was. I did have friends, but no close ones.

By lunchtime, I'd finally returned to earth. Crossing the courtyard behind the school to the cafeteria, I saw two guys walking toward me. One was tall and lanky with dark brown hair, the other was average height with sandy hair. Both sported neat haircuts, not the Beatles style a lot of guys wore these days.

"Excuse me. Are you seniors?" I said.

"Yeah, why?" the taller one replied.

"I'm working on a survey for the school newspaper and I need to ask senior boys a few questions."

They looked at each other and then at me.

"We've got a couple of minutes," the shorter one said. "My name's John Smith, of Pocahontas fame, currently president of the Drama Club. My colleague here is Mitch Davidson, co-owner of Harley-Davidson Motorcycle."

I giggled as Mitch punched John in the arm.

"And you are?" Mitch, the tall one, asked.

"She's the Frost and Tip girl, can't you see?" John said.

Honestly, sometimes I forgot what my hair looked like.

"I'm Angie Finley."

"You must be related to Deedee Finley, the beauty queen!" John gushed, holding his hands on his waist like a girl for a split second.

"Well... yes."

"I knew it. I knew it," he said, turning to Mitch. "I think she's even better looking than her sister, don't you?"

Apparently, Mitch noticed how embarrassed I was because he gave me a sympathetic look.

"Let her ask the questions, motormouth," he said.

So I did. And they answered them, although John kept up the comedy act the whole time. They both said they would register for the draft when they turned eighteen and neither would consider skipping the country to avoid going to Vietnam, but they were counting on college deferments. I thanked them profusely as I resumed my trek to the lunchroom.

"Nice meeting you guys."

"No, the pleasure is ours," John said, bowing at the waist.

"For once, you're right," said Mitch. "I'll watch for your article."

"Thanks. See ya."

"We sincerely hope so," John shouted. "If you think of anything else you need to ask, get in touch. We like to be touched."

Smirk, smirk.

When I got to the overcrowded cafeteria, it took me a minute to spot Stan at a table with two guys I didn't know. The lunchroom was always loud, but especially so during the overlap between first lunch and second lunch. Today the noise level was on the verge of deafening, so Stan and the other guys were practically shouting at each other to be heard.

I debated whether I should bother talking with him. My dander was still up. Way up. Part of me wanted to dump the story in his lap. I could find something else to report on. But I had to admit talking with John and Mitch had piqued my interest. Talking with guys so close to my own age about the possibility of being sent to Vietnam made the war seem more real to me.

And then there was the part of me that wanted to show Stan I was more than capable of being a reporter and not a typist. So I took a deep breath and approached his table, bringing his conversation with the other guys to an abrupt halt.

"I think we should distribute printed surveys to the seniors," I said, speaking loudly while trying to keep my voice civil. "That might be a lot quicker than trying to track them down one by one."

"Where've you been?" he said. "I thought you weren't coming."

His pals rolled their eyes and scraped their chairs as they vamoosed.

"I was interviewing a couple of seniors," I said.

"You were doing interviews?"

"Of course."

"But *I'm* doing the interviews. I need you to compile the..."

"Compile?" I said.

"You know, organize all the information, like how many guys say they'll register for the..."

"That's it!" I shook my head as I zigzagged between tables, Stan right behind me.

"Angie!"

I got in the serving line and slapped a tray in front of me.

"Angie..." he said, putting his hand on my arm.

"I told you," I cried, yanking my arm free. "I'm not your secretary!"

"But..."

"You compile your surveys. I'll compile mine."

I put a deviled ham sandwich, an apple and chocolate milk on my tray and moved forward.

Sliding my tray to the cashier, I paid my thirty-five cents, carried my food to a table in the center of the lunchroom and sat down so I could see the clock, Stan scrambling to keep up.

"I don't understand." He leaned on the table, a frustrated expression on his face.

Looking past him, I noticed Craig walking toward me. He

waved at some friends and slid into the chair next to mine, glancing from me to Stan, who made like Houdini and disappeared.

"Who's he?" Craig said.

"That's Mr. Stupid A. Moron."

"A?"

"Ass."

He hooted.

"He thinks he's a progressive guy," I said. "But when it comes to girls, he's straight out of the nineteenth century."

"You're cute when you're all riled up. Now, me – I'm straight from the twentieth century. And I'd really like to touch your hair."

As I put my straw in my milk he reached over and stroked the hair by my left ear, letting his fingers brush my cheek.

"I can't wait till Homecoming," he said, giving me a hungry look.

How does a girl swoon, I wondered.

"Of course, we don't have to wait. You free Saturday night?" he said.

"Uh…"

"Make that a week from Saturday. Just remembered I got something going on this Saturday. That okay with you?"

I started to say yes, then worried I'd come across as too available. I considered telling him I'd check my calendar, but gave in at the last second.

"Sure."

Which made him grin.

"I'll pick you up at seven. Maybe we can go to a movie."

"*Tres bien*," I whispered.

He winked at me and stood to leave.

"Hey, bozos!" he called out, strolling toward the exit where a group of football players was headed out the door.

~6~

The next morning I got to class early so I could speak privately with Dr. Kelley about distributing printed surveys to seniors. She was writing homework assignments on the blackboard, but set the chalk on the tray as she turned to face me.

"Great idea," she said, brushing white dust from her fingers. "Very efficient."

That's when Stan walked in. He hesitated just inside the doorway, hanging his head for a second, making me think he wanted to talk privately with Dr. Kelley as well.

Two other kids strolled through the door as she filled him in on the plan. Stan grunted and took his seat. I swear, anxious vibes radiated from his body all through class. He was waiting for me in the hallway as soon as the bell rang.

"So, you're running off surveys this afternoon," he said, raising his voice to be heard above the racket in the hallway.

"Dr. Kelley agrees it's a good idea to hand them out so guys can turn them in anonymously," I said, my voice a bit chilly.

"I'd like to help."

"Only takes one to run the mimeograph machine."

I pivoted and headed for geometry.

"Angie!"

My steps quickened.

"Angie, wait!"

He caught up with me, keeping pace beside me.

"Okay, I'm sorry," he said.

I came to a stop, a couple of big lugs nearly plowing into me from behind.

"Listen, Stan, there's no way we can work together as long as you keep…"

"I know, I know."

"Do you?"

"Yeah…"

"Do you know the definition of condescending?"

"I…"

"Prejudiced?"

"I'm not…"

"Yes you are."

He closed his eyes and grunted.

"Would you treat me that way if I were a guy?" I said.

"I was wrong. And I'm sorry."

"True. And true."

He smiled.

"I guess I need to join that new group – the National Something or Other for Women," he said, his face the very picture of regret.

"Organization."

"Right," he said. "Well?"

"Well, what?"

"Do you forgive me?"

Kids bypassed us like water flowing around a rock in Cross Creek.

I really, really wanted to be mad at him and make him suffer. He'd been a jerk. But he looked so sincere. And I didn't know many people who admitted they were wrong and actually apologized.

"Would it be all right if I help you?" he pleaded. "I mean, would you mind?"

Did he deserve for me to be nice to him? I wasn't sure. Then I remembered his real father was dead, so maybe I should cut him some slack.

~

I made a point of being on time for lunch that day so I could sit with Janet and Dottie. I didn't want to sound like I was bragging, but I needed to tell them about Homecoming before they heard it from someone else. They were in the middle of a vitally important conversation when I sat down.

"He got his hair cut?" Dottie said, taking a bite of meat loaf.

"Yeah, so he can be in a movie," Janet said.

"But the Beatles can't cut their hair," Dottie said, talking with her mouth full. "That's, like, blasphemy or something."

"Who got his hair cut?" I said.

"John," said Janet.

"He's gonna be an actor?"

"That's what it says in *Modern Screen Magazine*," she said. "I saw it at the beauty parlor."

I let them gossip a few minutes and then told them about Craig as I ate the mushy meat loaf and mashed potatoes.

"You lucky ducky," Dottie said. "I figured that's what was going on when you gave me the brush-off."

"Well, I didn't mean to, but..."

"I would've done the same thing."

Janet said nothing. She just spooned green Jell-O into her mouth.

"I'm working on Brad Davis. You know him?" Dottie said.

"No."

"He's a short sophomore who wears his pants up under his armpits," Janet said. "You know – the Key Club type."

"He's a nice guy," Dottie said, giving her a hurt look. "And I bet he'll be a high-paid lawyer someday. He'll make a lot more than a grease monkey, that's for sure."

Janet gave her an evil stare.

"Grease monkey?" I said.

Dottie wagged her head at Janet, then turned to me.

"This guy named Darrell Jones – he's a junior and he's got the hots for Janet."

"I can't help it if a loser falls in love with me," Janet said, her hand on her hip.

"He's not a loser," Dottie said. "In fact, I think he's sexy in his jeans and black leather jacket. You know, in a James Dean sort of way."

"James Dean is passé," said Janet. "And did I mention? He's also dead!"

"Well, are there any other guys who might be promising?" I asked.

"Are you cuckoo?" Dottie said. "We don't have multiple boys buzzing around us like you do. But I'm working on my mom to let me get contacts. And I don't care what she says – I'm going to bleach my hair platinum as soon as I get rid of these stupid glasses. I'll be the new Marilyn Monroe! All the boys will be pounding on my door begging me to go out with them! I'll have to give them tickets and have a drawing to see who I date first!"

She fluttered her eyelashes at us. Even grumpy Janet chuckled.

Dottie was on a roll.

"Yep," she said. "I'll have the Key Clubbers, the hoods, the athletes, the eggheads – jetcetera, jetcetera, jetcetera! They'll all beg to cop a feel of one of these giant kabungas!"

She did a little shimmy to show off her doorknockers.

I choked on my milk, some of which came out my nose. Janet and Dottie laughed even harder.

While I wiped my face, I thought how nice it was to see Janet in a good mood again. Just like the old days.

~

The mimeograph machine was a royal pain in the butt. I already had purple ink all over my fingers when Stan waltzed through the door of what amounted to a glorified closet in the teacher's work room. I was doing my best not to let the ink ruin my dress since I was wearing my black and white A-line.

"You really don't have any secretarial skills, do you?" he joked.

I gave him a warning look.

He helped me load my hand-written original onto the barrel and get the dumb thing going. The barrel turned round and round, filling the cramped space with its rhythmic hum as we printed a stack of wet, smeary surveys. When we were done, we wiped off the nasty machine and divvied up the surveys in the mailboxes of the senior homeroom teachers, along with handwritten notes I'd prepared asking them to pass them out.

After washing and rewashing our hands in the workroom sink, we walked out of the building together. I took a deep breath, trying to force the ink fumes from my lungs.

"I wonder how long it'll take for the purple to come off," I said, examining my fingers.

"So when do we get the completed surveys back?" he said.

"End of next week."

"That's cutting it close for *The Wildcat* deadline. We'll have to analyze them over the weekend."

"Next weekend? I don't know."

I was thinking about my date with Craig.

"Won't take long," he said.

"But..."

"How about Sunday afternoon?"

"Sunday?"

"I'll come to your house."

No way I was inviting him to my house.

"Let's meet at the Coffee Cup. It's a café where they serve breakfast all day," I said.

~ 7 ~

I was counting the hours till my first dream date with Craig. With only three more days to go, I was practically walking on air. But Wednesday brought me back to earth with a thud.

It started right after first period. As soon as the bell rang to change classes, Billy "Thing One" Wyler, was out the door like he'd been sneaking beers and couldn't hold it another second. Then Jack "Thing Two" Thompson said something to me as I walked out with Valerie. I stopped for a second to find out what in the world he wanted since he'd never said a word to me before.

"Uh," he said, staring at my chest, "I wanted to ask you..."

But it was like he couldn't remember what he wanted to say. And the way he was staring at me gave me the creeps.

"Ask me what?" I said.

"Yeah, uh, I wanted to ask you..." and he looked around as though checking to see if anyone was listening.

"I've gotta go," I said, backing away.

"But I haven't asked my question yet."

I shook my head and moved to sidestep him.

"I wanted to ask," he continued, jumping in front of me to block my path, "are you a B cup or a C cup?"

It was all I could do not to slap that ugly grin right off his face.

Then he careened down the hallway, bumping into students like a ricocheting pinball. I was still gritting my teeth when I turned the corner and found Valerie sprawled on the floor, obviously in pain, her books scattered everywhere.

"Valerie!"

I squatted next to her and set my stuff down, immediately thinking maybe Jack had bowled her over in his mad dash through the packed hallway. There were tears in her eyes but she was trying to compose herself.

"Are you all right?"

She didn't answer.

"Someone get a teacher!" I yelled at the do-nothings gaping like we were a sideshow.

"I'm okay," she whispered.

"No, you're not."

Then I noticed she was lying on a wet spot on the floor and there was an overwhelming sweet smell kind of like... baby oil. When I touched the dark tile, my fingertips came up greasy. It was plain to see she'd turned the corner and slipped on this stuff, whatever it was, and landed hard on her butt. I looked in both directions until something caught my eye about halfway down the long hallway. It was Billy and Jack, the Cretin Brothers. Billy whispered in Jack's ear when he saw me staring and they ducked inside a classroom.

It came together in my head: while Jack delayed me so I wouldn't walk with Valerie like I sometimes did, Billy hightailed it from history class. He waited for her. And just before she turned the corner, he dumped a bottle of baby oil on the floor. Maybe two bottles. I could feel my jaw clench as my geometry teacher, Mr. Owens, approached.

"Clear the hallway!" he barked, kneeling beside us.

"She slipped on this stuff," I said. "And it was no accident."

He touched the floor, then smelled his fingertips and rubbed them together.

"I'm ninety-nine-point-nine percent positive it's baby oil," I said.

You could see his brain clicking.

"I'm sure it was just an accident," Valerie said, struggling to stand.

The bell rang and Mr. Owens ordered me to guard the slick spot while another student found a janitor.

Valerie insisted she was okay, saying she didn't want to be late for second period. That satisfied Mr. Owens, who promptly disappeared into his classroom as I helped gather her books.

"You *know* this was not an accident," I said.

"I just don't want to make things worse," she whispered.

"Me neither."

She left me standing in the hallway, wondering what she meant. Did she mean those boys might really hurt her? I'd seen the horrible news reports on TV about racial attacks. Like the one just the other day where a white mob attacked black students trying to integrate schools in Mississippi. But it was hard to conceive of something like that happening in North Carolina. Still, maybe someone needed to speak up. But who? It was obvious Valerie wasn't going to do anything. Maybe it was my turn to take action. Although, I decided no one had to see me do it.

I loitered in the hallway until the janitor arrived and started mopping the floor. When all the students disappeared into their classrooms, I made a beeline for the front office.

~

As sweltering as the rest of the school was, the principal's office was like a walk-in freezer, cold air blowing from a window air conditioner – the only air conditioner in the entire school. You'd think it would be a relief from the heat but I shivered as the frigid blast hit me.

It was an ugly room with a pretentious mahogany desk and three tall file cabinets, each one topped by dusty philodendrons that hadn't been trimmed in eons. Yellowed diplomas hung on the wall and a threadbare navy rug filled the office with the sickening odor of stale cigarette smoke.

Mr. Lancaster was a serious man with a serious pot belly, a seriously bald head and a seriously large nose. His dark eyes looked small on that large, jowly face. They were imperious eyes and I was glad I was sitting down because my stomach was doing somersaults.

"So," he said, glancing at an open folder in front of him, "Angela... what is so important that you feel the need to interrupt my busy day?"

I swallowed uneasily.

"Well, there's this Negro student in my class..."

"We have quite a few Negro students in our classes now."

"Yes, sir, but this one is being bullied."

He raised an eyebrow at me and lowered his chin.

"Strange, I haven't heard a word about it. Who is this student?"

"Valerie Franklin. But, you see, she doesn't want to cause any trouble."

"And you do?"

"No, sir. It's just that…"

"If Miss Franklin hasn't come to me with any concerns, it makes me wonder why you're doing so."

"Well, it's just that there are a couple of guys in our class who I believe are bullying Valerie, trying to scare her, you know. Because she's black."

He tilted his head back so he was looking down his large, arrogant nose at me.

"Some specifics would be helpful," he said, an intimidating frown giving him the appearance of a cold-hearted dictator.

"Right. Well, on the first day of school some kids stole her book satchel and wouldn't give it back."

He made a show of checking his watch.

"Later, after first period, someone threw water on her face," I continued.

He drummed his fingers on his desk.

"And then, this morning, she was ambushed – someone poured baby oil on the floor – and she slipped and fell."

After giving me his undivided attention for about sixty seconds, it was obvious he was ready to move on.

"I appreciate your good intentions, Angela," he said, after pausing again to look at the file on his desk. "But I'm absolutely certain what we've got here are a couple of accidents, maybe a bit of horseplay. I don't believe any students at Lafayette Senior High would intentionally target someone in the manner you describe. And I don't believe for a minute that it has anything to do with race."

"But, Mr. Lancaster, can't we at least find out for sure what that stuff was on the floor?"

"Even if it was baby oil, as you suspect, it was most assuredly dropped by accident," he said, glancing at his watch again. "I want to thank you for your concern about a fellow student and for filling me in on the details."

He rose and handed me a hall pass.

"But..." I said.

He pressed the button on his intercom, calling his secretary as he waved me toward the door.

There was a pounding at my temples as I left the freezing office. How naive could I be, thinking the principal would care what I said.

I slapped the wall as I plodded along the empty hallway. Then I slapped it again, cussing under my breath.

So much for my bold move.

~

If I thought I'd had my share of unpleasantness for the day, I was mistaken. On my way to lunch I heard someone running up behind me.

"Angie, wait up!"

I recognized the voice and walked a little faster.

It was Mr. Boring as Broccoli in a plaid shirt that was a little too tight, his thin dishwater blonde hair sticking to his forehead.

He was out of breath as he pulled even with me. His pitiful, puppy dog eyes triggered a twinge of guilt in my stomach.

"I wanted to ask if...whether... you might consider, well, you know, if you might feel comfortable...well, you know, I uh… would you… would you… come, I mean go… to Home-coming with me?"

Crap and more crap. Why did he have to ask me? I mean, everyone knew by now I was going with Craig. Didn't they?

"I'm sorry, Junior, but I've already got a date for Homecoming."

His shoulders slumped. And although a smile was still pasted on his face, it wasn't a real smile. I guess it wasn't his fault he was shaped like a teddy bear and acted like one too.

"I figured you did," he said.

Even if Craig hadn't already asked me, I would've lied. Because no way, no how, was I going out with Limp as Lima Beans, no matter how sorry I felt for him.

I burst through the door to the courtyard like I'd been underwater too long and needed air. Which I did.

"Is that ace reporter Angie Finley?"

It was the two seniors I'd interviewed. I took a deep breath and racked my brain. Oh, yeah.

"If it isn't Pocahontas's boyfriend, John Smith, and his compadre, Mitch Davidson, co-owner of Harley-Davidson Motorcycles," I said in my best joking around voice.

"Gadzooks! She remembered!" John cried, slapping himself on the forehead.

Mitch smiled too like he was genuinely pleased to see me.

"We filled out your questionnaires this morning in home-room," he said.

"Appreciate that. It was my interview with you guys that convinced me we didn't have time to talk with enough seniors for our story."

"Well, the survey stirred up a lot of debate about the draft and going to Vietnam," he said.

"Yeah, we've got a bunch of sissies in the senior class," John added, affecting a limp wrist. "Including me! But don't tell anyone."

"Actually, I need to get a few more quotes for the article. You guys have five minutes you could spare?"

"Anything for the beautiful Angie Finley," John said. "Except, there's one minor problem. I have to be early for Calculus. So I'll have to take a rain check."

He trotted off, waving like a fool.

"Remedial sixth grade math!" Mitch shouted after him.

"He should be on *The Red Skelton Show*," I said.

"He thinks he is."

Suddenly I was a little self-conscious interviewing Mitch one-on-one. He suggested we talk on the way to his next class, so we strolled across the courtyard and into the building. He led the way up the stairs to the senior hall. I took notes.

Mitch didn't have beach boy good looks. In fact, something about him made me think of a political refugee from the Soviet Union or something, maybe the prominent brow or the thoughtful brown eyes. And he wore high-top basketball shoes, which stood out in a sea of loafers. Of course, I'd learned he was a starter on the basketball team.

I wrote down everything he said – he definitely planned on going to college and would apply for a college deferment, but still worried about being sent to Vietnam.

"I don't think I could kill someone," he explained. "Maybe I could've shot at people in World War Two, knowing Germany and Japan were trying to take over the world. But

I'm not so sure about what we're doing in Vietnam."

"If you were drafted, would you consider hiding out in Canada?"

"I don't like the idea of being a draft dodger."

"But getting a college deferment is dodging the draft."

"True. But it's legal. And I'm hoping the war will be over before..."

"Before you're forced to make a decision."

He nodded.

"Is that enough for your article?" he asked.

The hallway had filled, then emptied as seniors headed to their classrooms.

"Yeah, thanks. I didn't mean to take so much of your time."

"Time well spent."

He gave me this genuine look like he thought what I was doing was important. And, as I jogged down the stairs, a squeak of satisfaction escaped my lips. I liked having his respect.

~8~

Ugh. The hours dragged despite being busy with school work and research for my activist report. I'd also gotten a couple more interviews for the newspaper story, which made me feel good, but I couldn't wait for Saturday night and my date with Craig.

Friday morning the first two activist reports were presented. Immediately afterwards, Dr. Kelley gave us a quiz on Upton Sinclair and Nellie Bly. She said we could look at our notes to answer, so all we had to do was take good notes.

When class was over, I turned around to talk with Valerie. I felt so guilty about the awful attacks on her that I'd been doing my best to chat with her more often. I wanted her to know not all white people were beasts.

"How'd you do?" I said.

"I think I got them all right," she said. "I'm going to check out Sinclair's *The Jungle* from the library."

"I don't think I could ever eat meat again if I read about those filthy meatpacking plants."

She chuckled, which made her look younger.

"I also want to read more about Nellie Bly," she said. "I didn't know there was a woman investigative reporter in the nineteenth century."

"Interesting she's not mentioned in our history book."

"A lot of people aren't covered in our history book."

"You interested in becoming a reporter someday?"

"Maybe," she said. "I'm giving it a try right now, reporting for a small weekly newspaper."

"No kidding! Which one?"

"You've never heard of it. It's a Negro paper. *The Fayette-ville Message.*"

As we streamed into the hallway, I could feel hostile eyes watching us. But I refused to look around.

"Wow! I'm impressed. I've just started doing a little reporting too," I said. "Just the school paper, though."

"So I heard."

Stan trotted past us then.

"Don't forget," he called out. "See ya Sunday!"

God, what a Largemouth Bass! People might jump to the wrong conclusion.

~

Looking in the mirror Saturday evening, about two thirds of me thought I looked *chic* enough for my first date with Craig.

Of course, my black and white checked bedspread and my red carpet were covered with jeans, shorts, skirts, tops, belts – you name it. I must've changed 15 times. I had to look just right. He would be here any minute and it was important to come across like I hadn't given my outfit much thought, you know. I didn't want to appear to be trying too hard. So I'd settled on khaki shorts, palomino Weejuns and a matching belt and pocketbook. My new Carolina blue button-up shirt made me look like I went to UNC. Which is what I wanted.

But did it look like I was pretending to be a co-ed? Was it too obvious?

I rummaged through my closet again. Maybe the soft burgundy paisley top would be better. I held it in front of me, looking in the mirror. Maybe I should wear my new mini-dress. I snatched it from the closet and threw the paisley on the bed. The mini-dress was really cute. Navy blue with red and white sleeves. Much sexier. But it wasn't exactly... I don't know. So I chucked it onto the bed as well. Maybe my Sonny and Cher bell bottoms – that's what Deedee called them. I pulled them from the drawer, holding them against me as I studied my reflection.

That's when the doorbell rang. He was early!

Flinging the pants on the bed, I yanked my bottom drawer open, grabbing one sweater after another, tossing them on the floor. Pink? Tan? Yellow? No, no, no. Where was my navy sweater? Finally, I found it underneath all the others. I sniffed it. Only a little musty. I sprayed a shot of cologne in the air and waved the sweater through it. Then I tied it around my shoulders in a perfect, haphazard sort of way. I got my purse and took one last look. Lipstick. I needed more lipstick. I touched up my Frosted Pink and smacked my lips together, opening the door just as Mom was about to knock.

"He's here," she whispered, giving me this bug-eyed look.

In the living room Craig was talking with Deedee, who, unfortunately, was home on one of her rare breaks from college. Her jeans were so tight she must've laid down on her bed to zip them up – a trick she learned in the dorm. She'd also learned another trick – wearing a push-up bra at all times so she'd look as sexy as possible. I'm not accusing her of trying to steal Craig. I don't think she'd do that. But wasn't her long blonde hair enough? Did she have to touch up her lipstick and look like *she* was going on a date when it was *my* boyfriend coming over?

Craig turned and gave me his Hollywood heartthrob smile. He was wearing navy slacks, a light blue plaid shirt, with shiny pennies tucked into his freshly polished loafers.

"Well, don't you two make a cute couple?" Deedee cooed.

"Yeah," Craig said.

We needed to get out of there before any awkwardness reared its unseemly head.

"What time will you have her home?" Mom said, like she cared.

"Is eleven o'clock okay, Mrs. Finley?" he said.

"Call me Barb," she said, patting his arm. "Eleven is fine."

A black cocktail dress clung to her curvaceous body, a low scoop neckline showcasing her mighty cleavage packed in a Wonder Woman bra. Her orange hair was coiffed in the latest, teased-to-high-heaven style. Craig must've thought we were the Jezebel family.

We'd started out the front door when Deedee spotted his car parked on the street.

"Oh my God!" she shrieked. "A ragtop GTO!"

She rushed outside ahead of us, running barefoot across the grass. Mom followed. They both went on and on about how cool his car was.

"What year is it?" Deedee asked.

"A sixty-six," he replied. "My dad gave it to me for my sixteenth birthday."

"Love the red and white leather seats," Mom said, running her fingers across the upholstery.

I swear they were both flirting with him. I was about to die. He was so polite, answering all their questions. They both had to sit in it, of course. I began to think they might beg to go with us. But finally, Mom's boyfriend du jour pulled up in his long white Cadillac, honking the horn like he was in a hurry, so Mom and Deedee scattered.

Craig turned the radio on and we listened to *Wild Thing* as we drove down the street. My perfect hair was immediately undone, whipping my face as we picked up speed. But I didn't care. When we came to a stoplight, he looked me in the eye and sang along. I wasn't sure who he was calling a *Wild Thing* – him or me – but I was definitely feeling "groovy."

We drove for about twenty minutes and then pulled up in front of a white, two-story in the ritzy section of Haymount. He turned the radio down and revved the engine real loud, making the car vibrate.

"This is Sylvia's house – Dave's girlfriend," he said, like I knew it was a double date.

"Nice magnolias," I replied, noticing the professionally landscaped lawn.

Dave and Sylvia jumped in the back and Craig introduced us. Dave was on the football team and had that thick-necked, linebacker look and a short brown Beatles haircut. Sylvia was petite and top heavy with freckles and long, strawberry blonde hair. They were both friendly so I didn't have time to get nervous. We talked about going to see a movie. But Dave wanted to see *Fantastic Voyage* and Sylvia wanted to see *Harper*.

"You know, Raquel Welch is in *Fantastic Voyage*," Dave argued.

"Paul Newman's in *Harper*," Sylvia said.

"What's the big deal about Paul Newman?" he said.

"What's the big deal about Raquel Welch?" she said.

"Big *deals* – plural," Dave cracked.

Yukkity yuk yuk.

Craig winked at me as we drove down Raeford Road and the next thing you know we pulled into Putt-Putt. Now, I know that sounds kind of rinky-dink but it was actually a lot of fun. Dave and Sylvia teased each other. Dave razzed Craig. Craig made fun of Dave. And I didn't even have to pretend I wasn't very good at hitting the ball. So, naturally, Craig had to help me, just like in the movies. I think Sylvia suspected I was playing dumb. But, really, I wasn't.

After a couple of rounds, we played some pinball and then drove to the Tastee-Freez, the guys arguing over the new *Star Trek* TV series. Dave liked it, but Craig said it was cheesy.

"I think Spock is cool," I said. "And there's a woman officer on the bridge. A black woman."

"Spock is actually kinda sexy," said Sylvia, winking at me.

Craig scoffed at all of us, calling the show fakey.

"Talk about fakey," Dave said. "Half the shows on TV are fakey. *Bewitched*, *I Dream of Jeannie*, *My Favorite Martian*, and that stupid new show *The Monkees*."

"Yeah!" Sylvia said.

"Those shows are downright dopey," Craig said.

"But you watch 'em," Dave said. "I've seen you watch 'em."

Everyone laughed.

We sat in a little booth so our feet got tangled under the

table. Craig and I shared a banana split. So did Dave and Sylvia. Craig set his transistor radio on the table, giving me hot glances as he sang along with Neil Diamond's *Cherry Cherry*. Dave and Sylvia took turns spooning ice cream into each other's mouth, giggling and whispering the whole time. I kept wishing there'd be a chance for Craig to kiss me.

When we dropped them off, it was only about nine thirty. The radio blared *Younger Girl* as we drove away. Craig sang along. I fluttered my eyelashes and laughed.

I thought he was going to drop me off but he turned around and headed south on Raeford Road. I put my sweater on as we picked up speed. We finally turned off the highway into Lake Rim Park, bouncing along a rutted dirt road until we came to a clearing in some tall pines by the lake. The rippled surface of the water reflected a half moon rising in the east. When he turned off the engine it was so quiet we could hear the water lapping softly on the shore a few feet in front of us.

I brushed my hair with my fingers as he walked around the back of the car. Now I was nervous. And excited. And self-conscious.

He opened my door like a gentleman.

The crickets and frogs sang us a love song. I'm pretty sure it was *When a Man Loves a Woman*.

When we reached the water's edge, he leaned against a massive pine and held both my hands. Half of his face was lit by the moonlight and the other half was in shadow.

"My dad says you shouldn't kiss on the first date," he said.

"Thank goodness you didn't bring him along."

He grinned and moved his hands to my waist and pulled

me closer. I sighed as my body touched his. Then he kissed me very gently. It was incredible that a kiss could make me feel like my brain was no longer in control of my movements. I realized I was clutching his shoulders. But while his lips were soft, there was something solid below his belt. I was so surprised, I stepped back slightly so our bodies didn't touch and loosened my grip on his shoulders.

"Sorry," he said. "I didn't..."

"Craig," I whispered.

I just wanted to say his name.

He led me to the car and opened my door. Then he got in the driver's side. Instead of cranking the engine, though, he leaned over and kissed me again.

"You taste so good," he said. "And you feel so good. And you smell so good. So good, in fact, that I've gotta take you home right now."

While he made a big production of snapping the roof over our heads and locking it into place I tried not to show my disappointment. I admit – I wanted to make out.

He drove slowly until we got to the highway, then punched it so we squealed onto the pavement, the engine roaring. He slapped the gear shift into second as we picked up speed, then third, and finally, when he shifted to fourth, we were flying fast enough to get a speeding ticket if a cop had been around. It was obvious he loved driving his four-on-the-floor GTO.

We made it home in no time. He pulled to the curb in front of my house and killed the engine.

"You're not mad at me?" he asked, turning in his seat to face me.

"Mad?"

"I didn't mean to be so, you know. But you're…" he said, reaching over and taking my hand in his, "too…"

Then his lips were on mine. I felt like I was melting. It was the passionate, wet kiss I'd been dreaming of. His eyes were closed as he finally pulled away.

"Too… beautiful," he breathed.

When he walked me to my front door, he whispered in my ear.

"I'm going to dream about you tonight."

It would be an understatement to say that it was *me* who dreamed about *him.* I dreamed of his lips on mine. Of his breath on my neck. Of his hands on my waist. Of the half moon reflected in his eyes where I swam with a leisurely stroke, thrilling to the touch of the warm water on my bare skin.

And to think – he was taking me to Homecoming.

~9~

It took a while the next morning to find my floor. Clothes covered every square inch of my red carpet, I swear. That's where I'd tossed them when I climbed into bed and relived all the delicious moments of my first date with Prince Charming.

I was glad I didn't need to wash or roll my hair and sit under the hair dryer. After all, I was just going to meet Stan to work on those surveys. Wranglers and my comfy plaid shirt would do. I started to put my contacts in but stopped and looked in the mirror. Keep the glasses on, I thought. No makeup either. Not even a touch of lipstick.

I couldn't help but wonder if Craig would still think I was "too beautiful" now.

Mom was slumped over the kitchen table in her hideous Pepto-Bismol pink robe, smoking a cigarette and drinking coffee. If her beauty parlor customers could only see her now, the Sunday paper scattered in front of her and newsprint smudged on her cheek.

As usual on a Sunday morning, she was scanning the real estate listings. Why she thought she belonged in an exclusive neighborhood was beyond me. She was the furthest thing from those trim young women cooking colorful meals in well-appointed kitchens in the decorating magazines. Our kitchen, for instance, was as humble as hot dogs: pink formica table, matching chrome chairs with vinyl seats, dark wooden cabinets and faded potholders and kitchen utensils hanging above the stove.

Then again, she often complained about having to drive me to school every morning because we didn't live inside the city limits. Deedee and I were both allowed to attend out-of-district because our dad was in the Army. But that meant Mom drove me in the morning and I had to take a city transit bus instead of a school bus every afternoon. Personally, I preferred riding with adults even though I had to pay my fifteen cents every day.

"I'm walking down to the Coffee Cup to meet a friend," I said.

She grunted as she leaned back, eyes closed, stretching her arms above her head before returning to the Classifieds.

With a folder full of surveys and a spiral notebook under my arm, I started off. It was the kind of day when you know for sure that fall has arrived. The angle of the sun has changed. The light is crisper. The sky is bluer.

Craig's scent and the look in his eyes came back to me. And his sexy voice. I'd kissed boys before, but they'd just been puppy love smooches. Nothing serious. And even though I had no intention of taking an Introductory Class in Carnal Knowledge, as Deedee put it, I had to admit, with Craig's breath hot on my neck and his hands on my hips, it would've been hard to slow the train if we were headed down that track.

A skittering noise brought me back to earth. I watched two squirrels chase each other round and round the trunk of a tall hickory tree. It looked like a wild game of tag, but I suspected it had something to do with sex. The boy squirrel had the hots for the girl squirrel. Or maybe the girl squirrel was chasing the boy squirrel. Maybe he had beautiful eyes and long eyelashes. Maybe he had a fantastic fluffy tail. Maybe she dreamed about that squirrel and now she was chasing him down!

I chuckled as I continued down the street.

When I got to the restaurant, I was disappointed the outdoor tables were full. I didn't want to be trapped inside with smoke swirling around me. But then someone on the far side of the patio lowered his newspaper. It was Stan, his hair even messier than usual.

"Coffee?" he said as I sat down.

"Sure, but it's Dutch treat."

A skinny, white-haired woman, old enough to be my grandmother, set two menus in front of us and filled my brown mug with coffee.

We both ordered the breakfast special.

"We'd like separate checks, please," I said.

"All righty," she said, snatching the menus and scuttling off at top speed.

After setting my folder on the table, I added cream and sugar to my coffee before opening my notebook. Stan stared at me with an amused expression.

"What're you lookin' at?" I said.

"Your new look."

I crossed my eyes and stuck out my tongue, having temporarily forgotten how different I looked in my glasses. He laughed.

"Okay, down to business," I said.

So we prepared our surveys and lists. But before we could really get started, Granny the Speedy Waitress brought our food. We barely had time to move our papers out of the way before she slipped the plates in front of us.

I closed my eyes and savored the smell of eggs and bacon. There was also steaming cheese grits and an open biscuit smothered in gravy.

I sprinkled pepper over everything except the bacon, which I bit into first.

"Mm."

"We need some music," he said. "You heard the new Bob Dylan album yet?"

I shook my head as I chewed.

"It's called *Blonde on Blonde*. Some great songs."

I stirred my grits and took a small bite.

"You like Dylan?" he asked.

"Sure. But I guess the Beatles are my favorite."

"You know," he said, pausing to start on his eggs, "I read where John Lennon said he was influenced by Dylan."

"Well, yeah, along with a bunch of other people, including Chuck Berry and Buddy Holly."

"Sounds like you know something about music."

I shrugged as I tasted my biscuit. The gravy was nice and salty.

"I also like Joan Baez and Peter, Paul and Mary," he said.

"A folkie."

"Sometimes."

When we finished eating, we got to work.

"I can't believe all these guys are just gonna go along with the government," he said.

"What're they supposed to do?"

"They could do what my brother did. He burned his draft card."

"But he could get in big trouble for…"

"They had a peace rally and whole bunches of guys burned their draft cards," he said.

"But…"

"And I'm not gonna even register for the draft when I'm eighteen if this stupid war is still going on. In fact, I'm not gonna register even if the war's over."

"But you'll end up in jail."

"So?"

I sipped my coffee. What do you say to 'so?'

"SDS is planning a huge antiwar demonstration in the spring and I'm going," he said. "Thousands of guys are getting killed over there for nothing!"

"For nothing?"

"Nothing. When we're gone, Vietnam will still be run by Communists. Doesn't matter how many Americans leave their guts in the jungle."

"Stan," I said, glancing around to see if anyone heard.

Made me nervous about my dad too, even though he insisted he was out of harm's way.

"Sorry," he said.

When the waitress returned for the fourteenth time trying to hurry us off, I suggested we wrap it up.

"We going to your house?" he asked.

That was the last place I wanted to go. So we walked to the creek where I used to play. Most of the leaves were still green, although the dogwoods were already a rust color and loaded with bright red berries.

I showed him the big leaning oak I used to sit in. Because it tilted at such an angle, it was a cinch to climb. He couldn't resist and made quick work of scaling the trunk and scooting along the thick lower branch that ran parallel to the ground.

"Come on up," he called from his roost almost directly above me.

"We've got work to do!"

"Come on!"

With that grin on his face, it dawned on me that he was kind of cute in a non-cute sort of way. I turned toward the stream, noticing ribbons of light reflecting on the sparkling water.

Closing my eyes, I basked in the warmth of the sun on my face. But only for a moment before Stan's voice rang out again.

"Chicken!"

I could see we weren't going to make any progress until we got this out of the way. So I clambered up to my old perch, giving him a triumphant smile.

"A tomboy!" he said.

We sat silently for a couple of minutes, listening to the breeze whispering in the trees and the occasional trilling of songbirds nearby.

"By the way, how's your dad?" he asked.

Funny – none of my girlfriends ever asked that question.

"He's good, I think. In his letters, he says he's not close to the front."

I climbed down, which wasn't as easy as climbing up. He scrambled down after me and we sat on the grass in the sun.

"You know, glasses make you look intellectual," he said.

"You're so fulla bulla."

He grabbed his chest and threw himself backwards on the ground, groaning in mock agony.

"I'm wounded," he wheezed.

I couldn't help giggling. I could imagine him on stage, he was that good.

He opened one eye, then closed it again, moaning loudly.

"Shh! Someone will call the police if you don't *fermez la bouche*," I said.

"Firm up my butt?"

"It's French for 'shut up.'"

"Okay. I'm firming up my boosh."

He sat up, picked up his folder and parked himself next to me. We worked that way, side by side, until we got all the survey answers counted. And then I insisted I had to go home. He insisted we meet in the lunchroom the next day to start writing the article.

It was nice to see another side of Stan besides the pushy side. Oh, and the side that thought girls were meant to be secretaries for boys. I wasn't sure how we'd write the article *together*. But I had to admit, I was looking forward to seeing it in print. I pictured it on the front page. That was bound to impress Craig.

~10~

Stan seemed perfectly at home standing in the teacher's spot. Like he was a born speaker. He was even wearing a scruffy grey sport coat and black slacks, which made him look bizarre with those worn-out canvas tennies.

"Frederick Douglass might've become President of the United States if he'd been born, say, this year – in 1966. Which means he'd be old enough to run for president in the year 2001. Add another decade so he could get some political experience and he'd be in his mid-forties by 2012."

That's how he began his report Monday morning. But most of us had never heard of the guy, so it wasn't a shocking statement when he made it. It didn't take long, though, for the disapproval to rise like the blush on my face when I caught Craig undressing me with his eyes.

"This man," he continued, holding an open book above his head, "was the personification of courage and conviction."

What we saw was a photo of a handsome black man with a lion's mane of grey hair.

"No Negro will ever be president," Billy snarled, dragging out the word Negro to let everyone know that's not the word he normally used.

"Out!" Dr. Kelley snapped, glaring at him as she pointed at the door.

Stan waited as Billy took his time gathering his books and moseying from the room.

"He was the most famous civil rights activist of the nineteenth century," Stan continued.

Donna yawned loudly. Billy's buddy, Jack, on the far row, snorted like he was about to hawk a big gob across the room, prompting Dr. Kelley to point her finger at him and give him a threatening look.

"He was a man who freed himself from slavery," said Stan, "then worked to abolish it, continuing the fight for equal rights for the rest of his life."

A boy in the back of the room farted, which triggered a wave of snickering.

Stan paused for a second like he was considering punching someone's lights out, but then soldiered on. He spoke for over ten minutes, setting the record for the longest report.

After class he cornered me in the hallway.

"Well?" he said.

He knew he'd done good. He just wanted to hear it.

"Let me put it this way," I said. "If discomfort was rated like earthquakes, your report would've measured a seven-point-nine on the Richter scale."

He let loose with a belly laugh.

"Glad you didn't lose your cool," I said.

"I knew those bastards would try that."

~

I bumped into Dottie when I stopped by my locker before lunch. I'd just gotten my biology book out when Stan walked up, all smiles. He greeted me with the most idiotic question I'd ever been asked in my life.

"Can you take dictation?"

"Can I what?"

"You know, write down what I..."

"I know the definition of dictation."

I guess Dottie saw the fire in my eyes.

"I'll meet you in the cafeteria," she said, edging away.

"Wait up," I said. "This won't take a minute."

Then I turned my sights on Mr. Men are More Important than Women Bukowski.

"Funny, that's what I was going to ask you," I said. "Can *you* take dictation?"

"I didn't..." he said.

"Can you?"

"I..."

"Answer the question. Can you take dictation?"

"Angie..." he said.

Dottie didn't wait for me, disappearing like a wild chicken into the hallway.

"You big phony!" I said. "If all you really want is for a girl to take dictation for you, compile your statistics for you and do your typing for you, then I suggest you check with the typing teacher. I'm sure she can find a student interested in earning some extra money being your secretary."

He opened his mouth to speak but I wasn't finished.

"You can consider our collaboration over. *Fini!*"

I slammed my locker shut, snapped the lock in place and joined the throng of students cramming the hallway.

"Angie!" he called out, but I zigzagged between students to

catch up with Dottie.

"What was that all about?" she asked.

"Do you believe that guy?" I said, raising my voice to be heard over the din. "Do I take dictation? Hell, no! I will never take dictation!"

"What's wrong with taking dictation?"

Which stopped me dead in my tracks, nearly getting myself trampled before it dawned on me to keep moving.

"Dottie, Dottie, Dottie," I said, shaking my head.

And I couldn't believe how she and Janet acted at lunch. They both said I was overreacting. That I was blowing things out of proportion.

"Your problem," said Janet, "is that you've turned into Miss La-di-da."

Which caused me to shake my head once again.

"Are you telling me you'd be okay if he treated *you* as his lackey?" I said.

"He just asked if you could take dictation!" she said.

"Yeah, what's wrong with that?" Dottie chimed in. "Being a secretary would be a good job!"

"I don't want to be his secretary," I said, "any more than he wants to be *my* secretary! There's such a thing as *respect de soi!*"

Janet's hand landed on her hip. "Just because you've had two years of French doesn't mean you need to go all *parlez-vous* on us all the time!"

"Self-respect!" I cried. "I'm talking about self-respect!"

I jumped up and headed for the trash can, dumping the rest of my turkey and noodles on my way out, leaving them to talk behind my back.

~

Depositing my angry butt on a bench in the courtyard, I opened my notebook and began writing the article myself. I didn't need Mr. Nineteenth Century Bukowski. I used a quote from Mitch Davidson in my lead paragraph.

"Ain't she the purtiest girl in Dogpatch?"

It was John, the comedian, with a group of senior boys that included Mitch and some guys I didn't know.

I crossed my eyes and stuck my tongue out the side of my mouth.

"Hey, Daisy Mae!" John yelled. "Remember us when the Sadie Hawkins dance rolls around."

"I'll remember to give you the double whammy!" I hollered in my best hillbilly accent.

They cracked up.

"Like you'd know how to dance with a girl," one of the guys taunted John.

More laughter.

When the bell rang, I got up. But not to go to class. I was determined to hand my article in to Dr. Kelley before I left school. So I went to the typing room. It was filled with girls, naturally. Girls who were headed for office jobs right out of high school. The unsmiling typing teacher saw me as she was about to close the door.

"Yes?" she said.

"I was hoping to type a report I have to do?"

She was about to say no, I could tell. But then she looked at me for a second like she was sizing me up.

"In the back," she said.

It took me all of fifth and sixth periods, I'm such a bad typist. I kept having to untangle the typebars when they got stuck together and I must've used half a bottle of correction fluid. But when I handed the article to Dr. Kelley after school she nodded in approval.

"Can't wait to read it," she said, glancing at the first page. "Who gets top billing on the byline?"

"Ma'am?"

"Is it 'by Angie Finley and Stan Bukowski' or 'by Stan Bukowski and Angie Finley?'"

I exhaled sharply, not knowing what to say, as she looked over my shoulder.

"Stan, I was just discussing the byline with your fellow reporter here."

"The byline?" he said.

"For two smart kids, you both seem a little thickheaded today."

Why did I suddenly feel like a thief? But he deserved it, the rat.

"Is that...." Stan said.

"Your article, yes," she said. "Once I've approved it, I'll pass it along to Mike. But we have to decide how the byline will read. Should it have Angie's name first or yours? Depends on who did most of the writing and reporting."

Stan's eyes bored into me.

"Actually, we hadn't talked about that," he said. "And we might need to make a tiny revision before you read it."

"What revision?" I snapped.

"There's one figure I'm not sure I added up right."

"Well, you can check it. I've gotta go."

Figuring he might follow me, I double-timed it up the stairs and hid in the senior girls' bathroom. I could feel tears welling up and I didn't want Mr. Pretend Not to be Prejudiced to see me crying. No way. I went into a stall and used toilet tissue to blot my eyes, angry at myself for being on the verge of tears.

My feelings were so jumbled. I was furious but I also felt guilty – like I was the bad guy. All those 'buts' again. I'd worked hard on this project and Stan had been an arrogant swine. What made him think I should do his bidding? Like I didn't have a brain or something!

Finally, I rinsed my face. It burned me up that he was changing the article behind my back, telling Dr. Kelley it needed a "tiny revision."

I was heading out the front door to catch my bus when I heard my name. But it wasn't Stan, thank goodness. It was Craig.

"Hey, beautiful!" he called.

He was with another football player – both of them in short, fishnet jerseys and tight practice pants, their naked navels in full view.

"You coming to the game Friday night?" he said.

"Of course."

His friend slapped him on the shoulder.

"Oh, yeah, Angie, this is Eddie. Eddie, Angie. But don't get any ideas," he said, giving his burly teammate a little shove. "She's my girlfriend."

"All right, all right," Eddie said.

"We've gotta get back," Craig said, giving me a nod.

I waved and smiled. Let's see – did I hear him right? I was his girlfriend? I felt like my mother's devil's food cake rising in the oven.

~11~

Mr. Beguiling as Green Beans gave me yet another wounded look when I walked into homeroom on Thursday. That's when it dawned on me I should set him up with a girl. Maybe that way he'd stop making me feel like a meany.

"Hey, Junior," I whispered, sliding into my seat behind him.

He refused to turn around.

"I happen to know Linda Young doesn't have a date for Homecoming," I whispered.

He muttered something under his breath.

"Really," I said.

He swiveled in his seat and gave me this "yeah, right" look but glanced toward the far side of the room where Linda sat behind Billy the Butthead.

Okay, a small part of me felt guilty. But Linda needed a date and Junior needed a date. And I needed for Junior to stop lusting after me. He wasn't a bad guy really. He just bored me to tears. What he'd said to me that day about getting a reputation was probably true. He just didn't understand I preferred a reputation for being friendly to a black student. So, even though I wasn't normally the type to play cupid, I planted the seed, hoping it would grow into a decent tomato plant or whatever.

Valerie seemed quieter than usual, although that hardly seemed possible.

"You okay?" I whispered.

She nodded.

I'd been wrestling all week with telling her about my disappointing meeting with the principal. Maybe now was the right time. It might help to know someone cared.

"I talked with Mr. Lancaster about your fall," I said. "But I didn't tell him who I suspect."

She turned into a statue with blazing eyes.

I had the distinct impression people were trying to hear what we were saying – there was so much silence around me and a telltale lack of movement – so I wrote her a note: "Billy and Jack."

She opened it and read it, then wrote something on the bottom, folded it and slid it back to me.

"I know you mean well but you could accidentally cause more problems," the note said.

"How could..." I whispered.

But she closed her eyes and shook her head, like, she, too, suspected there were big ears close by.

~

Valerie must've felt a little guilty about our conversation because she was friendlier when I slid into my desk on Friday.

"Congratulations on your article," she said.

"Article?"

"In the school paper."

"Oh, yeah. I haven't seen it yet."

She pulled out her copy of *The Wildcat* and handed it to me.

"I'll get another one," she said.

It was right there on the front page: "LHS Seniors Ready to Serve." Not exactly a riveting headline. "By Angie Finley." It was just my name on the byline.

Stan slunk into the room at that very moment, so I tucked the newspaper under my books. But as soon as I made it to second period, I scanned the article. No changes. It was exactly what I'd written. No additions. No deletions. Not even a "tiny revision." So, if I'd won the battle, why did I feel like a pickpocket?

~

To tell the truth, I wasn't excited about watching the Wildcats, but I'd promised Craig. So I called Janet, Dottie and Linda and begged them to go with me.

We found seats at the top of the over-flowing bleachers, in the very back row. It was the last day of September and the air was cool and clear, with a few stars visible if you took the time to look up for a minute. Definitely more enjoyable than watching helmeted football players collide on the field and listening to endless cheerleader chants.

As we stood in line to buy popcorn at half-time I spotted Mr. Riveting as a Radish and a buddy of his. It was time for stage two of my seed-planting.

"Linda, you got a date for Homecoming yet?" I asked.

"I'm thinking of asking Jay Morgan," she said.

"You can't do that," Janet said. "You'll get a reputation."

"This is not the nineteenth century," I said.

"He'll think she's hot to trot," said Janet, her hand once again parked on her waist.

"He knows I'm not..." Linda said.

"Go ahead and see what happens," Janet said.

Like it or not, she had a point. Even though it was 1966, my mom said the only way she managed to get a credit card was for my dad – her ex-husband – to co-sign for it. Deedee said when she considered a job as an airline stewardess, she found out there was a mandatory retirement age of thirty-two. Plus, you couldn't gain weight or get pregnant. And it was true, no upstanding girl would call a boy on the telephone and ask him out, unless it was for the Sadie Hawkins dance.

"Besides," Janet said, "Jay spends half his life looking at the ceiling trying to stop a nosebleed."

She did a dead-on impression, cocking her head back, while trying not to walk into somebody as we stepped up to the counter to buy our snacks.

Heading back to the bleachers, I picked up where I'd left off.

"So," I said to Linda, "what if I sort of nudge a guy to ask you and let him know you'd say yes?"

"Like who?"

"Junior Duncan."

Her cheeks puffed out and she covered her mouth like she was about to upchuck.

"I've seen him eyeing you in history class," I said, stretching the truth like a rubber band.

"He's not bad," Dottie said. "Kind of nice, actually."

"Yeah," Janet said, "if you like guys from Dullsville."

"Oh, come on," Dottie said, obviously realizing the logic of my plan. "He's not that bad. And besides, his family's rich."

"Rich?" said Linda.

"You didn't know?" Dottie said. "His dad's a city council-man. My mom says he owns half of Fayetteville. In fact, if you don't want him, I'll take him."

"Now, wait a minute!" Linda said.

We all giggled as we crammed popcorn in our mouths, climbing the steps to our seats.

Because the Wildcats were so far ahead, Craig got to play part of the fourth quarter. He threw some nice passes and ran for yardage a couple of times. He looked so good out there in red and white with all those pads on. I screamed my head off for him. He spotted me from the sidelines in the final minutes and flashed me his stunning Warren Beatty smile.

"Doesn't Angie make you sick?" Linda said. "She wants to set me up with Junior Duncan, for Christ's sake, while she's got Craig Anderson in rut like a bull moose."

~12~

Homecoming was almost here. I had to shop for the perfect outfit for the parade and bonfire and the perfect dress for the game and dance. Mom and I were headed out the door Saturday when the phone rang. It was Dottie. She was organizing a girls-only roller rink outing for Sunday night. I told her to count me in. I love skating. It's the only time you can dance all by yourself in public without being labeled a lunatic.

My activist report was due Monday morning, but I'd been working along and along, reading, taking notes, writing. I'd already gotten Mom's portable typewriter out of the closet and put a new ribbon in it. I'd even typed a couple of pages. There was plenty of time to finish up.

Our shopping trip was a bit of a truce between Mom and me. She was so agreeable, buying me the most stunning red wool dress and matching jacket. The dress was short with cutout armholes, which would look good at the dance when I took off my jacket. We found some cute red pumps at Fleishman's. I didn't even have to beg. I also bought a new red sweater to wear in the parade. I might not be a cheerleader anymore but I'd be decked out in the team colors, which would make Craig happy.

Although she was in a spending mood in the department stores, we ate a cheap lunch at Biff Burger. That was fine with me, so I thanked her for the new duds.

"Well, it's a good investment," she said, giving me a motherly nod. "I figure we have to pull out all the stops since you didn't cut the mustard at cheerleader tryouts." She unwrapped her burger and dumped her fries on the wrapper. "I told myself to look at this as a new kind of challenge, luring in a handsome athlete without the use of pompoms. I think the wardrobe I bought you today should do the trick."

She squirted ketchup on her fries and dug in.

~

When I hopped in the car with Janet, Dottie and her mom after supper Sunday evening, I was on top of the world.

Linda and some other girls were already there when we walked in. They were skating around and around to *Wooly Bully*. The skating rink always played oldies. Colored lights in the ceiling reflected off the shiny wooden floor, making it feel like a party was going on.

We rented boot skates and sailed onto the floor just as *Love Potion Number 9* blared from the speakers. I streaked past my friends and swayed to the beat, singing the words. What a blast! We played follow the leader, doing funny dance steps and then I tried to skate backwards while Janet and Dottie held my hands.

"You stink!" Janet shouted.

And then I fell on my butt and they cracked up at my crack-up.

In no time at all, I was hot and sweaty, so I swung into the snack bar to get a Coke, nearly slamming into a middle-aged woman with short brown hair and glasses who gave me an evil look. Trying to avoid hitting her, I did a soft crash landing against the bar. When I turned around, there was Mitch Davidson, the tall senior I'd interviewed, looking highly amused.

"You laughing at me?" I said.

"Of course not. You're a regular Peggy Fleming."

I did a curtsy.

He clapped.

"You can do better, I suppose?" I said.

"Just dropping off my little sister and her friends. Just in time to see your audition for Roller Derby.

I had to laugh.

"By the way, congratulations on your story," he said. "Everyone wants to talk about the draft now. And the war."

Dottie and Linda zoomed up just as I was about to say thanks.

"Introduce us to your tall friend," Dottie said.

"This is Mitch Davidson. He's one of the guys I interviewed for the article in *The Wildcat.* Mitch, these are my friends, Dottie McGrath and Linda Young."

"*Enchantez!*" Dottie cooed.

"*Moi aussi,*" Mitch replied, not missing a beat.

"Same here," Linda said.

"Well, I've gotta make tracks," he said, looking at his watch. "I was supposed to be somewhere five minutes ago."

I gave him a little salute and slid down the bar to order my Coke. Dottie and Linda followed.

"Now, if you could put in a word with him, Angie," Linda said. "I could definitely imagine going to Homecoming with…"

"I think he's got eyes for Angie," Dottie butted in.

"We're just friends. He was just…"

"Listen, Angie," Dottie said, "I'm not as dumb as I look! In addition to these large boobs, I've also got large eyes."

I laughed in her face.

"You just can't comprehend a girl and a boy being friends, that's all," I said.

"Yeah," Linda said. "Easy for you to say. You're going to Homecoming with…"

"And you should see the cute dress I bought for the dance!" I said.

We got our Cokes and took over a booth, setting our bottles on the table. Janet and the other girls crowded in with us, our skates like bumper cars beneath the red formica.

"Big news, ya'll," Janet announced, puffing on a Parliament like she was Lauren Bacall or something. "Guess which tall, good-looking athlete is taking me to Homecoming."

Everyone squealed for her to tell.

She bobbed her head as she looked around the table. "Perry Adams!"

There were oohs and aahs all around.

"What happened to James Dean?" I asked.

"He's dead, remember?" she said.

I didn't care who Perry was. I was just happy Janet had a date. That must be why she could be friendly with me again. And from the conversation, I gathered he was a star on the jayvee basketball team – sure to be a starter for the varsity squad next year. Something I would've known if I were a cheerleader.

Everyone had a date except Linda.

~

After spending the evening at the roller rink, I was up late that night with my new friend, Susan B. "Failure Is Impossible" Anthony, practicing my oral presentation and finishing typing the written report. Unfortunately, there was a lot more work left to do than I realized. I kept messing up and having to retype whole pages to make it look neat. And I really wanted my presentation to be better than Stan's. I was up so late, I didn't hear my alarm clock the next morning. Mom assumed I was awake and didn't bother checking on me.

The clock on my nightstand said three minutes till 8:00 when I opened my eyes. A groan erupted from somewhere deep in my chest. I had to be sitting in my desk by 8:30. I'd never make it! And I was supposed to give my report first.

I rushed into the bathroom and brushed my teeth, thinking as fast as my groggy brain would allow. I'd have to skip breakfast. No time for a shower either. I washed my face and blotted it dry. When I looked in the mirror and saw what a mess my hair was, I panicked. It was going in fourteen different directions. I brushed madly, trying to get the snarls out, finally pulling it into a ponytail on my neck and clipping it with a big brown barrette. That would have to do. Next, I got my contacts ready. I put the right one in, no problem. But I had to start over with the left one. I was already trying to think of what clothes I could throw on when I dropped the lens on the green tile floor.

"Ready to go, Angie?" Mom bellowed from the kitchen.

"No!"

I squatted down to look for my lens.

"Don't yell at me like that, young lady!"

I closed my left eye so I could see more clearly out of my right eye. There it was on the floor, shattered into three pieces.

"Open up," she shouted, jiggling the doorknob.

Picking up the tiny shards, I turned the knob to let her in. She opened her mouth but then clamped it shut and rolled her eyes.

"I dropped my contact," I said, showing her the pieces in my hand.

"You're not dressed."

A frustrated growl escaped my mouth as I threw the bits of glass in the trash.

"You can be a little late this morning. And don't worry, we'll order a new lens."

"I have to get there on time, Mom. I'm doing my report."

She shook her head as she walked away, talking to herself as much as to me.

"In the great scheme of things, this can't possibly measure up to…"

But I stopped listening and got to work. I took my right contact out, put Erase under my eyes and lipstick on. When I put my glasses on, the white frames screamed "look at me!" So I decided to make it look like I *chose* to wear them. I put on my new fake Mondrian A-line – the one with the bright blocks of color. I ran into Deedee's room and found her white Mod cap hanging by her dresser.

"Mom, can I borrow your white boots?" I yelled.

I flew into her room, opened her closet and grabbed the boots. They were white patent leather go-go boots like the dancers wore on *Shindig*. Perfect. I pulled them on. A little big, but no one would know. I looked in the mirror. It looked intentional, not accidental, which was important.

"What are you doing wearing my new boots?" Mom barked as I jumped in the car.

"I asked if I could borrow them."

"Ask more loudly next time!"

Thank goodness she drove even more like a maniac than usual, daring other drivers to challenge a wild woman in a giant 1960 Buick Electra that was so banged up, another dent wouldn't make any difference.

The bell rang just as I skidded to a stop in the doorway of my homeroom. Of course, everyone stared. Even Dr. Kelley. Billy the Butthole made goofy glasses in front of his eyes with his fingers. Donna the Cheerleader Queen whispered under her breath for general consumption.

"They exiled her from England for bad taste."

Despite the snickering, I played it cool, crossing my legs as I sat down like I wanted to show off my shiny boots.

Beads of sweat popped up on my face and under my arms from all the rushing. Oh, no – I forgot my deodorant.

Dr. Kelley had reminded me on Friday that I was first up this morning. But she began lecturing on the abolitionist movement. I'm seventy-five percent certain she did it to give me time to compose myself. So I pulled out my note cards and studied them.

After about fifteen minutes, she announced that we would hear two reports – mine and Valerie's.

I stood at the front of the room behind the lectern and looked out upon my slouching classmates, busy scratching their heads, rubbing their eyes, yawning, picking their noses, whispering to each other or dozing with half-closed eyes. I don't know which is harder – speaking to people who aren't listening or speaking to people hanging on your every word. At any rate, my report had to be the best. Better than Stan's, for sure. And while I was sure Valerie's report would be well researched, she was too timid and reserved to give me much competition.

"When Susan B. Anthony was born, a woman's place was in the home," I began. "But before she died, she correctly predicted that women would get the right to vote. She didn't live to see the Nineteenth Amendment ratified, but she worked most of her life for women's rights."

I did my best to beat Mr. Two Face Bukowski, who, I have to admit, gave me his undivided attention. I explained how Susan B. Anthony never married, probably because she didn't want to be subservient to any man or be tied down with a bunch of children and housework. I explained how a woman didn't have the right to divorce even an abusive husband or the right to keep her own children if a marriage ended. I showed a few pictures. And when I was finished, some of the girls clapped. Stan did too.

Valerie flashed me an anxious look as I took my seat. Then she rose, walked to the front of the room and set some books on the chalk tray.

"It's hard for me to imagine being alive in nineteenth century America," she said in a steady voice that surprised me. "If I'd been born a hundred years ago I wouldn't be standing in a classroom at the age of fifteen, giving a report on someone I'd read about. Chances are I wouldn't have known how to read. Chances are I would've been one of the thousands of children forced to work twelve hours a day, six days a week, just to help their families put food on the table."

She looked around the classroom like she was really and truly speaking to each and every one of us.

"And chances are most of you in this class would've been in the same boat."

Someone whispered "yeah, right."

"Children as young as four or five years old were put to work," she said. "White children, mind you. Not just Negro children. Children were sent down into coal mines to push carts through small tunnels that grown men couldn't fit into. They were forced to break pieces of coal all day long. They had to do dangerous work in mills, many of them losing fingers in the machinery."

She had the class's attention.

"Girls our age had to work in sewing plants and factories. White girls. Negro girls. Immigrant girls. It was mostly the children of the well-to-do who had a childhood and an education."

"And then came Mother Jones. She became the mother to all the workers who were taken advantage of by the rich and powerful. She became our country's conscience."

She was on fire. Giving a sermon. Holding up images we all strained to see. A little boy with a finger missing. Skinny white children with sad faces blackened by coal. Young women who looked old in their twenties. Hollow-eyed men carrying tin lunch pails. And a picture of a fearless old white lady in a long black dress and hat leading a march down a dirt street.

When Valerie stopped talking I wanted to hear more.

The class was silent as she gathered her books and returned to her desk. And although I realized she'd seriously upstaged me, and maybe because of it, I led the way in giving her some well-deserved applause. Stan joined me. Then Linda and a few others. She'd outdone us all.

After class, we traded compliments. I asked her if she'd considered becoming a teacher, or maybe a preacher – she was that good. I didn't tell her how surprised I was. Who would've guessed?

~

When I entered Dr. Kelley's room after school that afternoon for *The Wildcat* editorial meeting I was greeted with raised eyebrows at my go-go girl outfit and white glasses, and some begrudging praise for my article. Of course, Mr. Bigshot Editor had to rub it in that Stan's byline wasn't on it.

"Wasn't that *your* story idea?" he said to Stan. "I thought you two were working together."

"We did," said Stan. "But Angie wrote the story, that's all."

Yvonne whispered something to Patsy as Mike and Rick exchanged suspicious glances.

"Anyway, we've got Homecoming this week," Mike said. "We're gonna need some good coverage of the game, the parade, the dance, the Homecoming queen."

Stan pretended he was falling asleep, snorting a couple of times like he was waking up from a nap.

"We'll get pictures of the queen and her court," Mike continued, ignoring him. "Yvonne, you interview the winner.

Rick, you do the write-up of the game."

"Yup," said Rick.

"Patsy, want to do a piece on the parade?"

"Sure."

"And then there's the dance. Jeez. We don't need a story on that, just pictures. Rick?"

"Sure. I can shoot everything. My girlfriend's always impressed when I'm the official photographer."

He laughed as he pointed an imaginary camera at Yvonne and Patsy.

"Now, what else for the next issue?" said Mike.

I cleared my throat.

"Well," I said, aiming for a confident tone, "I've gotten so much feedback about the military draft story, I'd like to do another one along that line. I was thinking of surveying senior girls on their career plans."

Dead silence.

"You know, how many of them are going on to college and professional careers after graduation, that kind of thing," I said.

"I like it," Yvonne said.

"Me too," said Patsy.

Rick sniffed. Mike looked at Dr. Kelley who nodded her head.

"Have at," Mike said, then turned to Stan. "And I suppose you have another brilliant story idea?"

"I'm gonna do a story on student activists," Stan said.

"You mean, like the Key Club?"

"No, I mean real activists – students involved in civil rights activities, antiwar protests, stuff like that."

Mike scowled. Stan cocked his head and sneered back.

"Sounds like a good story," Dr. Kelley said, "assuming you find any."

"Go for it," Mike finally said. "But I think we need to recruit some more reporters to cover stories students are interested in."

"Excellent idea," Dr. Kelley said.

I left the meeting quickly, already planning what questions to put in my new survey. But Stan called for me to wait up. I refused to look at him as we walked in silence along the corridor until he finally worked up the nerve to speak.

"You hate me."

"Correct."

Which caused him to wince.

"You were right, of course," he said.

I kept walking, wondering why he could be so broad-minded on the one hand and so narrow-minded on the other.

He held the front door open for me.

When we were about halfway to the street he latched onto my arm. He opened his mouth to say something and then closed it again.

"I've gotta go," I said, pulling away. An unpleasant feeling of déjà vu made me shake my head.

"Wait." He screwed up his face like he was in pain. "If I say anything again that…"

"You've had your three strikes and now you're out."

I headed for the bus stop.

"Angie…"

"Why should I talk with someone who treats me like his personal flunky?"

"I didn't mean to."

I shook my head as I reached the sidewalk where three Negro women were waiting. Maybe the same three who were there the last time I had words with Stan at the bus stop, I don't know.

"I was trying to do things like my brother does," he said. "He delegates, you know? He has people who help him. He doesn't do everything himself, know what I mean?"

I pushed my glasses up on my nose.

"I mean, there's this other guy who always handles printing the flyers they hand out. And several girls always make the sandwiches when they're having a rally. And..."

"Oh, Mr. Bigshot Antiwar Protester has the women folk do the cooking and cleaning!"

"Well..."

"Do the girls ever *speak* at SDS protests?"

"I..."

"You ever hear of male chauvinism?" I said, my voice getting louder by the minute. I didn't care that the three ladies were now staring. One of them was even nodding her head.

"I'm not a male chauvinist," he said.

"Actions speak louder than words!"

The lady who'd been nodding said "yes" softly.

"Okay, okay," he said. "You're right."

There was something about his face that reminded me of that bottle of Coke I opened at the last family picnic we had before Mom and Dad split up. We were sitting on an Army blanket at White Lake eating fried chicken, watching the glass-bottomed boat churn through the water, knowing Dad was moving out but trying to act like everything was normal.

I opened my Coke and there was no fizz. It was flat. And that's how Stan looked now, like he'd lost his fizz.

Fire must've been shooting from my eyes because he looked down as he rubbed the back of his neck.

"I'm willing to learn," he said. "And, one thing's for sure – I'll never open the door for you again."

"Ha!"

I was trying to decide whether to show him mercy when that little voice in my brain reminded me I didn't know any guys who thought of girls as their equals. The student body president was a boy. The presidents of the senior class, the junior class and the sophomore class were all boys. Girls were the class secretaries. Why would Stan be any different from all the other guys? At least he was willing to learn, as he put it. But I wondered how long it would take.

"You still hate me?" he said.

I made him stew a minute before I replied.

"It was temporary hate."

"That's a relief," he said, an earnest look on his face.

The Negro women edged closer to the curb as the bus approached. I didn't say good-bye, just moved forward as the ladies got on, one by one, and headed toward the back of the bus. I pulled my coins out of my purse and started up the steps.

"See ya tomorrow?" he said.

I glanced behind me as I reached the top step. He was standing a few feet from the door.

"Miss?" said the bus driver.

I dropped the change in the fare box and the driver closed the door behind me, pulling away from the curb. Through the windows, I saw Stan gazing after the bus.

Making my way down the aisle, I noticed the three Negro women had taken the big green seat in the very back. Their eyes were on me as they whispered to each other.

I'd always wanted to sit on that huge seat when I was younger. It stretched from one side of the bus to the other and looked like a fun place for a group of friends to ride downtown to go see a movie or something. But we all knew it was reserved for Negro riders, which is putting it delicately. Of course, they didn't have to sit in the back of the bus anymore. After all, this was 1966 and they could sit anywhere they wanted.

Steadying myself on the grab bar, I noticed a young black man in the third row, absorbed in a book. He wasn't sitting in the rear. Why were those middle-aged ladies sitting back there? I wanted to ask them that question. Where did Valerie sit when she rode the bus? That wasn't a question I ever had to think about. Because I was white.

There was a vacant spot beside the ladies – room for one more. Maybe I could sit there and strike up a conversation.

They saw me staring at them. Afraid they might think I was being disrespectful, I nodded my head politely and swung into an empty seat on the right side of the bus, about halfway between the front and the back.

~13~

Heaven on earth. That's what it was like the afternoon of the Homecoming cavalcade. The day was crisp and sunny, the sky so blue, it matched Craig's eyes. His red convertible had been waxed and buffed to a high sheen. I was so happy, I nearly busted out singing a Herman's Hermits song as we drove slowly down Haymount Hill while Dave and Sylvia waved red and white streamers from their perch atop the back seat.

Craig was a sight to behold as he gave me this oh, so masculine grin, one hand on the steering wheel, his blonde hair whipped by the wind.

There were other convertibles in the parade – a big burgundy Oldsmobile, a blue Plymouth, a yellow Buick and a navy Ford Fairlane – but none of them measured up to Craig's GTO.

The people walking along Hay Street weren't exactly cheering but we didn't care. We honked our horns and hooted and hollered anyway.

I'd gotten my replacement contact lens so I looked the part of a quarterback's girlfriend. I wore my new red alpaca sweater tied around my shoulders, a white button-up shirt and navy wool shorts with matching knee socks.

We cheered our lungs out at the bonfire too. It was gigantic! The flames shot at least twenty feet into the night sky. The pep band cranked out the fight song over and over. Craig joined his teammates as they were introduced to the crowd. The varsity cheerleaders did their bouncy-flouncy thing, showing off a lot of leg along with their saddle oxfords, proving they could spell complicated words like "Wildcats" and "victory." And we all did the bunny hop around the fire as the band played – you guessed it – *The Bunny Hop.*

When we pulled up at my house Craig leaped from the car without bothering to open the door. He jogged around and helped me out with a flourish.

"Your majesty," he said.

"*Merci.*"

"We're gonna win the game. I feel it! I feel it!"

Well, I could spell too.

"Give me an F," I shouted, fist in the air, "give me an E, give me another E, give me an L!"

"Hell, yeah!" he cried. "I feel it! I feel you!"

He picked me up and carried me around the front yard, swinging me this way and that. Then he let my feet go so I was standing in front of him. He slipped his arms around me.

"You looked so sexy beside me today in the parade," he said, pulling me closer.

He pressed his body against mine, kissing me full on the mouth. I tasted alcohol and wondered when that happened. He lifted my hair so he could kiss my neck. His other hand slid down my back and onto my butt. God, I was turned on, right there in my own front yard.

"My mom's probably watching through the window," I whispered, acutely aware of the streetlight shining on us.

He took a big gulp of air and pulled away.

"Sorry," he said.

He followed me to the front door.

"Okay, come down to the sideline at halftime tomorrow night so we can stand together for the coronation of the Homecoming Queen," he said.

"Right."

"Then after we whip their asses, I'll meet you in the cafeteria once I've showered and dressed."

"Gotcha."

"Promises, promises," he whispered.

I couldn't help but give him a coquettish look.

"Give me your hand," he said, seizing my left hand and pulling it toward him. "Gotta give you something."

He removed his class ring, then slid it on my ring finger, bobbing his head the whole time.

"Now, it's official," he said. "We're going steady."

My shoulders rose nearly to my ears as I grinned at him like a starstruck thirteen-year-old.

"I know it's way too big, but you can wrap the back of it with yarn or something."

He held my chin in his hand and kissed me. And he was off, bounding from the front porch onto the grass and doing fake football passes all the way to his car.

Once safely in my bedroom, I held out my hand, admiring the red stone and the ornate engravings that encircled the huge ring, feeling like a damsel who's found her white knight.

~

Friday morning when I walked into homeroom I was in a daze, looking forward to running my fingers through Craig's hair after the Homecoming dance that night.

Through the windows I watched as bright yellow maple leaves fluttered to the ground, mesmerized by the beauty of fall and the thrill of romance. Which, I realized, sounded a lot like the paperbacks my mom read before turning off her bedside lamp every night.

But then I saw Valerie standing by her seat, looking down with a horrified expression. I followed her eyes to a small wooden cross lying on her desk, charred black.

I immediately looked across the room where Jack and Billy, the Neanderthals on the far row, were talking as they looked innocently out the window.

"Dr. Kelley!" I cried.

People jockeyed for position so they could see as Dr. Kelley approached.

I pointed at the cross. Stan jumped on the seat of his desk to scan the room. Valerie stood motionless, as though any movement might trigger a booby trap. Bella Donna made insincere "tsk tsk tsk" noises.

"Stan, go to the office and tell Mr. Lancaster I need him right away," Dr. Kelley said. "And make it snappy."

We spent all of first period being interviewed by Mr. Lancaster. One by one, we were called into the hallway. When it was my turn, I reminded him of the earlier incidents. He thanked me with a dismissive nod of the head.

And that was it. Valerie held a book in front of her, but I didn't believe for a minute she was actually reading. Dr. Kelley asked her to stay after class. Stan and I hung back too.

"I need to talk privately with Valerie," Dr. Kelley said.

"You calling the police?" Stan asked.

"Mr. Lancaster doesn't think it's necessary."

"But..." he said.

"I need to talk with Valerie," she said, jutting her chin toward the door – a not so subtle invitation for us to split.

Stan and I waited in the hallway.

"I've got a bad feeling Mr. Lancaster isn't going to do anything," I said as people rushed by.

"Maybe *we* can do something," he said.

"Like what?"

"I don't know."

The bell rang.

"You free after school?" he asked.

"Uh, no."

"Right. I forgot. Homecoming." His voice was filled with disgust as he made a show of glancing at Craig's class ring on my hand. He quickly took his leave without a good-bye.

Although he said he never went to football games, calling them a waste of time, and he didn't have a lot of friends, Stan stayed abreast of school gossip. He knew I was dating Craig. And now he knew we were going steady. It was obvious he disapproved.

Valerie's eyebrows were furrowed like she had a headache when she finally came out.

"Valerie, I'm really sorry."

"Me too," she said, weariness in her voice.

"I..."

But nothing else came out of my mouth. She shrugged and headed to her next class. It was weird that the school day continued like nothing happened. And as weird as it was for me, it must've been terrifying for Valerie finding a burned cross on her desk.

~

Stan had apparently gotten over his huff because he was waiting for me later when I arrived in the cafeteria. He shadowed me through the lunch line.

"I saw Donna looking over at Billy and Jack this morning," he said. "Is she friends with those dingleberries?"

"I don't know."

"Maybe they talk about stuff."

As much as I disliked Donna, it was hard for me to believe she'd hang out with those losers. She fancied herself better than most people. She hobnobbed with football and basketball players. I'd seen her in Jerry Hinshaw's car in the parade, sitting so close, she was almost in his lap. She'd even tried to reel Craig in but he didn't fall for her bait.

"Maybe you could talk with her," he said.

"What're you – crazy? You don't understand. She's not gonna talk with me."

I put a sandwich and a banana on my tray.

"Well, then, let's find someone who's friends with her," he said. "I'm gonna do some P.I. work."

Then he sat down with some guys I'd never seen before. One of them was the boy who sat next to Billy and Jack in history. Okay, I could be a sleuth too. So I spent my lunch period pumping girls for information about Donna, using as much stealth as I could muster. I learned one morsel of information: Billy Wyler had a crush on Donna.

But the investigation would have to wait until at least

Monday because I had the biggest date of my life to get ready for.

I was in a huge rush to jump in the shower when I got home, but found a letter from Dad in the mailbox. I tore it open as I let myself in and headed for my bedroom.

Dear Angie,

I would enjoy reading your report on Susan Anthony. Maybe you could send me a carbon copy.

I know you were disappointed not to make the cheerleading team this year but my personal opinion is that it's a blessing in disguise. Focusing on your studies will be far more important as you get ready for college. Believe me, it'll be here before you know it! Maybe we can visit UNC next summer when I get home.

One more tidbit of advice from old Dad – watch out for the boys. Especially the ones who have a lot of romance on their minds. Deedee seems to want to get married and have children as soon as possible. But my impression is that you don't share her desire to rush into marriage and motherhood.

Everything's fine here. And being in Vietnam has at least one advantage. I'll get to see the USO Christmas show with Bob Hope, Phyllis Diller and Ann Margret!

Write me when you can. I miss you very much.

Love, Dad

Sounded like Dad was reading my mind. Or maybe he just had a good memory.

Mom and Dad got married right out of high school. Deedee was born about seven months later. What can I say? I guess they both had "romance" on their minds. But the romance didn't last. It was amazing to me that two people who had almost nothing in common couldn't see that from the beginning. Didn't she notice Dad was a homebody whose idea of a fun time was to read a book on the history of the English language and then discuss which words came from German, which from Latin and which ones came from French? And didn't he notice Mom was bossy and liked to put on party dresses and go dancing all the time? In their yearbook she was one of the prettiest girls at their high school and he was one of the best-looking guys. Maybe that was all that mattered back then.

I jumped in the shower, washed and rolled my hair and grabbed a snack to eat while I sat under the hair dryer for an hour. I also painted my nails red to go with my dress while I was getting my head baked.

When Mom got home from work, she tapped on the door while I was sitting in front of my dresser doing my makeup, giant rollers still covering my head like rolled bales of hay stacked in a field. She was smoking a cigarette.

"Mom! No smoking allowed!"

"You're such a sissy!"

She stepped into the bathroom, dropped her cigarette in the toilet with a hiss and returned. She sat on the bed behind me, looking at me in the mirror as I applied eyeliner.

"I can't do this with you watching," I said.

"Sorry, sweetie."

Uh oh. Bad sign if she was calling me sweetie.

"This won't take long," she said.

So I turned toward her.

"Angie, remember when we had the talk about the birds

and the bees?"

My eyes rolled of their own accord. I didn't mean to, I swear.

She looked at the ceiling and counted to ten under her breath.

"I want to give you something," she said, holding a small box toward me.

I took it but refused to look. I knew for sure I didn't want to know what was in that box. But I was about to find out anyway, whether I wanted to or not.

"I think we should pay a visit to my gynecologist next week so he can start you on birth control pills."

"What are you talking about?"

"Because I'm an established patient and because I do his wife's hair for free every week, including hair color and perms, he says he'll prescribe them for you, even though you're underage."

"I'm also not married, Mom. So it's against the law. I saw that on the news."

"Not if you need them for a medical condition. You know, horrible, painful, uncontrollable periods. He did that for Deedee too. I explained to him that the condition runs in our family. I have that problem too, you know. And the pill helps regulate the menstrual cycle and reduce the pain."

She pressed the palm of her hand against her belly and knitted her brows like she was hurting.

So that's how girls got the pill. There was an epidemic of painful menses going on at high schools and colleges across the country. Ha!

I turned my back on her and faced the mirror again, setting

the box on my dresser. I busied myself removing the rollers, tossing them one by one into an open drawer.

"You'll be sixteen soon and you'll be dating regularly," she said.

Each lock of hair fell from its curler, still holding the rounded shape.

"That handsome young man you're going out with tonight is obviously smitten with you. And I'm not blind. I see you're already wearing his ring."

I closed my eyes in embarrassment.

"For heaven's sake, Angie, I'm doing this for you!"

I could feel her eyes boring into me.

"Until we can get you started on the pill, I want you to use this spermicide," she said.

"Jesus, Mom! I'm not..."

"I didn't say..."

"I'm *not* going all the way with..."

"Angie! Don't raise your voice at me! I'm doing this for you!"

"Well, you can stop! I don't need this... this crap! And I don't need birth control pills! I'm not that kind of girl!"

"What kind of girl?"

"A slut!"

She stood beside me, looking directly at me instead of in the mirror.

"A girl who has sex is not a slut!" she shouted.

"Depends on who you ask."

"Well, I really, really, really don't want my daughter getting pregnant!"

"I really don't want to talk about this anymore. And I'm

not going to get pregnant!"

"Famous last words!" she huffed, hands on her hips. "I'd much rather have my daughter on birth control than having a baby in high school! I just wish the pill had been invented when I was your age!"

She probably didn't realize her words were an admission she would've preferred Deedee and I hadn't been born.

Of course, I knew that was how Deedee managed not to get pregnant. Everybody knew. That was part of the problem. If a girl was on the pill, word got around.

"Dammit," she shouted, "I expected you to thank me for being such an understanding, modern mother. But, no!"

She slammed the door so hard, my hat rack fell off the wall, dumping three hats on the floor. I squeezed my eyes shut and put my hands over my ears, trying to block out the sound of ranting and raving as she stomped through the house.

I remembered how Craig put his hands on me the night before in the front yard. My mother must've seen us. Must've. I opened my eyes and dropped that stinking box in the trash.

~14~

Game time. The stands were packed. The pep band was on its feet in the bleachers blasting the theme from *The Man from U.N.C.L.E.* The pounding of the drums vibrated through my shoes and up through my body.

The boys wore jackets and ties. The girls wore corsages on their suits or dresses. The florist delivered mine while I was arguing with Mom. It was a big white carnation with red and white ribbons, which looked lovely pinned to my red jacket.

There were lots of middle-aged alumni yukking it up, making fun of each other's pot bellies, lying to the women that they hadn't changed a bit since high school.

Then, as the stadium reverberated with a fast and furious rendition of the LHS fight song, the Wildcats burst onto the field through a giant paper banner in the end zone, ripping apart a fierce-looking cartoon Wildcat as the crowd went wild. We received the kickoff and proved we were one of the best high school football teams in the state. Of course, I use the term "we" loosely.

Janet looked like a little girl snuggling with her date. She came to Perry's armpit. Dottie was with a guy named Glenn who was almost as tall as she was. As for me, it was an honor to be the date of a football player for Homecoming, but that meant no boy to sit with during the game.

Janet and her Romeo sat on the "wherefore art thou" side of Dottie and Glenn. It was as obvious as her false eyelashes that Janet didn't want me to speak to Perry any more than was absolutely necessary. Like I'd even want to flirt with her new flame! I had a beau of my own. But even if I didn't, I wouldn't bat my eyes at somebody else's date. Not my style. Better to be the pursued than the pursuer. Although, come to think of it, that sounded kind of old-fashioned.

The game was exciting but I made sure I didn't cheer too loudly so I wouldn't work up a sweat. And I chewed some Juicy Fruit to freshen my breath as the clock ticked off the final seconds of the second quarter.

At halftime, the Wildcats led 14 to 7. The marching band took the field with its miles of braid, epaulettes and choreographed steps, playing an up-tempo version of *The Pink Panther* theme.

I rushed down to the sideline to stand beside Craig during the announcement of Homecoming Queen. He looked so fine in his uniform. The tight pants. The big pads. And I swear he was beaming as we walked arm in arm to our position on the field. He clasped my hand as we waited for the announcement.

"You look beautiful," he whispered.

"You too," I whispered back.

He chuckled and squeezed my hand.

The head of the varsity cheerleaders was picked Homecoming Queen, as expected. I couldn't help but notice Donna Touch-Her-Tosies in the stands watching everything, no doubt, fantasizing that she'd be wearing that crown in a couple of years. She was with Jerry Hinshaw, a starter on the varsity basketball team. Sitting with them was a girl I'd seen with her a couple of times – Myra something or other.

The only real bummer of the entire game happened late in the third quarter. Our star wide receiver took a hard hit and had to come out of the game. Another player, number eighty-three, was sent in to take his place.

I heard Perry and Janet talking on my right.

"Isn't number eighty-three one of the Negro players?" Janet asked.

"Yup. Don't know what the coach is thinking," he replied.

Our quarterback tried a running play which backfired, the Wildcats losing yardage. Then he threw a pass to the sub, who caught it. But as the black player hightailed it downfield, two defenders tackled him, slamming him hard to the ground. Which was bad enough, but then there was a frenzied pile-up. First, it was purple and gold jerseys. But then our red and white jerseys piled on as well. The referees blew their whistles, but they didn't seem to be in a hurry to force the guys to get up.

When the last player finally pulled himself up, number eighty-three didn't move.

"You don't ever wanna be at the bottom of a pile in football," Perry said. "Especially if your skin is the color of coffee grounds."

My muscles knotted up as we waited for the trainer to run onto the field from the sideline. He squatted down next to the boy, blocking our view.

"Maybe they yanked his balls off," Perry whispered, snickering.

Janet shushed him.

Finally, the trainer helped the guy to a sitting position and then to his feet, draping the boy's arm over his shoulder. He limped off the field to tepid applause from the crowd.

I let out a breath, realizing then that I'd been holding it.

Then another sub – a white kid – was sent onto the field and play resumed.

Craig got to see some action in the final minutes when the starting quarterback needed a rest. I pulled my cheerleader voice out of mothballs when he completed a fifteen-yard pass. We won the game 24 to 14.

~

The theme for the Homecoming dance was Island Paradise. Meaning the cafeteria had undergone quite a transformation. The walls were decorated with fake palm trees, seagulls flying over sandy beaches, surfers riding the waves, and even a volcano spewing lava. Real coconuts and seashells were scattered on the refreshment tables. A band played the Beatles' *I Want to Hold Your Hand* as I left my jacket at the door with some girls dressed in hula skirts and leis.

The first person I saw was Linda. My attempt at matchmaking had been successful. She was with Junior Tedious as a Turnip Duncan. But she looked happy, so maybe Junior wasn't all that bad. And I have to admit he looked better than I'd ever seen him – a few pounds lighter and his face wasn't as pimply. I hadn't noticed until then, but Linda had dropped a few pounds herself. Either that or she'd squeezed herself into a tight girdle.

I chatted with the other girls waiting for the Homecoming Heroes. When they arrived en masse, reeking of a dozen different kinds of men's cologne, Craig took time to slap the backs of his teammates as he introduced me to a bunch of them.

The punch bowl was his first priority. As he guzzled his second cup, Janet appeared, still attached to Perry like English Ivy climbing a loblolly pine.

"Perry, this is Craig Anderson," she said, not even acknowledging my presence.

Perry nodded.

"Perry's on the jayvee basketball team," she said, gazing up at him.

"Cool," Craig said, taking a swig from his cup.

The band went into overdrive for *My Baby Does the Hanky Panky*.

"All right!" Craig said, turning to me. "Time to dance!"

As he pulled me onto the dance floor, Janet started wiggling her butt, finally untangling herself from her date.

"If there's one thing I'm good at, it's doing the hanky panky," she called out.

Craig didn't even notice she was looking at *him* when she said it. But I did. And so did Perry, whose Adam's apple bobbed as she turned her Lolita look on him and boogied to the beat.

When the band finally slowed the tempo, I was ready. It was the same song the crickets sang for us that night at the lake – *When a Man Loves a Woman*.

Craig held me close as the lights dimmed. I savored the moment, trying to hang onto it as long as possible. I concentrated on his hand on my waist, the way his other hand held mine close to his chest, the way his body pressed into mine as he sang the words in my ear. I wanted to remember this moment. I had goose bumps and he knew it.

Then the band charged into *Devil With a Blue Dress*. And guess who materialized beside us like a loud, bossy blue jay.

Donna was way overdressed in a royal blue velvet, empire waist dress with silver accents. Her yellow hair was piled high in big swirls that must've taken an entire can of Aqua Net hairspray to cement into place.

"I just have to have one dance with your date, Angie," she said. "You don't mind, do you?"

I stepped back.

"It'll give me time to freshen my lipstick," I said.

Craig looked like he wasn't sure how to handle the situation. I just smiled and waved. *Devil With a Blue Dress*, indeed. She probably requested it. But it gave me a chance to catch my breath.

I scarfed down a cookie on my way to the ladies' room. Then, as I touched up my lipstick in front of a bank of mirrors, I heard two senior girls whispering to each other on their way out the door.

"I'd say it's mission accomplished."

"Well, we made it very clear they weren't welcome," the other one replied.

Looking around the cafeteria when I came out, I realized there wasn't one single black student there. I mentioned it to Craig as he handed me a cup of punch. He shrugged.

"How many Negro players are on the team?" I asked.

"Uh, three, I think. No, make that four."

I scanned the lunchroom again – very slowly this time – but there were no black players.

"Stop hogging the punch bowl, Anderson!"

It was Eddie, Craig's beefy teammate.

"Anything more interesting than Ginger Ale in it?" he said, winking first at Craig and then at me.

"Are you kidding?" Craig said.

"I can fix that," Eddie said, patting his chest.

Craig held his cup out and Eddie obliged by pulling out a silver flask and sharing some of its contents.

"Don't be so stingy," Craig said.

He looked over my head to make sure nobody was watching as Eddie tipped the flask a second time.

Craig gulped it down and pulled me back onto the dance floor as the band started into *I Can't Get No Satisfaction*.

~

If it hadn't been so chilly, it would've been fun to put the top down on our drive home. The sky was filled with stars, making the evening all the more romantic.

"You know what I'd do if we were older?" Craig said, not waiting for me to reply. "I'd take you to my apartment. We'd sit on the sofa by the fire and sip wine from long-stemmed glasses."

I giggled.

"Although, if you wanna know the truth, I'd prefer beer from beer glasses. And then," he said, giving me a slow, meaningful wink, "I'd kiss you."

I could see us in a New York high rise with a view of the Empire State Building, sitting on a sectional sofa holding fancy stemware filled with something golden and bubbly. Music would play in the background on a built-in stereo system, the lights turned down low so you could see the skyline through the windows.

"Whaddya think?" he said.

"*Tres romantique.*"

"Yeah. What you said."

He turned on the radio and pushed buttons until he found some soft music. And when we pulled onto a side street he turned off the engine, leaving the radio on.

There was a pounding in my ears as his lips touched mine. He kissed me like he craved the taste of me. But when he tried to pull me closer, the gear shift poked me and the music wasn't quite enough to transport me to his bachelor pad.

He sighed. "I need a larger apartment."

I had to laugh.

When we pulled up in front of my house, I debated whether to invite him in. Mom was out on a date with an insurance salesman named Walter. I knew I shouldn't, but I had to admit I really wanted to make out. So I asked him in. We popped the caps of two bottles of Coke and took our jackets off before sitting side by side on the couch.

"Did you see my article in *The Wildcat?*" I said, thinking we should at least make a little conversation.

"Mm-hm."

He set our Cokes on the coffee table.

"Well, what did you..." I said.

"It was great."

And without further ado, we were horizontal on the sofa and he was breathing loudly as he kissed my neck. There was a tingling that immediately spread over my entire body. But I didn't want him to think I was giving him the greenlight to put the pedal to the metal, so when I felt his hand moving toward my breast, I hit the brakes.

"Craig," I whispered.

"I just can't resist you."

Resist *me?* Wait a minute. It was *me* who couldn't resist *him!*

"You're just so gorgeous," he said.

"My mom will be home soon."

He popped up like a jack-in-the-box, pulling me up too. I smoothed my hair as he followed me to the side door.

"How about we drive down to the beach next weekend?" he said.

"The beach?"

"Just for the afternoon."

He sensed my fear, I guess.

"I promise not to lose control, okay?" he said. "Maybe a kiss or two now and then, though."

I couldn't help but smile.

"I'll pick you up next Saturday at ten."

He gave me a sweet kiss, holding my face in his hands.

"Bring a bathing suit and a towel," he called as he jogged down the driveway.

"It's October, dummy!" I said to myself as I closed the door, adjusting his oversized class ring on my finger.

~

Sunday morning I decided to reply to Dad's letter. After writing the story for the school paper, he'd been on my mind.

Dear Dad,

I'm sending you a carbon copy of my report on Susan B. Anthony. I never realized how awful it used to be for women. I know we've come a long way since then, but sometimes I feel like there's still a long way to go. I've noticed at school some boys act like a girl's place is behind a typewriter or a stove.

I'm also sending you a copy of the school newspaper. As you can see, I wrote a front-page story! Pretty cool, huh? I think you'll be interested in what the story's about too.

I went to Homecoming with a very nice boy named Craig. He's in the 11th grade and is a second string quarterback on the football team. It was a blast and the Wildcats won! But don't worry, I'm taking your advice to watch out for boys with romance on their minds. You're right – I don't want to end up getting married too young.

It would be fun to visit UNC when you come home. I'm thinking I might major in journalism.

Hope everything there is okay. I'm sure you'll enjoy seeing Ann Margret!! Every time I turn around she's on the cover of some magazine at the grocery store. And who wouldn't want to see Bob Hope and Phyllis Diller? Maybe she'll talk about Fang!

Love,
Angie

Obviously, I made sure not to say anything that would worry him. Sometimes parents didn't need to know everything.

~15~

Monday morning Linda ran up to me in the hallway, gushing about what a wonderful time she had on Friday night and how Junior wasn't so bad, really, and did I know he'd had a crush on me since sixth grade – gross – but he was over it now, and how she appreciated my engineering her very first date. And on and on. And while our mouths were running a mile a minute she asked me about Craig and I was so excited, I blurted out that he'd invited me to drive to the beach with him. Her eyes nearly popped out of their sockets.

"Just to have lunch at an oceanfront restaurant and stroll along the shore," I added, realizing I'd put my mouth in Drive without putting my brain in gear. "Please don't tell anyone, Linda."

"Of course," she replied.

Silly me! Stan caught me coming out of class and said he heard me telling Linda I was going to the beach with someone.

"I know it's none of my business, but…"

"That's right."

"Craig Anderson?"

I shifted the books in my arms.

He shook his head in obvious contempt. "You don't want to go to the beach with that jockstrap."

"Stan!"

"You do know he's one of the guys who tossed Valerie's book satchel the first day of school."

"No way."

"I saw him."

"You lie!"

"And mark my words, he'll end up a potbellied, middle-aged businessman who owns a chain of furniture stores and has a big house with a wife who drives a station wagon and stays home with their three kids when she's not doing volunteer work for some hoity-toity ladies' club."

I rolled my eyes.

"He'll probably also cheat on his wife with younger women," he said, flapping his hands in the air.

"You're so funny, you oughta be on *The Ed Sullivan Show* – right between the jugglers and the talking mouse."

"I'm serious. Very middle class. Definitely not an intellectual."

"And what's wrong with owning a chain of furniture stores?"

"Nothing, nothing. It's just that..."

"I can't believe I'm even listening to you. And, by the way, he did not throw Valerie's book satchel."

I took off like a running back charging downfield, threading my way between linebackers, Stan trailing behind me.

"Don't get mad, Angie. I'm just trying to..."

"Poke your nose into my business."

"True. But what do you two talk about?"

"None of…"

"*Do* you talk?"

I walked faster.

"I guess he likes to discuss ideas, current events?" he called after me, finally giving up the chase. "Bet he listens to bubblegum music!"

The ultimate insult.

"See you at lunch?" he yelled.

~

I couldn't keep my mind on geometry. While Mr. Owens blabbed on and on about obtuse angles, I was focused on a cute angle. Har har.

But what *did* Craig and I talk about? Did we talk? Of course we talked. We talked about… his car. We talked about… other guys' cars. We talked about music. I think. And he was definitely not one of the monsters who played hot potato with Valerie's book bag! Stan didn't know anyone on the first day of school. He just saw some guy who looked kind of like Craig, that's all.

The library was quiet at lunchtime. That's where I went to avoid Stan, the Insufferable Buttinsky. So I got a lot of work done on my second article for *The Wildcat*.

I had distributed surveys to senior girls about their plans for life after high school. And I'd interviewed half a dozen of them to get some quotes. About two thirds of them said they were planning to go to college and get a job afterwards. The rest said they were already looking for jobs and weren't going to college. But ninety-nine percent of them admitted they'd quit as soon as they got married, whether it was college or a job. Finding Mr. Right was their top priority. Ugh.

That night I called Janet to ask if she'd like to help me organize a girls' bowling night. She thought it was a great idea. I ran down a list of names, including Myra, the girl I'd seen with Donna at the Homecoming game. I called Dottie too. But I warned them not to invite *any* boys because I really didn't want them staring at my backside. I just wanted to have some fun with the girls. Of course, my real motive was to find out if Myra could tell us anything about Donna Holier Than the Rest of Humanity Jenkins.

I didn't talk with Stan again until I ran into him on my way out of school the next day. He was slouched on the concrete wall at the top of the front steps, leaning against one of the pillars on the front portico. He didn't look his usual fearless self. Beyond him, the maples were just starting to go bald on top, their yellow leaves still clinging to the lower branches.

We exchanged nods and he fell in beside me. Just as we reached the bottom step, a gust of wind scattered a pile of golden leaves, sending them skimming across the walkway in front of us, like a flock of migrating birds startled into flight.

"Billy's got a crush on Donna," I said.

"So, maybe he's trying to impress her."

"You find out anything from the guys?"

"Only that they like to joke about wearing white sheets."

"I'll be talking with a friend of Donna's. Maybe she knows something."

He nodded.

"Did you find any student activists to do your story on?" I asked.

"I'm thinking of asking Valerie if she'll let me interview her."

"Valerie?"

"Yeah, I was downtown the other day and I picked up a copy of *The Fayetteville Message* and saw her byline on a front page story about a civil rights rally at Fayetteville State College."

"But..."

"That got me thinking – she's doing her part, you know. Writing news stories on civil rights events. Hell, just coming to this school should be enough to qualify. She needs combat boots just to come to class."

"Maybe. But she won't do an interview with you. If there's one thing I know about Valerie, it's that she doesn't like the limelight."

My bus rumbled toward us.

"Well, I'll keep you posted if I learn anything from the girls," I said.

"Wait!"

He opened his history book, handed me a record and shifted from one foot to the other. It was a Bob Dylan 45 – *All I Really Want to Do*.

I wasn't sure what to say so I nodded at him, trying to remember the words.

The three black ladies I'd seen before weren't at the bus stop. Too early for them, I guess. So I boarded alone, dropped my money in the box and headed down the aisle, noticing the back seat was empty. I wondered what would happen if a Negro passenger boarded and saw me sitting back there. Just then a young black man seated at the halfway point glanced up at me for a fleeting second. But it was enough to put a halt to my little fantasy. I slipped into the seat across from him to let him know I was cool with sharing the boundary between the back of the bus and the front of the bus.

When I got home I listened to the song three times, staring at the record as it turned round and round, thinking of that look on Stan's face. Clever way to apologize. And it was true. We always had something to talk about. Although sometimes it was more like arguing than talking. So all he wanted to do was be friends with me, as Dylan put it. Fair enough.

~

The activist reports continued with Donna's pathetic profile of Elizabeth Cady Stanton, who I'd never heard of until her dad charged into class that day. She gritted her teeth as she talked about the woman who helped organize the first women's rights convention in the US a couple of decades before the Civil War, and later in life wrote the women's Bible that her dad despised. But what caught my attention was when she said Stanton was a long-time partner of Susan B. Anthony, that the two worked side by side for women's rights.

As I was leaving class Dr. Kelley returned my report on Anthony. I was stunned. She gave me a lousy "B." Written in red ink across the top: "Excellent report except you never mentioned Elizabeth Cady Stanton, who was Anthony's collaborator, friend, confidante and sometime speechwriter for decades. You must not have read enough."

I was bent out of shape for days, firstly, because of such a pathetic grade, secondly, because I'd missed the connection between the two women in my research, and thirdly, because

I was irritated the women Donna and I reported on were collaborators.

~

Friday night finally arrived and a big group of girls showed up at the bowling alley. The smoke was thick when we bee-bopped into the joint, giggling like a gaggle of sixth grade geese, shaking our tail feathers to Wilson Pickett's *Land of 1000 Dances* blaring from the speakers.

It was me, Janet, Dottie, Linda, Craig's sister, Sherry, and Myra – the girl I wanted to interrogate on the sly – along with a few other girls. We got two lanes right in the middle and made complete fools of ourselves, eating those wonderful greasy, bowling alley French fries and drinking way too much Coke.

We fed coins into the jukebox like we were playing slot machines, choosing songs by the Beatles, The Supremes, The Dave Clark Five and Mitch Ryder and the Detroit Wheels. We sang along with our favorite songs and danced to the fast ones against the backdrop of crashing bowling pins.

Every chance I got I sat next to Myra, who wore her auburn hair in a shoulder-length flip with long bangs, accentuated by dark cat-eye glasses. Finally, during our second game, I heard her mention Donna's name.

"I love to bowl," she said, "but some of my friends don't."

"Who doesn't like to bowl?" I asked.

"You know Donna Jenkins, right?" she said.

We nodded nonchalantly and hooted when Dottie threw another gutter ball.

"Well, Donna's too stuck up about some things," Myra said. "She thinks she's too good for bowling. Says it's working class."

"Working class?" Janet cried, stubbing out her sixth or seventh cigarette. She and Myra had at least one thing in common. They both smoked.

"Yeah, and she won't ride the bus downtown with us because she says the bus is low class!"

"I ride the bus all the time," I said.

"So do I!" said Dottie, prompting a wave of vigorous head nodding.

"Well, not Donna," Myra continued, exhaling smoke as she talked. "She says there's too many..." and she leaned forward, making the shush sign, her finger touching her lips, "niggers, as *she* puts it."

"You must be kidding," Dottie said. "That's how I go shopping, to the movies, jetcetera, jetcetera. I mean, what else are you supposed to do until you're old enough to drive?"

"Well, Donna has her mom or dad drive her," Myra said. "Her older brother used to drive her sometimes but he's in Vietnam now. She says they're gonna give her a car for her sixteenth birthday, so she'll never have to ride the bus. She says she wants a pink Mustang. And her parents spoil her so much, I wouldn't be surprised if she gets one."

"Lucky her," Janet said, blowing smoke rings in the air.

"Her and Billy Wyler," I said, trying to sound like I knew a secret.

"He's pathetic," Myra said. "Like a lovesick hound dog, forever trying to make Donna think he's strong and manly."

"Like, what kinds of things does he do?" I asked.

142

"Oh, if you only knew," she said, her eyes wide.

"Knew what?" Linda said.

Myra looked around and lowered her voice.

"Well, I don't know if it's true but he said he was gonna start up a junior KKK."

"You're kidding," said Sherry.

"But I'm not really sure Donna's all that impressed," Myra said.

"Has he attacked any black people?" I asked.

"He says he has, but I don't believe it, myself."

"It's your turn, Angie," Dottie yelled.

"Yeah, let's bowl!" Janet said.

I almost told them to skip my turn, wanting badly to continue the conversation but realized it might be rather obvious. So I stifled my frustration and stepped to the line, bowling ball in hand. Of course, the girls razzed me without mercy.

"Aim for the gutter, maybe you'll hit a pin," Janet yelled.

"We're watching your butt cheeks, Angie," Dottie shouted.

I smirked at her over my shoulder, then gave it my best shot. Amazingly, I knocked down nine pins. The tenth one wobbled and wobbled and finally fell. I jumped up and spun around, clapping my hands, sticking my tongue out at my friends.

"Pure luck," Dottie shouted.

Everyone laughed as I pranced back to our seats so Janet could take her turn. But then I saw a group of boys watching me and cheering. It was Craig and three of his buddies.

"Angie!" he called out.

His friends punched his shoulders and laughed. They

looked like they'd had a couple of beers. I thought about my tight pants and how my boobs must've bounced when I was jumping up and down.

"We gonna bowl or we just gonna stand around drooling?" one of them yelled.

"I'll be there in a minute," Craig said.

The other guys dragged the loudmouth away to rent some shoes.

"Hi, Craig," Dottie chirped.

"Hi, Craig," Linda said.

"Hi, Craig," the rest of the girls sing-songed together.

He laughed and motioned for me to come closer so the others couldn't hear.

"I just had to see you," he said.

"How'd you know I was here?"

"Sherry told me. Let's have a Coke together."

"Well, I've gotta leave soon," I said. "And I want to finish my game."

"Oh, okay, no problem. I understand. Ladies bowling night."

He didn't look hurt but I wondered if he'd expected me to jump at the chance to be with him.

"You've got great form," he said, giving me another one of his slow winks.

I bobbed my head like I was proud of my strike and waved at him as I headed back to my lane.

"Ten o'clock tomorrow morning," he called after me.

Dang. I hoped the girls didn't hear. I couldn't believe I was actually driving to the beach with him in the morning.

~16~

My alarm clock rang at seven-thirty – early for a Saturday morning. But I had to give myself plenty of time to get ready. Contacts, hair, makeup, clothes. I dropped my bathing suit and towel in my beach bag although I couldn't imagine where we might go swimming. The ocean would be freezing.

Part of me had hoped Mom wouldn't let me go – maybe twenty-five percent – saving me from myself, you know. What a birdbrain I was. She thought it was a fantastic idea. She said the Andersons were a good family, that Craig's dad owned car dealerships in Fayetteville, Raleigh and Chapel Hill. That he was on the board of directors of Lafayette Savings and Loan. She said his mom was an officer in the Junior League and they lived in Vanstory Hills. It was like she'd done research on them or something.

When she might've had time was a mystery to me. She was working long hours opening her second beauty salon. When she was home, she spent a lot of time on the phone, which was always available now with Deedee away at college. Mom wanted to open more salons – a whole chain of them – so she could make enough money to buy a house in the hoity-toity section of Haymount or Vanstory (neighbors with the Andersons, maybe,) have a maid and fly off on an island vacation twice a year with one of her middle-aged beaux. I suspected that mothering kind of got in the way.

I put my sunglasses and a pack of Juicy Fruit in my pocketbook and glanced at my watch. It was 9:30.

Mom blew smoke at me as I walked through the kitchen door. She was at the table having her usual breakfast of coffee and cigarettes. My mother, the beauty shop tycoon, looked like a witch. Her "does she or doesn't she?" orange hair stuck out in all directions. She hadn't washed off her makeup before she went to bed and now, with mascara and eyeliner smeared around her eyes and her ratty pink robe hanging open in front, she resembled a bedraggled Lucille Ball in one of her ridiculous TV skits.

"Take this with you," she said in her husky morning voice, setting a small, familiar box on the table. She coughed several times like the effort of talking was nearly too much for her.

I started to say something but thought better of it. What good would it do to get into another argument? I poured Corn Flakes and milk in a bowl and orange juice in a glass.

"Read the directions while you're eating," she said, tapping long ashes from her cigarette into a bean bag ash tray.

She groaned as she rose from her chair, then shuffled from the kitchen, leaving the ash tray, her mug, the newspaper and the box on the table.

I dumped the nasty contents of the ash tray in the trash, then put it on top of the fridge and ate my cereal in silence, staring at the blue box. Pulling it across the table, I looked more closely. "Applicator included." Jesus. I didn't want to know any more so I dropped it in the trash on top of the stinking cigarette butts.

At ten o'clock, on the dot, the doorbell rang.

Craig gave me a lopsided grin as he took my beach bag.

"I'll have her back no later than nine, Mrs. Finley."

I jerked my head around in horror. I didn't want anyone to see my mother in all of her Sunday morning glory. But she had a blue towel wrapped around her hair like she'd just stepped from the shower and she was wearing a flowing blue paisley caftan. Her face was clean and she had lipstick on. I was so relieved.

"Please call me Barb," she said, doing her best to overcome her smoker's voice. "Angie, I put some emergency supplies in your bag, just in case. You know, suntan oil, Solarcaine. Now, *bon voyage*! That's French for have fun at the beach or something like that."

She giggled and gave us a syrupy look, then disappeared into the hallway.

"Great day for a drive," Craig said, ushering me through the front door.

The sun was so bright, it hurt my eyes. As soon as we settled into the car I slipped on my sunglasses.

"You look like a movie star," he said.

He put his shades on too and revved the engine. Funny, I did feel like I was in a movie. Hadn't I seen one with Robert Goulet driving through the countryside in a convertible singing a love song to an attractive brunette beside him?

We stopped to get Cokes and drove down Highway 87.

Even with my sunglasses on, I was blinded by the light. The sunshine was so intense and the shade was so deep, I couldn't see into the shadows until we actually drove into them. Which was kind of surreal. But it didn't slow Craig down. He seemed to know every inch of the road.

"Isn't it beautiful?" I said.

The trees were cloaked in brilliant colors that looked more like stones sparkling in the sun – ruby, amethyst, topaz. We took a curve on the outskirts of town and raced through a shower of dazzling leaves that swirled around us. It was one of those moments when you think the world is a magical place, full of promise, and you're just happy to be alive.

After a bit, he turned the radio on but I was determined to talk. And I wanted to talk about something in particular.

"Remember the first day of school?" I said.

"How could I forget?"

He pumped his eyebrows and turned the volume down a bit.

"Did you see those boys playing keep-away with the book satchel?" I said.

"Not till those dipsticks hit me in the face with it. I was talking with a friend and – wham! – it landed right here."

He touched his right cheek bone.

"Really?"

"Yeah. Pissed me off," he said.

"I couldn't believe they were being so hateful."

"I couldn't believe they were allowed out of elementary school," he said.

And then he turned the volume up as *Rescue Me* came on.

There was never any doubt in my mind that he might be in the same phylum as Billy the Bacteria. Craig would never do something so cruel. But if he'd just held onto the bag and not thrown it back to the pond scum. Of course, who was I to talk?

"What's your favorite group?" he asked, raising his voice over the music.

"Well, the Beatles, for sure, and maybe Bob Dylan, although he's not a group."

He replied with a prune face.

"You don't like Dylan?" I asked.

He shrugged his shoulders and continued tapping his fingers on the steering wheel.

"Why not?" I said.

"His voice stinks, for one thing."

"And for another?"

"I like something with a beat. Like this one."

He cranked the radio even louder, singing along as Fontella Bass belted out the chorus of *Rescue Me*, looking over at me and bobbing his head.

Just like Robert Goulet and the brunette.

We got to Wrightsville Beach at lunchtime and ate in a restaurant with a postcard view of the ocean. White tablecloths, the aroma of garlic sauce, sea oats on a low dune swaying in the breeze just outside our window. And beyond that – the deep blue sea.

My eyes were drawn to the long, straight edge of a cold front running diagonally across the sky, driving a wall of clouds before it, as though the air itself was a bully forcing the clouds into submission.

There were only a few people walking along the sand. No bathing suits in sight. The beach was a different world in October.

It was obvious Craig wasn't new to The Docksider, giving the host his name and commenting that he'd reserved his favorite table overlooking the beach. He ordered for us after asking me if I liked seafood. The waiter brought us mounded platters of fried shrimp, boiled shrimp, crab cakes, scallops and raw oysters.

"I knew you'd look sensational by the ocean," he said, giving me this satisfied look.

I fluffed my hair for him.

"So, where you planning on going to college?" I said.

He dipped fried shrimp in cocktail sauce one after another and popped them in his mouth, answering as he chewed.

"UNC."

"Have you decided on a major?" I was determined to talk.

"Oh, I don't know. Probably business administration." He dumped an oyster down his throat.

"You planning on being a tycoon?" I teased.

"Yeah, something like that." And he laughed.

"What kind of business?"

"Well, Dad says he could help me get started in something. Maybe a car dealership."

He dipped a crab cake in ketchup and took an enormous bite.

"You like cars, don't you?"

"Man, I love cars," he said, his words all tangled up with crab meat.

"What's your favorite car?" I asked, taking a sip of my iced tea.

"I love my GTO. And I wanna buy a Dodge Charger."

"You like antique cars too?"

"They're okay. But they're too round, you know? Except possibly I wouldn't mind owning a miniature '57 T-Bird.

Hard-top convertible, of course."

Maybe if I just shut up he would ask me something. I put a boiled shrimp in my mouth and watched the whitecaps on the waves as they rolled in. He kept feeding his face.

"You never told me what you thought of my article on seniors and the draft," I finally said.

"Article?"

"You know, in *The Wildcat.*"

"Oh, yeah. It was good."

He was still inhaling food like he hadn't eaten in days.

"Well, when you're eighteen, will you register for the draft?" I asked.

"Sure." He covered his mouth and burped. "Scuse me."

"What if you have to go to Vietnam?"

"I'll get a college deferment. Then Dad says he can get me into the National Guard. That way, I won't have to go."

Simple as that.

"You want any more?" he said, eyeing my plate, still mounded with seafood.

"No, go ahead."

Finally, when both platters were empty, he leaned back in his chair and grunted as he patted his stomach.

"Man, that was top notch," he said. "How about some dessert? They make good strawberry shortcake."

Not having any brothers, I found it hard to believe a guy could eat that much food in one sitting. I tried to picture him with a pot gut. But after seeing his belly button that day when he was in his practice jersey, it was inconceivable.

"Maybe later."

I thought we'd walk along the beach after lunch, but

instead, we drove half a mile south to a high-rise apartment building called Oceanside Tower.

"We own an apartment here," he said.

He carried my bag while I tried to pretend I wasn't about to have a heart attack.

We rode the elevator to the fourth floor and entered an apartment like what you might see in *Ladies Home Journal*. I didn't let on how impressed I was. There was a large kitchen with a bar separating it from a dining area and living room. The living room opened through sliding glass doors onto an oceanfront balcony. Off to the left were a couple of bedrooms and bathrooms. It was decorated in a very beachy keachy way – conch shells and starfish on the tables, driftwood paintings on pale blue walls, rattan furniture with aqua cushions and Berber carpeting the color of sand.

"Let's walk on the beach," I said, desperate to get out of there.

He laughed like he was reading my mind.

We walked south, facing into the wind. I zipped up my jacket, rolled up the bottoms of my khaki pants and stuck my hands in my pockets. It felt good to dig my bare feet into the sand. Craig walked on my left and draped his arm over my shoulder. The sound of waves breaking on the shore was exhilarating.

"I love the beach," I said.

He moved his hand from my shoulder to my waist and tugged me closer.

"Your hair is so pretty, blowing around like that," he said.

"So's yours."

Well, that's all he needed to pull me down on the sand. I

squealed as we rolled over and over. When we stopped, we were lying side by side on our backs. He pulled me to him and presented me with a perfectly delicious kiss that gave me tickle bumps all down my right side. There was something magical about his kisses. Each one made me want another.

But I jumped up and ran, daring him to catch me. He grabbed me around the waist, lifted me up and swung me around, pretending he was going to drop me in the surf. I screamed, holding onto his neck, afraid he might actually toss me into the freezing water. He found my ear with his mouth and made a loud, smooching sound. Then he yum-yummed all over my neck until I thought I would die.

That's how we made our way back up the beach until we reached the boardwalk to the apartment building. A grey-haired couple got on the elevator with us and gave us disapproving stares. That sobered me up a bit.

As soon as we entered the apartment, Craig said it was time to go for a swim.

"Yeah, right," I said.

"There's a heated pool," he said. "So slip on your swimsuit. You brought one, didn't you?"

I nodded.

"Cause I'd be crushed if you had to swim in the nude," he said, laughing at his own cleverness.

He picked up my beach bag and handed it to me, gesturing for me to use the master bedroom while he changed in the other one.

I should've brought my one piece. I felt naked in my pink bikini. And my white terry cover-up didn't cover very much.

When I opened my door, he was standing there in royal

blue swim trunks, looking for all the world like the Greek god, Adonis. He was tan and his chest and shoulders were muscular, but not too muscular. There could never be a more perfect body. No lie. It made me shiver just looking at him, which caused my cheeks to overheat.

The small, kidney-shaped pool was in a building adjacent to the apartment tower. Large windows on the ocean side let the sunshine in but fogged over so you couldn't see out. Blue and white tiles decorated the floor around the pool and there were several large plants in the corners. It was nice and warm and empty, every sound echoing under that high ceiling.

Craig swam a few leisurely laps while I leaned against the side in the shallow end. How nice it must be to have money, I thought. We came to the beach once a year in July and stayed two blocks from the shore in the leaky old Belview Motel, complete with a Coke machine by the office door and mold behind the beds. "You're at the beach!" Mom would say. "What more do you want?"

He swam up to me, putting his hands on my waist as he looked down at my breasts. He had to be the most unselfconscious person I'd ever met.

"That is one fine bathing suit," he said.

"Likewise, I'm sure."

And then he pulled me tight against him and nibbled my earlobe.

"Craig," was all I could say.

He sang The Dave Clark Five's *Do You Love Me,* soft and low.

"Do you love me?" he whispered.

'Oui.'

I came to my senses as we rushed to the apartment, towels wrapped around our wet bodies. He picked me up once we were inside the door and carried me into the big bedroom with the ocean view, laying me roughly on the bed. I was in a full-blown panic. I'd said 'yes,' although it wasn't 'yes' to sex. He might've seen it differently, though.

"Craig," I said, my voice sounding shrill.

He ignored me, grabbing my beach bag and tossing it on the floor where it landed upside down. That's when he saw the little blue box. Only a blind person couldn't see the word "Spermicide." I must've had a stricken look on my face because he raised his eyebrows.

"Emergency supplies?" he said, quoting my mom.

I clamped my eyes shut, trying to figure out what to do. It was one thing to make out with your boyfriend. Quite another to bring contraception along like you were ready to give up your virginity. Contraception that your mother stashed in your beach bag!

He laughed as he dried me off with his towel. And before I knew it he was lying with me on the bed, kissing me. One kiss led to two. Two kisses led to three. Three kisses led to four. With fingertip accompaniment.

"Craig..."

"Just let me touch you."

"But, Craig..."

"Angie, I love you."

He kissed my neck and a part of me wanted him to keep going.

"Angie, let me make love to you," he whispered.

"I can't."

I meant for my voice to be firm but it sounded weak.

"Angie, Angie..."

He unhooked the back of my bikini top. I gasped, wrenching myself to a sitting position, holding the top against my chest.

"Stop," I cried.

"Angie..."

I got up and headed to the bathroom, taking in his reflection in the mirror as I shut the door. His eyes were closed and he was shaking his head. I leaned against the door and wondered what Susan B. Anthony would do if she were alive in 1966 instead of 1866? Probably take birth control pills.

I wasn't sure if he'd ever want to see me again, but he was sweet on the way home. At the door, he held my chin in his hand and kissed me as if to say "tell me when you're ready."

We stared into each other's eyes, but said nothing. I was so confused about everything that I started crying as soon as he was gone. I cried until my eyes were swollen.

~17~

When Stan called the next morning I was still in bed. Mom told him I was sleeping, thank goodness. But I was awake. My sleep had not been what you'd call restful. I kept dreaming of Craig. I dreamed we made love on the beach, waves washing up around our naked bodies. God.

What greeted me when I looked in the mirror on this morning after our very close call, was red, puffy eyes and a big pimple on my nose. Gross.

I swiped a Coke from the fridge while Mom was in the shower and hid out in my room reading a novel I was supposed to do a report on. But Stan didn't give up. He called again around eleven and Mom told him I was up.

Why was he calling me? To find out if I'd had sex with Craig? I told Mom I didn't feel like coming to the phone. But she opened my door and ordered me out.

"I'm not your answering service!" she barked.

I stood next to the telephone chair in the hallway. My mother called it the gossip chair. It was like a little mahogany desk with a small attached table for the phone. It's where Deedee practically *lived* before she went to college, sitting there for hours gabbing with one boyfriend after another, then immediately calling her girlfriends to brag about her boyfriends. She knew everyone's phone number by heart and had the fastest dialing finger in the south.

But I refused to sit down. I had nothing I wanted to gossip about.

"Stan, I'm sorry, but I'm not feeling good today."

"Catch a cold at the beach?"

From where I was standing I could see the framed eight by ten of Dad in uniform on my bedroom wall. Watch out for boys with romance on their minds, he said.

"Did you and Craig have... a lot to talk about?" he said.

I pulled the receiver from my ear and looked at it, hearing Stan's voice in the distance. "Angie? You there?" I gently placed the handset back on the phone.

It rang again right away but I ignored it and returned to my room, closing my door softly. Mom knocked a moment later and yelled "phone!" But I stretched out on my bed and stared at a crack in the ceiling. A while later the ringing started again. Mom tapped on my door, then opened it and poked her head in.

"A boy named Stan asked me to please tell you he's sorry. That he didn't mean to act like an ass on the phone."

I didn't go to school on Monday. And I didn't go on Tuesday. I told Mom I was sick to my stomach – that I was having diarrhea. I guess she figured it was okay if I stayed home a couple of days.

But I really was sick. I was suffering from mortification aggravated by humiliation. I'd agreed to go to the beach with Craig when I knew what he had on his mind. I'd done some heavy-duty flirting and then... well, I'd said no. He must think

I was a cock tease. I'd heard boys use that expression. Now I knew what it meant.

Everyone would think I'd gone to bed with him. Why had I blabbed to Linda? And Stan must think I was a hussy. I wished I could move to Hawaii. No one would know me there and I could get a fresh start as a surfer girl.

I watched *General Hospital* and *As the World Turns* and read Anne Brontë's *Tenant of Wildfell Hall* for two days, recommended to me by Dr. Kelley. Which left me scratching my head that Helen could fall for such an egotistical, self-indulgent cheater.

But on Wednesday morning, Mom barreled into my room at seven o'clock, singing *When the Red Red Robin Comes Bob Bob Bobbin' Along*. It was so painful, I had to cover my head with my pillow.

"You've stayed home long enough!" She yanked the covers off, forcing me into a fetal position. "I'll pour cold water on you if I have to."

I rubbed my eyes.

"Up!" she thundered.

"But, Mom, I didn't wash and roll my hair last night."

"Tough toenails."

"But..."

"Get moving!"

Just when I thought I'd gotten rid of her, she poked her head back in the door and said, "Oh, and by the way, I'm picking you up after school to go see my gynecologist."

I sat bolt upright. "No!"

"Yes!"

"I'm not spreading my legs for anyone!"

She slammed the door and I collapsed on my bed. No way I was going to get birth control pills. And I couldn't go to school. I was shamefaced.

~

When I walked into history class, I could feel everyone's eyes on me, despite my best efforts at invisibility. My hair was pulled back in a big clip. I was wearing a brown corduroy jumper, a long-sleeved tan turtleneck, brown tights and loafers. I wanted to be warm. And brown.

Stan leaned over. "You get my message?"

He sounded so sincere, I must've really looked sick. I nodded.

There was a tap on my shoulder and I looked around. Valerie whispered to me – something she never did in class.

"You okay?"

I faked a smile.

"Is that sand on her shoes?" Donna whispered to no one in particular.

Someone snickered. I pretended not to hear, cringing as I realized the whole school knew.

Dr. Kelley lectured on slavery. But I couldn't concentrate. About halfway through class, a folded note appeared in front of me.

"I'm starting an SDS chapter. Want to join? Stan."

I couldn't remember what SDS stood for but I did remember his brother was involved. Let's see – draft card burnings, protests. I watched him out of the corner of my eye. He had his hands behind his head with his elbows sticking up in the air, leaning back in his seat. His hair, as usual was a tousled mess. Still, he didn't look insane or anything.

When the bell rang, he was at my side as soon as I reached the door.

"You can help me recruit members," he said. "I want to have an organizational meeting on Saturday."

"You're nuts."

Valerie caught up with us and walked on the other side of me.

"Hi." That's all she said, but she stared at me like she was looking for a rash on my face.

"Angie and I are starting an activist group," Stan told her. "Wanna help?"

"Angie and I?" I said, coming to a halt.

They both did an about face and Stan gave me an uncertain half grin.

"What kind of group?" Valerie asked. "I mean, what's your cause?"

"Starting with the war, then maybe civil rights, you know," he said.

"Might want to pick just one," she said, like she knew what she was talking about.

"Wanna join?" he asked her.

"Watch out, Valerie," I said. "He's talking about burning draft cards."

She raised her eyebrows and puckered her mouth like she was impressed.

"Gotta go," she said.

"Me too," I said.

"No draft card burnings," he said as we walked away. "Peace rallies, that's all."

~

At lunch, Janet and Dottie sat down across from me. They tried to stare me into speaking but I held out. Janet fired the opening salvo.

"You look like shit."

Dottie slapped her on the shoulder.

"Well, she does," Janet said.

"Thanks."

"And I hate to say it, but that's one nasty pimple," she said.

"Janet!" Dottie cried.

Janet inspected my failed attempt to hide it with makeup.

"Well?" she said.

"Well, what?" I said.

"You know."

"No, I don't know."

"Don't play dumb."

She and Dottie both fixed their eyes on me, their elbows on the table. I took a bite of my chicken salad sandwich and shook my head. Should I say anything about the beach? Whatever I said would be broadcast to the whole school.

"Did you go?" Dottie asked, eyes bulging.

They waited. I chewed.

"Come on!" Janet demanded.

"We're your friends," Dottie said.

"Yes, we drove down to the beach. And no, he did not score a touchdown. Is that what you want to know?"

"A field goal, maybe?" Dottie whispered, leaning closer.

"We had lunch overlooking the beach at a nice restaurant."

"And?" Janet said.

"And we walked along the beach."

"And?" Dottie said.

162

"And we went swimming at an indoor pool."

"And?" they both said.

"And then we drove home."

"Is that all?" Dottie said, her voice so high-pitched, she sounded like a 45 record played at 78 rpm.

"Hell, no, that's not all," said Janet.

Dottie giggled and hugged herself.

"You're right, Janet," I said. "That's not all. We also kissed a couple of times."

She wagged her head sarcastically like she didn't believe a word I said.

Dottie ate a forkful of her stinking sauerkraut and I took a bite of my apple. They both watched me chew until I couldn't stand it any longer.

"Listen," I said, "I'm actually telling the truth."

"Uh," Janet said, turning her head as though she were looking for assistance, "can we get a lie detector over here pronto?"

"Well, you can believe what you want to but we did *not* go all the way."

They looked at each other and rolled their eyes.

Of course, I wasn't about to tell them how close we came.

It was then that I saw Craig approaching our table. The chicken salad sandwich did a little cock-a-doodle-doo in my stomach.

"Hey, good lookin'," he said, sitting in the chair next to me.

"Hi," I said, straining to avert my face slightly so he couldn't see my zit.

He nodded at Janet and Dottie, after which they snuck secret glances at each other.

"Wanna go out Saturday night?" he asked me. "I got me a hot rod Pontiac and a twenty-dollar bill."

"Sure, Mr. Williams."

"You got my meaning," he said, grinning. "I'll pick you up at seven."

Then he hopped up and left me sitting there with my face flushing fourteen shades of red.

"Be still, my beating heart," Dottie gushed.

"Mr. Williams?" Janet said, watching him walk away like she wanted to get her hands inside his shirt.

"Old Hank Williams song," I said, not bothering to explain the lyrics of *Hey, Good Lookin*. Now didn't seem like the best time.

As if the inquisition by Janet and Dottie wasn't enough, Stan got in my way as I was leaving the cafeteria, still consumed with his activist group idea.

"First meeting Saturday, eleven o'clock, the Coffee Cup," he said.

I motioned for him to move.

"First project is planning a peace rally," he said.

"You're..."

"Crazy, I know," he said, his eyes blazing with conviction.

"I was gonna say loco."

~

When the final bell rang that afternoon I made myself scarce so Mom couldn't find me for that dumb doctor's appointment. I escaped through the gate behind the girl's baseball field and caught a different bus that dropped me off a couple of miles from my house. I took some back streets to my favorite little creek. It was a long walk, but I was in no hurry to get anywhere, that's for sure. The leaning oak would be the perfect place to hide.

The afternoon sun filtered through the branches, giving the woods a dappled look, like a watercolor painting in bronze, copper and gold. It was lovely and peaceful. Sitting on the streambank, it was as though the water gurgled and whispered just for me. Like the birds in the trees twittered for my ears only. Gradually, my muscles unknotted. I closed my eyes, turning my face to the autumn sun, and took a slow, deep breath.

I finally calmed down enough to realize I could withstand my mother's melodramatic tirade when I got home. There was no doubt in my mind she would crank up the volume. But there would be no trip to the gynecologist for birth control pills. Not now, anyway. It would be like admitting that having sex was a priority – a necessity – in my life. But I knew in my heart there had to be so much more than the physical thing. Though I had to admit it was easier said than done. I sympathized with the pea hen mesmerized when a peacock flashes his magnificent tail. That's how I felt when I was around Craig. Like some primitive hormonal urges took control of my brain.

My puffy eyes had finally stopped stinging and I figured I'd survive the whispers and the gossip. But I decided to make my next date with Craig a team sport. At lunch the following day I would suggest we get a group together and go bowling. That way I wouldn't have to be alone with him. Because about ninety-seven percent of me didn't want to tempt fate.

~*18*~

Attending Stan's so-called organizational meeting wasn't exactly my idea of a happening event. I had just about decided not to go and make my apologies later when my mother insisted on watching the evening news while we ate supper Friday night. We sat on the couch, TV trays in front of us, eating tuna casserole. And although I liked Walter Cronkite as much as the next person, watching the news made me sigh a lot. Nearly every story was about the war.

That night's broadcast was no different. There was a report on the continued bombing of North Vietnam. A report on one of our planes being shot down, its crew missing, maybe dead. A story about Defense Secretary Robert McNamara saying even though US forces were killing thousands of Viet Cong every week, the north seemed to have an endless supply of troops. And a scary report about one American Army unit trekking through the jungle, getting shot at, suffering from heat exhaustion as a helmeted correspondent interviewed the men, then talked directly into the camera. All so depressing.

During a cigarette commercial, Mom added to the melancholy mood with a bit of family news.

"Your cousin Merle got his draft notice this week," she

said, lighting up another Winston.

"I thought he was going to college."

"Aunt Doreen said she begged him to enroll so he could get a deferment, but Merle wouldn't listen."

"He just graduated from high school this spring."

"Doreen couldn't choke back the tears on the phone."

Mom's casserole was suddenly even less appetizing than usual. I excused myself, telling her I'd be back to wash the dishes when the news was over.

I looked at Dad's portrait on my wall as I closed the door to my bedroom, hoping to block out the unpleasantness blaring from the TV. In the photo, he wore his khakis and a garrison cap, his Airborne insignia visible above one pocket, his name above the other, along with various patches and ribbons. Serious, handsome and young. It was taken when he was about twenty-five. He reminded me of the soldiers I'd seen on the news.

~

When I showed up at the café Saturday morning, Stan had two strange boys with him. And I do mean strange. The tall, skinny one smelled sour, like his jeans had been hung on the clothesline on a humid day and taken too long to dry. He winked at me while we were eating. The short one with dirty hair focused his eyes on my chest like he was using X-ray vision to study my nipples.

We discussed having a peace rally over Christmas break. But I felt like we were fifth graders pretending to be adults. Stan wrapped up the "meeting" after about thirty minutes. Not exactly a promising start to the local SDS chapter.

The Dirty Old Men in Training headed to the bus stop

while Stan and I walked the other way. There was a nip in the air so I stuck my hands in my jacket pockets to keep them warm.

"Maybe we could offer free refreshments," he said. "That might get more people to come to the next meeting."

I really wasn't into it.

"Could you head up the refreshment committee?" he said.

"The refreshment committee?" My voice was full of indignation.

"Just kidding, just kidding." And he laughed.

I punched his shoulder and let him walk me home, pulling my collar up against a tail wind that seemed to push me along.

For once, Stan didn't talk much. Maybe he sensed my mood. But when we arrived at my front door, he handed me another record. Peter, Paul and Mary's *Blowin' in the Wind*.

"When I stepped outside this morning I knew this was the perfect day to give you this," he said. "Written by Bob Dylan. From one activist to another."

"I'm not an activist."

He shrugged.

I'd heard the song on the radio, of course, but I'd never given it much thought. In the privacy of my room, I listened closely. Dylan raised a good question: how many deaths does it take till you realize it's too many?

~

At my suggestion, Craig invited three of his football buddies and their girlfriends bowling with us. He was a pretty good bowler – he broke 200 once and came close twice. The pins exploded every time his ball slammed into them at a hundred miles an hour. I didn't humiliate myself too badly.

His friends were nice enough, although their girlfriends weren't quite as friendly. The guy named Eddie – the one with the flask at the Homecoming dance – kept *accidentally* backing into me. So I knew something was up even before he followed me to the ladies' room, waiting for me to come out so he could tell me that when Craig and I broke up, he wanted to take me out. What a dipstick, I swear!

We dropped by The Torch drive-in afterwards and Craig put his arm around my waist and walked me around the parking lot, showing me off. Which, of course, didn't endear me to all the other girls there, having been in their shoes not so long ago. We finally got back in his GTO and laid rubber squealing out of the parking lot.

"All the guys are jealous of me," he said, his head bobbing like one of those dime store doggies you see in the rear window of an old Chevy with fender skirts.

He gave me that seductive look of his with one hand on the wheel. I wasn't sure I liked playing the role of athlete's trophy.

"I want to apologize for going too fast at the beach," he said, suddenly serious.

I'd been dreading talking about it, hoping maybe he wouldn't say anything.

"Craig, I might've..."

"My fault," he said.

He took my hand in his and we drove to Rowan Street Park. As soon as he cut the engine, he turned toward me and I knew what was coming. So I opened my door and made a dash down the hill to the giant blue concrete whale I used to play on when I was younger. I jumped on the tail and ran up onto the whale's back, which was about six feet off the ground. Craig was right behind me. It hadn't occurred to me until that moment that it was a Sperm Whale. Jeez. Of course, there was only one way down and he was blocking my path.

"Gotcha," he said.

We were both laughing there in the dark, standing on that big goofy whale. He reached out and I let him take my hand and pull me close.

"I've been dreaming about your velvety skin," he whispered.

He kissed my neck and I tingled all up and down my left side. He could tell how turned on I was because he kissed me there again.

"Craig," I whispered.

"Hm?"

"I'm freezing."

"Well, come on then. I know how to fix that."

He led me carefully down the slope of the whale's back and fins. Then we ran back to his car and jumped in, breathing hard.

I thought he was going to crank the engine but he leaned over and planted a kiss on my mouth, caressing me through my sweater. I definitely wasn't cold anymore.

He moved his hand higher. I pushed it away.

"Craig," I whispered.

My nose began to run. It's like he had a one-track mind. Couldn't we have fun doing something together and not visit Grope City?

Suddenly an animal noise just outside the car brought the proceedings to a halt. Then a blinding light flashed in our faces. Craig jerked away from me, fumbling in his pocket for his keys. A tapping on my window made me nearly jump out of my skin. A man's voice called out.

"Is he hurtin' you, miss?"

Holding my hand in front of my face, I strained to see through the light shining directly in my eyes. We heard the sound again close by. But now that I didn't have Craig panting in my ear, I recognized it as an animal bleating.

"It's the goat man," I cried, rolling down my window several inches as Craig finally found his keys.

"Are you all right?" the man said, a little white goat behind him.

He was the extremely elderly black man who lived in a shack on the edge of the park. All the kids called him the goat man because he kept a few goats and some chickens. He entertained the children by quoting whole passages from the Bible.

"I'm okay," I said.

Craig started the car but then changed his mind, killing the engine, opening his door and charging around the front of the vehicle toward the old man.

"What the hell are you doing threatening us like that, you old..."

"Craig!" I cried, opening my door and jumping out as well.

"It's a good thing I don't carry a gun," Craig snarled.

"Craig, calm down! Everything's fine."

The little white goat bleated again, stepping closer to the old man.

"Looked like the young lady was in some torment," he said in a soft voice.

"I'm fine," I explained. "Although I understand how you might've thought that. I'm sorry we scared you."

"Scared *him!*" Craig barked. "He's the one who scared us!"

"Everything's all right," I said, then turned again to the goat man. "Thank you for your concern. We're going home now so you can have some peace and quiet."

He looked into my eyes as though he needed to confirm whether I was telling the truth, then nodded.

"Come along, Blossom," the old man said to his goat, walking down the hill into the park, lighting his way with the flashlight, the goat trailing behind.

Craig shook his head and cursed under his breath as he walked around to the other side of the car and climbed in again.

"Let's go!" he snapped, revving the engine.

We drove home in silence. It took that long for him to calm down.

When we pulled up at my house he walked me to the front porch. I wished Mom had left the porch light on, but she probably turned it off on purpose to give us privacy.

"Too bad the stupid goat man butted in," he said. "Get it? Butted in?"

He chuckled and I tried to.

Then he pressed his hard body slam up against mine as he sent his tongue on a mission to find my tonsils.

"We're perfect together," he whispered when he came up for air.

He kissed me non-stop for an eternity, his hands kneading my buns like they were loaves of bread dough. When it was over I escaped inside, collapsed against the door, turned the lock and wiped my mouth with the back of my hand. I was so tired. And, to top it off, my chin was raw from beard burn.

Before finally drifting off to sleep, I remembered my first visit to the park when I was eleven. I was standing with some other kids, listening to the goat man talk about his life. He told us he was a hundred years old. I don't know if he knew his real age, but if that was true, then he was born during the Civil War. He *looked* a hundred years old, that's for sure, his dark skin wrinkled up like a raisin, with thinning white hair and half his teeth missing. But he had a warm voice and kind eyes.

~

And then I had a stroke of luck. Bad luck. I came down with mono. I slept pretty much night and day for the next few weeks, feverish and limp. Right through Thanksgiving. When I was able to stay awake, Mom got all my books and assignments and I tried to catch up. I was almost feeling well enough to go back to school when Christmas break arrived. It was the season of the year when my birthday got lost in Christmas debt.

Craig called several times. So did Stan. Valerie called. And Dottie. Even Dr. Kelley called to see how I was doing. Janet called too, but I wished she hadn't.

"So, who gave you the Kissing Disease?" she said. "As if everyone doesn't already know."

I was too tired for a witty comeback.

"According to the grapevine, your boyfriend is a walking germ factory."

"I've gotta lie down now, Janet. Thanks for calling."

Before she could say another word, I hung up, wishing I'd been asleep when she called. Although I'd already wondered how I contracted mono, I had tried not to lay the blame at Craig's feet. Or his lips.

I did lay down after her call, drained from that short conversation. One thing about it, I could take a nap anytime because I had zero visitors. Although I certainly understood why no one wanted to come near me.

Craig flew out to Colorado with his family on a ski trip for the holidays. He dropped off a Christmas present on the front porch one day without even knocking. It was a gift set of Estee Lauder cologne and bath oil. Must've been his favorite scent. And he had the florist deliver a huge bouquet of flowers.

Stan was going to California to spend Christmas with his brother.

Deedee came home from college but it was more than just a Christmas vacation. She broke the big news that she was engaged and was quitting school temporarily. We all knew that meant permanently. She was planning a September wedding, after Dad got home, and was already shopping for a wedding gown. Her fiancé played tackle for the Wolfpack and was graduating with a degree in business administration and a job selling pharmaceuticals with his dad's company. She said his parents were making a big down payment on a starter house for them in Raleigh. Three bedrooms, two baths, central air conditioning and wall to wall carpeting.

It was hard to say who was prouder – Deedee or my mother, who I heard telling someone on the phone "one down, one to go."

Two days before Christmas the doorbell rang and Deedee tapped on my bedroom door.

"A boy is here to see you," she said.

Looking in the mirror, I saw this homely girl with stringy hair and dark circles under her eyes looking back at me.

I washed my face and put Erase under my eyes and some light lipstick on. I took my baggy pajamas off and threw on some jeans and a blue turtleneck sweater, although my jeans were now unfashionably loose. I wiped my glasses off and pulled my hair into a ponytail on my neck. Then, as casually as possible, I walked into the living room where I found Stan sitting on the couch with a flat present beside him.

He jumped up when he saw me, his forehead pinched with worry.

"Sorry I look so awful," I said.

"You don't look awful. I like the way you look in glasses."

No point in arguing when someone lied through their teeth to be nice.

"Would you like a Coke?" I said.

"Sure."

I brought us each a bottle and we sat facing each other – him on the couch and me in the gold armchair with my feet tucked under me.

"You feeling better?" he asked.

"Yeah, thanks. I'm ready to come back to school. So, how's the peace rally shaping up?"

"I decided to wait a while."

He took a swig of his Coke like he didn't really want to talk about it.

"I thought you were in California with your brother," I said.

"I'm leaving tomorrow. But I wanted to give you this first."

He handed me the present which was wrapped in pink

birthday paper with a big yellow bow on it. Obviously a record album.

"Open it," he said.

I tore the paper off. Simon and Garfunkel.

"Thank you, Stan."

I studied the album cover.

"Want to listen to a song or two?" he said.

He used his thumbnail to slice the plastic cover open, then put the album on the turntable. We listened to the whole thing, front and back – all the moody songs of *Parsley, Sage, Rosemary and Thyme*. I stared out the window at the colorless sky, then at our nubby teal carpet, then at the white ceiling. Every once in a while, I snuck a glance at Stan who had closed his eyes after the first few songs. It was so odd to see him look so quiet and peaceful.

When it was over, neither of us wanted to break the spell so we just sat quietly. Finally, he cleared his throat.

"Happy birthday," he said.

"How'd you know?"

He raised his eyebrows several times like Groucho Marx. Then he jumped up and put on his jacket.

"I'll write you," he said.

"You not coming back?"

"I'll be back in time for school to start."

His mouth smiled but not his eyes. He paused at the door and looked at me like he was going to say something else but chewed his lip instead. He wished me a quiet "Merry Christmas" as he trotted down the steps.

I watched through the window as he walked down the street. Tiny snowflakes swirled in the air, melting as soon as they touched the ground. It was a snow tease. The kind of snow I used to get excited about when I was little, thinking I'd soon be outside building a snowman or sliding down a hill on a piece of cardboard. But now I knew it was just a light flurry and that it wouldn't stick.

I played the album again in my room, lying on my bed, staring at the ceiling until I fell asleep, dreaming about sewing a shirt with no needle work.

~

Christmas break was long and tedious. I did get my driver's license, though. And to show off, I drove when Janet, Dottie and I went to see *The Sand Pebbles*. They called Mom's car a tank on the way downtown, making fun of me when the car conked off at a stoplight because I let the clutch out too fast. Then they drooled over Steve McQueen all the way home. But I didn't feel much like talking after the movie – it reminded me too much of Vietnam.

One day, just to get out of the house, I walked to the Coffee Cup, took a booth inside and drank coffee while I tried to read. I glanced up after a few pages and saw Mitch Davidson looking at me from the front door. He waved and headed for my table.

"What're you reading?" he asked, sliding in across from me.

"Oh, something for English class."

He took the book and made a show of flipping through it.

"Ah, *Pride and Prejudice*," he said, handing it back. "All I can say is: I'm glad things have changed since then."

"Yeah, but there's still too much focus on finding a 'suitable husband.' Of course, back then, most women didn't have much choice."

He ordered coffee and a Danish from Granny, the Speedy Waitress and we talked about Austen's book. I have to admit, I was surprised he'd read it.

"So, what're you reading lately?" I asked.

"*On the Road* by Jack Kerouac. Heard of it?"

"Nope."

He proceeded to tell me how stimulating the book was, about the search for revelation, about the travels of these intellectual friends. And about the "improvisational" writing style.

"Of course, it's more of a guy book," he concluded with a shrug.

I asked him about his college plans and he told me he was going to UNC and planning on becoming a filmmaker. Which I thought was fascinating. I'd never known anyone who talked about *making* movies. I only knew people who talked about *starring* in movies. He talked about directors like my girlfriends talked about actresses. I felt like I'd been transported to an adult planet.

During his second cup of coffee he asked about me. Fancy that.

"Well, the only thing I'm sure of is – I don't want to get married. At least not in the next fifteen years."

Now, why I said that is beyond me. It just popped out. But it was true. It had been bubbling up inside me as I read *Pride and Prejudice* after having read about Susan B. Anthony. Like her, I didn't want to lose my identity and become Mrs. Arthur

P. Somebody. But why I admitted this to Mitch was a mystery. Maybe my brain had weakened while I was sick.

He nodded, although I wasn't sure if he approved or just didn't know what to say. And I realized I didn't care. Which was nice. Maybe that's why I'd been so honest.

"It's refreshing to hear a girl say that," he finally said.

"Do you think a girl and a guy can just be friends?"

"We're friends, aren't we?"

"*Mais oui,*" I said. "Of course."

"Anyway, my policy is to let the girl make the first move," he said.

Which was a novel idea.

Then we talked about our families. His mom and dad were both college professors. That's where he'd watched a lot of movies – I mean, films – at college film nights.

When I told him about my family he said my mother sounded like a modern, liberated, divorced businesswoman and my dad sounded more old-fashioned because he didn't believe in the war but was over there anyway.

Our stimulating conversation lifted my spirits, leaving me feeling somehow more fulfilled just for having talked about things that mattered.

When I got home, I was surprised to find a letter from Stan. He said he was having a good time, that his brother was talking a lot about the antiwar rally SDS was helping to organize in New York. And then there was this part:

I told Nick I really want to go. And he said he's cool with that. He even said he could drive me. I asked him if we could take someone with us and he said that would be okay as long as they have permission. Do you think your mother would let you go?

Now I knew for sure Stan was off his rocker. What was it he said? I'd make a good activist? Well, I had other trains to catch. Even though I wasn't interested in holy matrimony, that didn't mean I wanted to spend my entire life working for a cause like Susan "Do-Gooder" Anthony and have no personal life.

~19~

Mom gave me some new clothes for Christmas, which I chose the week before at Belk's and she wrapped and put under the tree. I missed the Christmases of my childhood, back when my dad was there and we ripped red and green paper off our presents and were surprised at what was inside. On the other hand, I got to choose my own stuff. And it was a good thing I did my own shopping – my new duds were a size smaller than what I'd worn before I got sick.

She also set up an appointment a few days later for me to have my hair frosted again so I'd look good to start school in January. When I said I wasn't sure I wanted to frost it again, she lit into me.

"After being sick with mononucleosis, you need all the help you can get, missy. And you need to make sure you wear makeup every day. Your complexion still looks kind of yellow."

So, even though I had my doubts, I ended up spending the better part of an afternoon in the beautician's chair.

The first day back at school, I wore my new pink alpaca sweater, matching knee socks and a grey and pink plaid skirt. I also wore extra Erase under my eyes so the dark circles wouldn't show. Maybe it was my imagination, but everyone seemed to be giving me a critical once-over.

When Valerie walked into homeroom, she was wearing a new wool coat. It was tan, knee length with large brown buttons down the front. Not exactly what you'd call fashionable, but I complimented her on it anyway.

"I got it for Christmas," she said quietly.

She carefully unbuttoned it and pulled her arms from the sleeves, but continued sitting on it, kind of like an open-faced turkey sandwich.

"Don't you want to hang it up?" I said, remembering how she sometimes hung her old coat on a hook by the door. "Especially since it's new."

She shook her head and gave me a little shrug.

"So what else did you get for Christmas?" I said, trying to smooth over what seemed like an awkward moment.

"This was my present," she said, then changed the subject. "Are you feeling a hundred percent now?"

"Pretty much."

The bell rang and Dr. Kelley welcomed everyone back from Christmas break, giving me a special nod. Then she had a couple of students distribute mimeographed sheets listing upcoming reading assignments and test dates while she launched into her lecture on disenfranchisement of former slaves after the Civil War ended – poll taxes, literacy tests – all that unpleasant stuff.

I had to stay after class to talk with her about making up some missed assignments. She handed me a list and just as I turned to leave, she spoke again, keeping her voice low.

"Valerie's coat was stolen from her locker a few days before Christmas break," she said.

Which made my arms and legs feel weak for some reason.

"I talked with her parents," she continued. "They're concerned about her safety. Mrs. Franklin said they thought she might get the cold shoulder going to school here, but they were surprised she's been harassed like this."

"So that's why she got a boring new coat for Christmas," I said.

She nodded. "Do you have any idea who's been…"

"Billy and Jack," I said.

Her second period students began pouring into the room. She nodded at me in dismissal and I headed for geometry class.

Craig was waiting for me at lunchtime when I entered the cafeteria, tanned and handsomer than ever, if that's possible. He carried my tray and sat with me for a few minutes until it was time for him to go to class.

"Man, I missed you," he said, giving me a hungry look without getting too close.

"How was the skiing?"

"It was a blast. Listen, are you over… I mean, are you feeling better?"

"Yep."

"You sure?"

"Don't worry," I said. "I'm not contagious anymore."

So he asked me out and I said okay. But as soon as he left, I thought about that word "contagious." He was worried I'd give *him* mono? As much as I hated to admit Janet might be right, I was pretty sure I'd gotten it from Craig. After all, he was the only boy I'd kissed.

Then Stan plopped down across from me.

"You get my letter?"

"Yeah, that was really nice of..."

"Well?"

"Well, what?"

"The protest," he said.

"Listen, Stan, there's no way my mom's gonna let me go gallivanting off to New York for a humongous antiwar rally."

"What if my brother calls her?"

"No offense or anything, but I don't want to go."

"Of course you do! Hell, it'll be the experience of a lifetime! And, besides, we need all the people we can get!"

"I'll write my dad and see what he thinks."

He cocked his head and screwed up his mouth, but didn't argue. I'd gotten him off my back. At least temporarily.

~

That was the week the pressure began about the high school beauty pageant. Mom wanted to take me to Raleigh to shop for an evening gown. She said I absolutely had to have the perfect dress. Deedee said one thing she'd learned was not to have your hair done at the beauty shop, that the judges didn't like beauty shop hair. Which pissed Mom off something fierce, considering herself a beauty parlor magnate.

Everyone had to have a sponsor. Each homeroom elected two girls to represent the class. On Friday, Donna and I were elected from Dr. Kelley's homeroom, leaving me with mixed feelings. On the one hand, it might've been helpful if I hadn't been elected at all. That way, I wouldn't have to worry about it. On the other hand, I would probably have been shamefaced at losing out again. Plus, I really didn't like being on any team with Donna.

Janet finagled a sponsorship from the Art Club. Dottie was

representing the Future Teachers Club, which was too funny. I think she joined just for that purpose. And suddenly everyone got more than a little secretive about where they were shopping.

But I was jolted back into reality that afternoon as we changed classes for sixth period. I saw a knot of kids gawking at something in the locker room. I joined the craning necks and saw what looked like the white-hooded head of a Ku Klux Klansman staring out at us from inside a locker. It took me a minute to realize it was Valerie's locker.

The evil suspects were nowhere around. I saw Donna whispering with a girlfriend and Linda giving Junior an uneasy look.

Valerie was absent the next day and Dr. Kelley looked positively grim.

"Class, you all know by now what was found in Valerie's locker yesterday," she said. "I must say I'm exceptionally disappointed and angry that Valerie has been threatened like this by a fellow student." She shook her head slowly. "And, as you all know, this is not the first time she's been harassed. This kind of hateful behavior has no place in our school. No place in our country." She swept the room with her eyes, going up and down every row, looking into each student's eyes. "I want to ask anyone who knows anything about it to please see me privately. I promise any information I receive will remain completely anonymous."

I looked over at Billy and Jack, innocent as baby snakes. Just as I turned back toward Dr. Kelley I noticed Donna stretching and turning her head this way and that. I peeked out of the corner of my eye and saw Billy wink in her direction.

It was at that moment I decided I had to do something, even if it was wrong. Something more than going to the principal.

I spent most of my lunch break in the girls' bathroom. And when Donna and her friends finally came in, as they always did before going to class, I was waiting in the far stall. I joined them in front of the mirrors, leaning over one of the sinks like I was sick. Donna ignored me.

Closing my eyes, I put my hand on my stomach. As they sauntered toward the door I straightened up.

"Donna?"

She turned.

"I hate to bother you," I said, "but I need some help."

"I don't wanna be late for class."

She and the other girls snickered.

"It won't take a second," I said, sounding as pitiful as possible.

"Go on," she told her friends.

As soon as the door closed, I ditched the sick act and got right to the point.

"I think Billy and Jack are terrorizing Valerie."

"And why, pray tell, are you sharing this with me?" she said, heading for the door.

"Because I need your help."

"My help?"

"Yeah. To catch them."

She raised her nose in the air and sniffed loudly several times, turning her head this way and that.

"You been smoking grass?" she said.

"I think they're trying to impress *you*. So if they're building up to something bigger, you might get in trouble too."

She gave me a cold stare.

"Of course, any time a Negro family moves into a white neighborhood, they're bound to make enemies," she said.

That threw me for a loop. But I didn't let on that she'd broken the news to me.

"I don't know anything about those morons," she said. "But if I should learn anything, I'll be sure to let you know."

She was mocking me. But I was prepared.

"You know, it's possible I might be able to get you some mileage out of turning those creeps in."

She tapped her foot, a bored expression on her face.

"What if you were painted as a heroine for a story in the school paper? Or even the Fayetteville paper?" I said.

She looked at the ceiling.

"I mean, it might make some boys very interested in you," I said.

"It also might make some boys hate me for the rest of my life. I might even end up with a white sheet in *my* locker."

She tilted her head back and looked at me with her hooded Elvis eyes before doing a one-eighty and leaving me standing there.

~

When Craig picked me up Saturday evening he looked sharp in his red and white letter jacket. He raved about my new mohair sweater and about how I was sure to be in the Miss LHS court. He said everyone knew I was the prettiest girl at school but the judges always crowned a senior so I'd have to wait to be queen. I was embarrassed just listening to him.

We went to a pizza place on Bragg Boulevard where we met Dave and Sylvia. I insisted on a double date, just to be safe.

Right after we sat down Sylvia said in a low voice: "Isn't that guy over there on your football team?"

She glanced at a Negro boy wearing a small white apron clearing tables.

"Yeah," said Dave.

"Isn't that number eighty-three?" I said. "The one who got injured in the Homecoming game?"

"Yep," Craig said.

"What's his name?" I asked.

He shrugged.

"Freeman," said Dave. "Coach calls him Freeman."

The guy picked up his tub of dishes and hustled right by us on his way back to the kitchen. Neither Craig nor Dave said a word to him.

"Coach mainly calls him bench warmer," Craig said, sharing a laugh with Dave.

I wasn't listening as the conversation veered off in another direction. I was thinking that maybe Craig was the kind of guy who wouldn't do anything to hurt a black person's feelings. Then again, he wouldn't say or do anything that might be construed as being on their side either. Like saying "hello." But I couldn't help but recall our unpleasant encounter with the goat man.

After the guys stuffed themselves sufficiently, Dave suggested we all go to his house to play cards. He lived in a newer home in Vanstory Hills, one of the fashionable neighborhoods my mother had on her "to covet" list. As soon as we walked in, it was obvious nobody was home.

The living room resembled a pictorial in *Better Homes and Gardens* magazine. It was all creams and whites with bright splashes of color. An abstract painting in orange and blue hung above the modern sectional sofa. There was a fire already burning in the fireplace, which gave the room a warm glow and made me suspect going to his house wasn't a spur-of-the-moment idea.

We did get cards out and we did actually play a game of Canasta at the kitchen table. But that was so we could drink Coke spiked generously with some kind of whiskey that Dave poured with his back to us. It wasn't long till he and a giggling Sylvia disappeared down the hallway, his arm draped over her shoulder.

Craig fixed us two more glasses of Coke and whatever, then led me to the couch in the living room. He sat down beside me and clinked his glass against mine, making a toast.

"To the most beautiful girl I know!"

He put his arm around me and we gazed at the crackling fire. He gulped from his glass and told me to drink up. I took a sip but I was already feeling more than a little sideways.

"So, tell me about your ski trip," I said.

"The snow was perfect," he said, kissing behind my ear.

"I've never been skiing. It must be exciting."

"Almost as exciting as kissing you."

He set our glasses on the lamp table and put his hand on my breast, giving me this steamy French kiss. He was picking up right where he'd left off the last time. It was his hurry-up offense.

"Craig…" I said, pushing his hand away.

"I missed you, Angie."

"Time for me to go home."

But his eyes were so seductive, I felt like I only existed in those blue pools of lust.

"Kiss me," he whispered.

I hesitated.

"Kiss me," he repeated.

I closed my eyes and kissed him, my head swimming. It was like trying to resist eating chocolate-covered cherries at Christmas. I knew I shouldn't eat them because I'd get fat and my face would break out, but they were so sweet and delicious, it was like torture not to. And that's how I felt with Craig.

"I need to go home now," I whispered.

He rose from the couch, pulling me with him.

"Angie, you love me?"

I didn't respond. So he wrapped me in his arms and swayed back and forth burying his face in my hair.

"Yes, you love me. And if we love each other, it's okay if…."

"Craig, it's like that's all you can think about."

"I can't help it. I want you so bad."

~

Once I was safely in my bedroom I tried to sort out my feelings. Maybe Craig was just more honest than I was. Maybe I was too hung up. One thing was becoming crystal clear: he wasn't going to be satisfied until he scored.

I imagined the next time we went out. We'd go to a movie

or something and then it would be a rerun of the popular game show "Squeeze That Breast." He was wearing me down. Getting me used to the idea bit by bit. Before you know it, his hand would be down my pants. And I felt like it was my fault. I'd given him the go-ahead right from the start. If I'd just said no when he asked me to drive down to the beach with him. And if my mom hadn't stuck that spermicide in my beach bag. God!

Confused. That's what I was. Just being around him made me feel like my body was buzzing. I really liked dating Craig, except for the dread that welled up inside me about the wrestling matches.

~

Monday morning Donna made history by passing me a note.

"Meet me same time, same place."

She came into the bathroom alone, wearing a form-fitting olive green turtleneck sweater dress. And she didn't beat around the bush.

"I've been thinking about what you said," she began. "And there's one thing you've got that I want."

"Such as?"

"Such as Craig Anderson."

I couldn't hide my surprise. But she went on like we were discussing a business deal.

"If you dump him in such a way as to open the door for me… well, then, just maybe I might be able to dig up some dirt on the two gentlemen in question."

My mouth may have hung open slightly, I'm not sure.

"You know where to find me," she said and flounced out the door.

~20~

Hanging in front of my closet, my new evening gown was a sight to behold. Pale blue-green, with a bodice fitted down to the hips and a flared skirt. Mom said it would show off my figure better than a baby doll style and would look more *au courant* than dresses with a regular waistline. It had a scoop neckline that Mom and Deedee agreed was cut just low enough to show a little cleavage, but not too much. My mother had paid dearly for it. But she was satisfied there wouldn't be another dress like mine in the Miss Lafayette Senior High pageant.

Thirteen-year-old me would be doing cartwheels of joy at the prospect of preening in that dress in front of the whole school. But sixteen-year-old me was filled with doubt. I was certain that Indira Gandhi was never in a beauty contest.

Craig's class ring sat front and center on my dresser. It would look tacky with my evening gown. It was actually a relief to have the big heavy thing off my finger.

I decided to wear my hair in my usual style, down on my shoulders, which annoyed Mom, who had made appointments for all three of us at her new Tallywood salon.

Around eleven that morning, as I was washing off the facial she'd given me, the phone rang. It was Stan.

"I'm working on some signs today advertising the New York protest," he said. "Wanna help?"

"Today?"

"Yeah. I could pick you up."

"Well..."

"I got my driver's license."

"Oh, happy birthday," I said.

"Yeah, I've got the car for a little while."

"Well, I'm kind of busy today. You know, the beauty pageant."

He made a noise somewhere between a snort and a groan.

"I have to..." I began.

"You have to spend the entire day primping so you can put yourself on display tonight like a piece of meat at the butcher shop."

I twirled the phone cord around my finger.

"Why on earth would you want people to think of you as a pea-brained beauty queen?" he said.

"Beauty queens aren't..."

"It's so irrelevant! There's so much important stuff going on. Have you watched the news lately?"

"I..."

"Do you know that asshole, Senator Stennis, is calling for stepped up bombing of North Vietnam? *And,* he's asking that a hundred thousand more American troops be sent over there! A hundred thousand more! So that even more Americans can be killed. And you're busy gussying yourself up with a ton of makeup so you can compete with other girls to see who's the prettiest?"

He was practically yelling. I didn't know what to say. He

was right. Why *was* I in the beauty pageant? Because it was expected. It was the normal thing for a girl to do. Like wearing nail polish, lipstick and high heels.

"Sorry, Angie. I didn't mean to yell. It's just that beauty pageants are so….you know…"

"Old-fashioned?"

"Moronic."

There was an uncomfortable silence.

"I sure have a knack for running off at the mouth," he said.

More silence.

"Okay, okay," he said. "I'm a self-righteous know-it-all."

"I've gotta go," I said.

"Angie, wait."

More silence.

"See, it's like this… everyone already knows you're…" he said, sounding really uncomfortable. "I mean, you could shave your head bald and… well, I mean, you don't need a crown, you know, to prove anything."

I heard a thud through the phone like maybe something hit the wall on his end.

"How about tomorrow?" he asked.

"Tomorrow?"

"To work on the signs."

"I don't know."

"I'll pick you up at two." And he hung up before I could say another word.

So I was in a sour mood as I headed to the shower. I'd been struggling with my feelings ever since school started in the fall. Why would I want to parade around on stage while judges rated my hair, my smile and my bra size?

Standing in front of the mirror in my blue terry robe and glasses, I stared at my reflection. It would take about fifteen minutes to wash and condition my hair. I'd have to spend twenty minutes rolling it, an hour under the hair dryer, then leave it in curlers for another half hour to cool down before styling it – my usual routine. What a ridiculous waste of time! Why would any human being want to spend that much time on hair?

Pulling some brown locks from beneath the frosted strands, I studied myself in the mirror. With glasses and no makeup I realized how like *me* I looked. I wondered what Craig would say if he could see me now? Would he still say we were perfect together? Would he still say I was "too beautiful?"

I poked my head out of the bathroom just long enough to make sure Mom and Deedee had left for the beauty parlor. If either of them were in the house, their noses would give me away.

Under the sink, behind the Ajax and the Sani-flush, Miss Clairol's "Warm Chestnut Brown" waited for me. I hid the box there after my last meeting with Donna, not knowing if I'd ever have the nerve to actually use it.

I waffled right up to the very second I began squirting the dye, my hands shaking so bad that brown drips spattered my robe and the floor. An hour later I was a brunette again.

But, after turning this way and that, carefully examining my reflection, I decided it wasn't enough. Not nearly enough. I yanked the drawer open and pulled out Mom's professional styling scissors. Before I had time to chicken out, I grabbed a hank of hair on the left side of my face and – whack! – cut it along the chin line. I let the hair fall to the green tile floor and proceeded to cut a big hunk from my right side. Then I took the scissors and cut clumps of hair from the back. If Craig really loved me, he'd have to love me with short, brown hair. He'd have to love me even if I wasn't the prettiest girl at Lafayette High. He'd have to love me for the deep down me, not just the on-the-surface me. Did that make sense?

Suddenly a huge sob erupted, my whole body shuddering as tears ran down my face. Then Mom was banging on the bathroom door.

"Angie! Are you all right?"

Which made me cry even harder because I knew what would happen when she saw me. The reality was much worse than I expected. When I opened the door, she paused there in the hallway to take it all in – the clumps of hair everywhere, the scissors on the vanity, my jagged, dark hairdo. Then she exploded like a land mine, hurling her purse and keys, knocking the telephone off the table, everything crashing to the floor.

"What is the matter with you? Are you insane? Look! At! Your! Hair! Just look at it! You've ruined it! Ruined it! Are you out of your mind?"

I stared at the wet hair in the sink, so dark, it looked almost black against the white porcelain.

"Answer me!" she shrieked.

Her hands balled up into fists at her side and for an instant I thought she might hit me.

Deedee appeared behind her in the doorway, a freshly lit cigarette in hand.

"What in the world are you screaming about, Mother?

The neighbors will hear."

"Just look at her!" Mom yelled, flailing her arms above her head.

"Holy shit, Angie," Deedee said, her eyes bugging out. "Tonight's the beauty pageant."

"She knows that!" Mom roared, sweeping past Deedee into the living room. "Dammit, dammit, dammit, dammit, dammit!" she yelled at the top of her lungs. "She's trying to punish me! I buy her the most expensive dress I can find and this is how she thanks me!"

Deedee stared at me as Mom stalked through the house cursing.

"Mom, the neighbors," Deedee said.

"I don't give a damn about the neighbors!"

Deedee turned her attention back to me.

"You look like a freak," she said, taking a drag on her cigarette and blowing smoke in my face before disappearing into her room.

Mom paced in circles around the living room, mumbling angrily to herself. Then she returned to the hallway and picked up the telephone, setting it back on the phone table.

I closed the door as she dialed a number so hard, I thought the rotary wheel might break into pieces. But she was right outside the bathroom door so I heard every word.

"I know she's booked, but I need you to cancel her three o'clock hour," she said.

I reached up with my right hand and touched my head. God, what had I done?

"Just call 'em and reschedule. Tell them she had an emergency!" Mom shouted.

I scooped up locks of hair and laid them on a tissue on the counter.

"This *is* an emergency!" she boomed.

When we walked into the salon, it felt like the violet walls were closing in on me. It didn't help that the air was filled with hairspray and the sickening odor of perm solution. Despite the air conditioning, four hair dryers along the far wall were cooking the polluted air into a toxic stew that made me want to gag.

Her best beautician stood ready and waiting at her work station. Jill was in her twenties and knew all the latest styles. When I took off my scarf, she raised her eyebrows and nodded as she walked around me, lifting strands of hair.

"What do you think?" Mom said, lighting a cigarette – further contaminating the air.

"How about a Sassoon style?" Jill said. "The Mod Look. She's still got enough hair for it."

They talked to each other like I was a poodle coming in to be clipped.

"And maybe she can wear some false eyelashes to make her eyes look bigger," Mom said, "which might possibly make people think the look is intentional."

So that's how I got my geometric hairstyle. It was parted on the left with both sides sweeping down nearly to my chin, the hair in back much shorter than the sides. Jill shampooed me, put on a conditioner that made my hair look ultra shiny, then used her chrome blow dryer to shape it. Mom insisted it should be lacquered into place with hairspray, but Jill patiently explained that this style was meant to move and sway. So she left it soft and natural.

Walking to the car, I felt naked. My neck wasn't used to being exposed to the cold. I thought of Stan's comment about me being bald and still looking good. At least, I think that's what he said. But Deedee's greeting slapped me back into the real world.

"Judges don't like short hair," she said as we entered the kitchen.

Mom ignored her and started ordering me around.

"You need to get busy and do your nails. And when you're done with that, I'll help you apply the false eyelashes I brought home from the salon."

"Mother, judges don't like false eyelashes," Deedee said.

"What they don't know won't hurt 'em," Mom shot back.

"But..." Deedee said.

"They're not those extra-long ones. No one will know."

"I will," I said.

Mom gave me a stern look like I'd better not cross her and pulled the tab off a can of Schlitz.

~21~

Every step of the way I kept thinking about strategies to avoid going on stage. I thought about ripping my dress, faking a sprained ankle, putting my finger down my throat so I'd throw up. I considered taking some of Mom's Ex-Lax. But I got to school on time.

Talk about a surreal scene. Girls pretending to be women in classrooms on the 100 hall – giggling and chattering away, all dressed like fairy princesses or Las Vegas showgirls with concrete hair. And the smell! White Shoulders mixed with Evening in Paris mixed with Chanel No.5 and Estee Lauder, layered with a ton of Adorn, Miss Breck and Aqua Net hairspray. Boy, did everyone look absurd in their evening dresses and long white gloves sitting in little desks! As I walked into my assigned classroom I heard a girl ask someone if the pimple on her forehead was too noticeable.

And what a hullaballoo my new look caused. Janet's mouth hung open but then she clamped it shut and spoke through clenched teeth.

"Are you trying to steal my hairdo?"

I fidgeted with my evening bag, trying to figure out what to say. We didn't look like twins or anything but I understood her reaction.

"Oh my God!" Dottie cried, as she and Linda rushed over. "Oh my God!"

I hardly recognized her. Her glasses were gone and her honey blonde hair was piled in big ringlets on top of her head. She wore a ton of makeup and a pink evening gown that showcased her twin peaks.

"Quit with the 'Oh my Gods,'" Janet snapped.

"Oh my God!" Dottie said again, ignoring her and gawking at my dress. "You look like an actress at the Academy Awards!"

Janet groaned like she was about to explode, then whirled around and stalked across the room in her high heels. She joined a group of girls I didn't know, planting her hand on her hip and ruining the silhouette of her white baby doll evening gown.

"Angie, you look like you just walked off the pages of *Seventeen* magazine," Linda gushed. "*Vogue* magazine, even!"

Across the room, next to a picture of penguins on an ice floe, I noticed Deal-Making Donna glaring at me.

I couldn't believe it. I'd hacked off my hair and dyed it brown trying to look worse and, thanks to my wily mother, this is what I got?

I excused myself, taking my silver clutch with me to the bathroom.

The mirror confronted me with the truth. With this fashion magazine haircut, this expensive dress and this professional makeup job, it was possible I might actually be chosen as a runner-up. But would that be so bad? My eyes began to sting. I'd been rejected for cheerleader. Did I really want to be rejected again? And did I really want to test Craig's love? If he failed the test, I'd be offering him up on a silver platter to Donna Juana herself.

When I reached for a tissue in my bag I saw my glasses case.

Craig was counting on His Girlfriend being chosen for the queen's court. It was a badge of honor for him, right up there with his letter jacket. The more I thought about it, the more ticked off I got. I don't think he even read my articles in *The Wildcat.* He never asked what I thought about anything. Suddenly, I let loose with a very unladylike snort.

I removed my contacts and dropped first one, then the other on the dirty floor and stomped on them with my silver high heels, grinding them into the tiles. Then I put my glasses on, staring at my reflection as I swallowed hard. The white frames and thick lenses looked perfectly putrid with my dress.

Taking them off, I stashed them in my bag and rejoined the other girls, trying not to squint. I was a case of nerves.

Finally, number 47 was called and I trooped off with five other girls. We'd rehearsed on Friday and it was pretty simple: the announcer called our names and numbers, one by one. All I had to do was hold my number as I walked to center stage, stand for a count of ten and then turn and walk to my designated position, which was marked with an "X" of masking tape on the floor, and then wait until all the girls in my group did the same. When the last girl finished, we all turned and exited on the other side of the stage.

Deedee told me to keep a smile on my face every second and not to hurry. She said if I thought about Craig watching me, that would help me have a more natural smile. And I knew he was in the audience bragging to anyone who'd listen that his girl was the best looking.

My body trembled as my group waited in the wings. I got my glasses out and laid my bag on a table. Two other girls were called and then it was my turn. "Number forty-seven, Angie Finley," the announcer said. "Angie is a sophomore, sponsored by her homeroom."

My glasses nearly landed on the floor as I fumbled to put them on. Should I do this? Being in a beauty pageant wasn't evil. What in the world was I doing? I didn't have to be an activist and a perfect human being. I didn't have to give up my boyfriend in exchange for information from Unreliable Donna of the Ulterior Motives.

Still, it was more than that. I wanted Craig to see beyond the surface. To feel something for me besides lust.

"Number forty-seven, Angie Finley," the announcer said again.

I adjusted my glasses and hurried onstage, feeling like I was jumping out of an airplane without a parachute. I was immediately blinded by intense spotlights, which we didn't have in rehearsal. I froze for a moment as my eyes adjusted. Then I walked to center stage. Even with my glasses on, I couldn't really see the audience, but I could tell the gym was packed. There was polite applause.

It was like Stan said. I felt like a juicy steak on display at the meat market. Did I have enough marbling? Or would the shoppers like the T-bone to my left? Or the little filet mignon sashaying onstage behind me? She was a senior and had a big fan club yelling their heads off, whistling and hooting. She grinned from ear to ear like this was absolutely the highlight of her entire life. I blinked several times, trying with all my might to keep from crying.

~

Mom said nothing but Deedee didn't hold back.

"Good God, Angie! I was so ashamed! My sister up there on stage wearing idiotic glasses and a look on her face like she'd eaten broccoli for supper and had a bad case of gas!"

I sat in the back seat, staring out the window, trying to breathe through the cloud of smoke in the car. Both Mom and Deedee were smoking but this was one time I didn't feel like challenging them.

"What were you thinking?" she said, her voice filling the car like a blender crushing ice.

"And they had to call you twice!"

My head throbbed.

"Do you have any idea how stupid you looked? I mean, every other girl managed to smile. But you! You had this... this... grimace on your face like you'd had baked beans with onions and needed to fart!"

Mom took a corner too fast, forcing my head against the window.

"Mom spent a wad on that dress. A wad, with a capital W! You do know how much she spent, don't you?"

Still my mother said nothing.

"And there were the shoes, the gloves, that expensive strapless bra!"

She fired at will all the way home. She was still on the attack as we walked into the house.

"I mean, even if you did *accidentally* break *both* contacts – which is a crock of shit if I've ever heard one – but even if you did break them, you didn't have to put on those god-awful glasses. I didn't see one other pair of glasses on that stage tonight! Not one! Every other girl who wears glasses and can't afford contacts went without them! Except you! You dumbass!"

My mother slammed the door behind us but Deedee reloaded and continued firing.

"Not enough that you went and ruined your hair! No! You had to wear glasses too!"

I escaped to the bathroom and Mom disappeared into her bedroom. Deedee called her fiancé and vented her spleen to him. I was glad she did because it meant she wasn't yelling at *me* anymore, plus it tied up the phone. I didn't want anybody calling me.

With my evening gown back on its hanger and my face freed from all that makeup, I climbed into bed, pulled the covers up and turned off the lamp. But sleep was hard to come by. I was sure all my friends were talking about me. Moron. That's what they were calling me right this minute. Lunatic. Psycho.

And Craig? I imagined him looking at me in that amorous way. I remembered how it felt when he touched me. How my skin turned into a mass of gooseflesh at the merest brush of his fingertips. And now, no doubt he was humiliated. His girlfriend had made a fool of herself in front of everybody. It occurred to me that I could sneak out of the house and find him. I'd slip my hands under his shirt, caress his bare chest, kiss his mouth. I'd let him do the same to me. More, maybe.

The tears fell silently as I realized how intensely I wished I hadn't done it.

~

When the doorbell rang the next day, I was genuinely perplexed to find Stan on the front porch. I'd forgotten all about the signs.

"You ready?" he said.

His grin disappeared though when he took a closer look and saw I was as grey as the overcast sky.

"Well, if you wanna know the truth – no."

"I can wait."

I just wanted to stay in my room and hide. And maybe – just maybe – Craig might call.

"Stan, I'm sorry. Really. I'm just not doing too well today. Plus, my mom's mad at me."

He looked crushed. He'd gotten his license and I could tell he wanted to show off, even if it was only in his mom's old station wagon.

"Can we make the signs next weekend?"

"Sure," he said. "But why's your mom mad at you?"

"The beauty pageant was last night and… well, it's a long story."

He smiled, which threw me off.

"I sure was proud of you," he said.

"What?"

"For what you did."

"You were there?"

"Yeah."

"But you hate beauty pageants."

He nodded slowly, puckering his mouth self-consciously.

"Proud of?" I said.

"Your protest."

"My…"

"Yeah. The glasses. The hair. Brilliant."

I tried to absorb what he was saying.

"Much more effective to show up and wear your glasses and brown hair than not participate at all. What a great way to thumb your nose at the whole beauty pageant thing. But only someone as good-looking as you could make it work."

Then he looked down, but not before I noticed a blush rising in his cheeks.

"The rest of humanity thinks I'm an idiot," I said.

"Nah."

It was my turn to look down.

"It was very cool," he said.

He let me off the hook once I promised to help with the signs the following weekend. I watched through the window as he walked down the driveway past Dad's daffodils, which, despite temperatures in the thirties, were in full bloom. I remembered Dad telling me the pretty yellow flowers were a symbol of rebirth and new beginnings. Which made me feel better as Stan drove away.

But not for long.

Janet called that afternoon. "What's your problem?" That was the gist of her questions. I think she finally decided I'd gone over the edge.

Dottie actually felt bad for me, like a sympathetic girl trying to support a wacko friend. She's the one who told me that Donna of the Pointed Falsies got into the top ten. She didn't make the queen's court, but I knew she'd be absolutely insufferable. I cut both conversations short thinking Craig might call. But he never did.

Mom condescended to speak to me that night.

"Just so you know, I will never buy you another pair of contacts," she said when I came into the kitchen searching for food. "You want another pair – you'll have to buy them yourself. If what you want is to be an old maid..."

"Look where your beauty got you!"

"You ungrateful, spoiled brat! I've tried to help you be the prettiest girl at school."

"Maybe I don't want to be the prettiest girl at school!"

"Good grief, Angie. How do you expect to snag a good husband?"

"I don't want a husband! Why would I want to follow in your footsteps?"

"I just picked the *wrong* husband!"

"Dad's a...."

"He's not ambitious enough. He doesn't make enough money. And he's..."

"I can make my own money."

"Right."

"*You* do."

"Pfft!" She shook her head like I was a fool.

"Mom, you're so contradictory. You talk about finding a rich husband like a woman is all helpless or something. But you have your own business. You make your own money. You're liberated and you don't even know it."

"I don't want to be liberated! I've been trying to land a husband ever since..."

"Well, I'm not you!"

She tapped a cigarette out of the pack and lit it, sucking nicotine into her lungs.

"Fine. Fine. Just don't come asking me for another pair of contacts or a dress for another beauty pageant! But, mark my words, you'll be sorry."

I took some chips and onion dip to eat in my room where I could stew in private. She made me so mad. But she also made me question my sanity. I mean, what was I thinking – sabotaging my chances in the beauty pageant? Screwing up at cheerleading try-outs? If I kept this up I might really end up like that nineteenth century women's rights worker bee. No romance. Just work, work, work, while the other girls had all the fun, fun, fun.

I turned on the radio, trying to escape, but *My World Is Empty Without You* was playing on one station. I turned the dial to another station but it was playing *What Becomes of the Brokenhearted?* Good question.

~22~

It was Stare at Angie Day on Monday. I heard the whispers. I saw the finger pointing.

Donna was holding court when I walked into history class, her mile-high beauty pageant hairdo still cemented into place. Valerie's nose was buried in a book. Stan watched me take my seat and gave me this peppy look when I glanced his way. Linda came and stood by my desk and went on and on about my hair.

"Angie! You look like a college co-ed."

"With those cool glasses, an *intellectual* co-ed," Stan said.

I gave him a butt-out glare.

"But why'd you wear the glasses Saturday night?" said Linda.

"Yeah, number forty-seven," Donna said, filing her nails. "Don't tell me – that's all the rage in Red China this year! The Red Guards wear glasses when they're on the attack."

There were snickers on the far side of the room.

"I lost my contacts," I said, clearing my throat as I gave her a meaningful look.

She squinted at me for a second and then looked like she was doing some mental math.

"Dottie had to practically feel her way onstage 'cause she

knows better than to wear her dopey-looking glasses in a beauty pageant," she went on, obviously putting on a show for her fans. "And I must say, she did look a lot better than usual. Though, of course even without her glasses she looks like Lynn Redgrave in *Georgy Girl*. A little too big and a little too plain, if you know what I mean."

She chuckled as she looked around the room.

"But, at least she's a natural woman," Stan said, which wiped the smile off her face.

Craig did his best not to even look at me at lunch. When he and his friends left for afternoon classes, he pretended not to notice I was there, listening to his transistor radio through his earpiece like he didn't give a damn if it was confiscated.

Donna watched me from where her clique had congregated in the center of the cafeteria. I motioned with a turn of my head for her to follow him. She said something to the girl beside her and exited by the same door Craig used.

I stared at the pile of flaccid noodles on my plate. There was still a tiny grain of hope that maybe Craig really did love me like he said he did. That maybe, just maybe, he'd give Donna the brush-off and ask me out again.

Janet and Dottie landed across from me, making a ton of noise.

"He took his shirt off last night," Dottie gushed.

Janet gave her an impatient look.

"Well, he's got a sexy chest," Dottie said.

"Who?" I said.

"Robert Conrad – on *The Wild Wild West*," said Dottie. "He's sooooo good-looking."

Janet shook her head. "You know, it's really pitiful to

fantasize about a celebrity who's probably got more women than he knows what to do with."

"I can fantasize if I want to," Dottie said, looking hurt.

Janet ignored her and turned her sights on me.

"So, how long till you get your new contacts?"

I shrugged.

"You look like a nose-picking bookworm in glasses, you know," she said.

"Thanks a lot," I said.

"Janet! She looks good in glasses," Dottie said. "And what about me? I wear glasses!"

"Your eyes look so big, they remind me of a giant squid," Janet said, jutting her jaw at Dottie.

Dottie scowled and turned to me.

"Don't let her bother you, Angie. She's just..."

"What happened to you over the summer?" Janet cut in, turning to me again. "You used to be normal. You have a bad acid trip or something?"

"Janet!" Dottie cried.

"I know," Janet said. "You hired on with the FBI to infiltrate some church youth group. So you have to make yourself invisible."

"Shut up," Dottie said.

"Don't tell me to shut up," Janet said. "She's *my* friend."

"With friends like you, who needs enemies?" Dottie snapped, jumping up and crossing her arms, towering over Janet. "In fact, why don't you make like a kite and fly away!"

"Why don't you make like a fork and get bent!" Janet shot back, then stalked off, leaving her tray on the table.

I knew Dottie probably wondered why I put up with Janet.

But I'd developed this guilt complex as we went through junior high. I mean, my parents divorced, which a lot of people thought was embarrassing, but *her* parents were bound and determined to stay together till death do them part. And they sometimes seemed intent on death arriving sooner, rather than later, considering all the liquor they went through.

But the reason I stopped going over to her house during eighth grade had to do with her dad. I spotted him one night sitting in a lawn chair in the back yard, a drink in his hand, watching us through Janet's bedroom window. Without thinking, I blurted "a peeping tom is sitting out there in the dark watching us, Janet!" She yanked the curtains shut and laughed, saying "that's just my dad." But then she knew that *I* knew her dad was a pervert. I just hoped he wasn't a pervert with her.

Of course, the older we got, the more rivalry became a factor. So our friendship soured and her quick wit turned into barbed attacks. But I wasn't about to tell Dottie any of that. It's possible Janet thought I might spill the beans, but I would never do that. So all the slights stayed on the back burner, simmering and simmering until there was no liquid in the pot.

I headed for the trash cans.

"Angie, wait," Dottie said, close on my heels. "She's jealous as all get out. She wanted so bad to be named a runner-up in the beauty pageant. She worked so hard, you know? And I think it really pisses her off that you seem to take your looks for granted. I mean, she would die to have a boyfriend like Craig. But you… you don't think it's any big deal. Know what I mean?"

Little did she know what a big deal it was.

"Listen, I've got an idea," she said. "Why don't you come over Friday night? Spend the night. We'll do something fun."

Looking at Dottie's face, for some reason I could see her as a young mother with three kids. She'd fall for the first decent guy who came along. She'd never make it to college because she'd get knocked up in her senior year and she'd probably be *happy* being a wife and mother and find it fulfilling. Man, I didn't want that to happen to me!

"And we can talk about what we're gonna wear to the Sadie Hawkins dance," she said as we rushed across the courtyard, our breath forming little clouds in the freezing air. "Have you asked Craig?"

All this time I'd assumed Craig would go with me but I hadn't asked him yet. It was the one time of the year girls were supposed to chase after the boys. Everyone dressed like hicks from Li'l Abner and they crowned a king and queen – Li'l Abner and Daisy Mae. I'd planned to put my hair in braided pigtails and paint freckles on my face. But all that was out the window now.

"Not yet," I said.

~

I knew my strategy worked when I saw Donna in homeroom the next day. She was in full gloat mode, bragging about what she was wearing to the Sadie Hawkins dance. Her mother was making her a real Daisy Mae outfit and there was no doubt in my mind it would be an eye-popper. She didn't say who she was taking, telling everyone it would be a big surprise, but I already knew.

As if that wasn't enough, Stan was blabbing a mile a minute at full volume.

"They demanded an end to the draft!"

"Who?" Junior asked.

"A bunch of student organizations meeting in Washington," said Stan. "Including SDS – Students for a Democratic Society. My brother was there."

"Not gonna happen," said Junior.

"Might," said Stan.

"No way, Polack," said Billy from his seat by the windows.

"Like you even know how to read the newspaper, Einstein."

I was stunned when I realized it was *my* mouth talking, like I was in third grade or something.

"Sticks and stones may break my bones," Billy sing-songed, "but words will never hurt me!"

He and Jack busted out laughing.

My mouth wanted to call him a few choice names but my brain finally took control, telling me to zip it.

Stan passed me a note when class got underway.

"That's the first time anyone has ever come to my defense. I'm touched."

"In the head," I wrote and passed the note back.

~

I was taken by surprise when Craig sat down with me at lunch, my heart skipping a little beat. Even more surprised at the guilty look on his face.

"Angie?" he said.

He was so gorgeous. Was it too late?

216

"Someone else asked me to go to the Sadie Hawkins dance," he said.

I nodded, scraping my upper teeth on my lower lip. Maybe I could lean over and whisper in his ear that I could make him a better offer, that I wanted him to take me to the beach again and this time...

"And I..." he said, pausing for a moment, "I'm thinking..."

If only he would tell me how much he loved me. That looks really didn't matter. That he loved my soul.

"I'm thinking I might..." he said.

But suddenly, his eyes didn't look quite so blue.

"It's okay, Craig." I pulled his class ring from my handbag and set it on the table.

He squinted at me for a long time. A very long time, until I finally had to look down at my milk carton.

"God," he said. "You did it on purpose, didn't you?"

I pushed my hair behind my ear, trying to figure out something to say.

"Everyone thinks I dumped you," he said. "But it's the other way around, isn't it?"

He screwed up his mouth, shook his head and grabbed the ring, pocketing it as he walked away.

Word got around fast that: (a) Craig and I were history; and (b) Donna was taking him to the Sadie Hawkins dance.

Of course, now that I didn't have to dread the wrestling matches, that's all I could think about. His hands on my body. His lips on my lips. The two of us rolling on the beach. I knew I was a victim of wounded pride, but that didn't make it any easier.

~

Just when I decided Donna wasn't going to keep her end of the bargain she poked me in the back as I was leaving the cafeteria.

"Meet me," she whispered.

First thing she did when she arrived in the girls' bathroom was to look under each stall door.

"I've been told to watch the eleven o'clock news tomorrow night," she said. "Might be a big cross burning."

And she headed for the door.

"At Valerie's house?"

"You get a gold star and a concrete cookie," she said without turning around.

~

"Damn! I didn't really think they'd go this far," Stan said.

I found him as he was getting into his mom's old clunker after school.

"We've gotta warn Valerie and call the police," I said.

"Let's talk with Dr. Kelley first."

So we hustled back inside, dodging cars as they pulled out of the parking lot. We found her in the classroom, stuffing papers into her briefcase.

"Where did you hear this?"

"I can't say," I said.

"What if it's just a rumor started by someone talking big, trying to stir up trouble?"

"That's possible," Stan said.

"And then again, it's possible the Franklins are in real danger," I said.

She snapped the briefcase shut and sighed as she put on a black wool coat and buttoned it slowly. Then she pulled on black leather gloves and picked up the briefcase and her purse.

"Let me handle it," she said. "I'll warn the Franklins and I'll contact the FBI."

She turned off the lights as we left the room and locked the door behind us.

But I wasn't convinced we should just leave matters in Dr. Kelley's hands. Neither was Stan.

~

Unfortunately, spending the night with Dottie didn't lift my spirits. Or calm my nerves. But I'd promised her and didn't want to hurt her feelings by backing out. Especially after she came to my defense with Janet.

We froze our butts off at the drive-in watching *Doctor Zhivago*, which just made me more lovesick for Craig. I felt like Zhivago's wife when she realizes he's making it with Lara of the Long Blonde Hair.

And I didn't get a wink of sleep, not because it was a sleepover, but because I had a serious case of the jitters about Saturday night.

~23~

How do you tell your mother you're going to a cross burning? The answer: you don't. You pretend you're going to the Sadie Hawkins dance with Stan. Of course, that prompted a lot of crowing from my sister who said she wasn't the least bit surprised Craig dumped me after I turned myself into Plain Jane.

With my overalls, orange checked shirt, straw hat and, of course, my glasses, plus my worn out, green plaid car coat, I really did look like a hayseed. Stan resembled a lumberjack in work boots, rolled up jeans and a red plaid flannel jacket and matching hat with earflaps.

"Have a good time!" Mom called out as she rushed around getting ready for her date with Hank, the real estate salesman. I'd heard her telling Aunt Doreen that she dumped her last beau because he tried to tell her how to run her business. And, boy, if there's one thing my mother won't tolerate, it's a man trying to boss her around, even if he's good looking and makes a lot of money.

But Hank wasn't as tall as she was, which was a sure sign she wasn't really interested in him. Something told me she planned to give him some kind of inducement, if you get my drift, so he would forego his listing fee to sell our house.

Stan and I did a passable job pretending we were going out on a date but we were both nervous and hardly said a word once we were in the car, which looked as uncool as we did. His mom's hideous '57 Rambler station wagon was the perfect date-mobile for the Sadie Hawkins dance, which, ironically, we weren't going to.

We parked the car two blocks from Valerie's street and hoofed it the rest of the way.

It was a modest white frame house with drapes drawn in the picture window. Looked like all the other homes on the street – neat and tidy. There were lights on inside and an old car in the driveway.

We took cover behind some big holly bushes at the end of the house. Thank goodness, Stan brought a couple of old Army blankets. We sat on one and wrapped the other one around us, huddling together. The air was so cold it hurt my nose to breathe. We'd only been there a few minutes when I realized I couldn't feel my toes. The middle of February was not the best time to sit on the ground in the dark.

Not long after we settled in, we heard a car approaching. We both tensed, but it passed on by.

"What if a cop spots us?" I whispered, fingering the camera I'd tucked in my coat pocket.

"I don't know."

"What if Billy and Jack see us?"

"You wanna go back to the car while I keep watch?"

"No."

"What if they really do burn a cross in the front yard?" I whispered.

"We go to a neighbor's house and call the police."

I realized my right leg was bouncing and pulled both legs tight against my chest.

We sat silently, leaning against the cinderblock foundation. I didn't even know whether Valerie had brothers or sisters. Why had I never asked about her family?

A loud pickup drove by and we both stiffened. I pulled my Kodak Instamatic out of my pocket, but stuffed it back inside when nothing happened.

I don't know how long we'd been there but it already felt like forever. My butt was numb and I couldn't feel my fingers anymore. Stan must've noticed my shivering because he put his arm around my shoulder and tugged the blanket tighter around us. I found myself snuggling against him, tucking my gloved hands under my armpits. His right hand squeezed my upper arm, pulling me close. He was like a furnace.

And that's when I thought I heard something. Like a twig snapping. We held our breath. Nothing. Maybe it was just a squirrel out past his bedtime. We were like submariners running silent, not wanting to give our position away to the enemy.

Then another snap. Someone was definitely nearby. What if they saw us?

Headlights lit up the street as a vehicle rumbled closer, moving in slow motion. Then it was dark again like the lights had been switched off. We sat still as statues listening as the car came to a stop, its engine idling.

It was then that I began to question my sanity. What on earth made me think we should sneak around and watch a cross burning?

Expecting voices and footsteps, my whole body jerked

when I heard glass breaking instead, like a baseball going through a window. A split second later, there was another crash of shattering glass, followed immediately by squealing tires like someone hauling ass from the starting line of a drag race.

I shrugged the blanket from my shoulders and jumped up, yanking my camera out of my pocket as I ran toward the street.

"Angie, wait!" Stan cried, right behind me.

I aimed the camera at a dark pickup truck fishtailing down the street, snapping pictures, pushing the lever and snapping again as fast as I could. I took several shots, knowing it was unlikely I'd get even one decent photo in the dark. Then I noticed flickering orange light dancing across the Franklin's front yard. I was about to whirl around to take a look when a man charged straight toward us from the house next door, zooming by at full speed, his overcoat flapping behind him. Suddenly, another man loomed out of the darkness, dressed like the first guy in dark slacks and an overcoat. He saw us, stopped a few feet away and aimed a flashlight in our faces.

"Put your hands up!" he shouted.

With the light in my eyes, it took me a second to see he was holding something in his other hand. My heart was about to pound its way out of my chest when I realized it was a gun.

"Who..." Stan said.

"Turn around and put your hands in the air, *now!*" the man cried.

The frigid air was suddenly filled with the telltale odor of smoke.

"I don't...." Stan said.

The guy in the front yard yelled at the top of his lungs, "The house is on fire!"

"Drop the weapon, miss!" the man with the gun barked.

"Weapon?" I said.

It finally registered that he was referring to my camera. I was about to obey when a deafening blast knocked me off my feet, throwing me to the ground as though a giant fist had punched me from behind. I was flat on my face, ears ringing. Someone said something but I didn't understand the words.

My body couldn't move and my brain was in neutral, my cheek resting on frozen blades of grass lit by a flickering glow from somewhere nearby.

I don't know how long I lay there, but when I raised my head, dizziness overwhelmed me. Still, I had this urgent need to get up. Slowly pulling myself to a sitting position, I stared in disbelief at what looked like a war zone. Flames leapt into the air from the Franklin home. The roof was gone, as were two outer walls. Bits of wood and glass were strewn across the yard, along with household furnishings and personal belongings – a kitchen chair, a shattered mirror, a broken rocking horse. God, it looked like a bomb had exploded.

"Valerie!" I screamed, my voice seemingly trapped inside my head.

Anguish filled my heart when I realized anyone in that house could not possibly have survived.

Then I saw Stan lying on the ground a few feet away. I called his name, but there was no answer. I crawled on hands and knees across the icy ground. Kneeling beside him, I touched his shoulder, noticing blood on his temple. His eyes slowly blinked open.

"Stan?" I whispered, tears streaming down my face.

He didn't reply, giving me a dazed look. Then he turned his head toward the source of the light, his eyes growing wide at the sight of the flames.

Beyond him, I saw the two men in trench coats. The one who'd pointed his gun at me was sitting on the ground, speaking haltingly into a walkie-talkie. Closer to the house, the other one was flat on his back, and appeared to be staring up at the smoke-filled night sky.

I found my camera beside Stan's foot and tucked it back in my pocket as strobing red lights announced the arrival of a police car, a fire engine and an ambulance, in quick succession. Even my muffled ears could hear the sirens wail.

The trench coat guy appeared at my elbow. He said something to me with pinched eyebrows, I'm not sure what.

"Valerie and her family..." I cried.

He ignored me, speaking again into his walkie-talkie.

Then a fireman and two medics swooped in, giving us a cursory check. They carried the other trench coat man away on a stretcher and the ambulance sped away, lights flashing and siren blaring.

"What about the Franklins?" I shouted.

Still no reply. The tight-lipped trench coat guy helped Stan to his feet, then herded both of us to the curb. He made us sit on the concrete beneath a streetlight. Then, without warning, he pulled Stan's arms behind his back and slapped handcuffs on him. I let out a yelp when he did the same to me, then bellowed at the top of my lungs.

"Was anyone inside?"

"No!" the man snapped before he was drowned out by

another police car roaring up the street, siren blaring, lights flashing.

I lowered my head, trying to compose myself, deeply relieved the house was empty. Stan, close on my left, leaned his shoulder into mine to comfort me.

We were not alone in the street. A cluster of neighbors had gathered, many in robes and slippers, gawking at the flames, watching as firefighters battled the huge, hopeless blaze. I noticed all the neighbors were white. I heard someone say "Molotov cocktail." I also heard a woman's voice saying "they kept to themselves," and a man's voice saying "the yard was neat as a pin."

I watched too, witnessing the very moment the flames jumped from the Franklin home to the roof of the house next door.

My teeth chattered as firemen uncoiled hoses and rushed about. Soon, a freezing spray of water bombarded the burning structures, filling the air with thick, foul smoke. What had only a short time ago been a peaceful winter night, was now a scene of chaos – walkie-talkies squawking, men's voices shouting, red lights flashing, orange flames lighting up the night sky and the ground littered with debris.

Then a dark sedan pulled up. The terse cop, or whatever he was, marshaled us into the back seat, then slid into the front passenger seat. The driver, another guy in a tan trench coat, had to cut through someone's yard as another firetruck pulled up near the first one, its siren wailing and red lights adding to the nightmarish scene.

No words were spoken as we sped away. I was in a state of shock. But after a few minutes, I worked up the nerve to ask if the man taken away by ambulance was all right.

"I have no information," he replied, turning his head slightly.

"You don't really think we had anything to do with..." I said.

"Save it," he said.

In short order, we arrived at a small nondescript brick building not far from the police station. Two intimidating men in slacks, white shirts and ties met us in the parking lot and escorted Stan to a room just inside the entrance. Stan didn't look at me, his face a stony mask as the door closed. The brusque cop who'd held a gun on us guided me toward the back of the building into what looked like an interrogation room on a TV show – grey walls, a grey table in the center of the room and several tired green leather office chairs. There were no windows.

It scared me that Stan and I were separated. It also set off alarm bells that we still had handcuffs on.

A severe looking woman wearing a brown dress stepped into the room as my escort sat me down at the table. He asked my name, my age and my address, then walked out, a legal pad in hand, closing the door behind him.

"Can I call my mother?" I said to the woman.

Although I loathed the idea of explaining everything to Mom, the thought of being locked up scared me to death.

"Soon," the woman replied, her voice a monotone.

So I waited, leaning forward in my chair because my hands were still cuffed behind me. I tried to think what I'd say to my mom on the phone. She would be so upset. So worried. Even though she had this tough façade, I remembered how she cried watching the news right after I started seventh grade.

She was on the couch, Dad was in the big chair and I was flipping through Deedee's stack of *Modern Teen* magazines, hoping since I was there first, I'd get to pick what show we watched after the news was over. But the lead story drew my eyes to the TV.

Four girls had been killed when a Negro church blew up in Birmingham, Alabama. Walter Cronkite told us three of the girls were fourteen years old, one of them was eleven. And then he introduced a man to read an editorial he wrote for the Atlanta newspaper. It was about a black woman holding a little shoe from the foot of her daughter who died inside the church. But it was also about how all of us were to blame, not just the bombers.

Then I heard sniffling and turned just as Mom wiped tears from her cheeks, trying to hide her emotions. When she saw me watching her, she hurried from the room, leaving her cigarette burning in the ash tray.

Dad rose wearily from his chair and turned off the TV.

"Those girls were about your age," he said, staring, not at me, but out the front window. "This has been a sad year."

I thought he was talking about all the terrible racial violence of 1963. Little did we know it was about to get even sadder – that a couple of months later, President Kennedy would be assassinated and that in the spring, Dad would move out, leaving a gaping hole in our family.

Finally, the trench coat man returned, no longer wearing his trench coat, yanking me back to the present. He was accompanied by a woman who looked like a secretary, a pen and notepad in hand. My handcuffs were finally removed so I was able to sit normally. I rubbed my wrists as my tight-lipped guard and his secretary sat across from me.

"I'd like to call my mother," I said, startled when my voice came out sounding like a frightened child.

"I need to ask you a few questions. Is that all right?" he said, using a more sympathetic tone.

"I guess so."

"First, I'm FBI Agent Armstrong."

Of course. FBI.

"You need to answer truthfully. Do you understand?"

I nodded.

After asking me what school I attended, he got right to it, his secretary taking notes.

"Why were you at the Franklin home this evening?"

"A classmate told me there might be a cross burning there tonight. We – Stan and I – told our history teacher, Dr. Kelley, about it. She said she would warn the Franklins and notify the FBI. But we wanted to make sure whoever was threatening our friend, Valerie, was caught."

"Valerie Franklin?"

"Yes, she sits behind me in history class."

"Why did you think someone would really burn a cross in her yard?"

"Well, she's the only Negro student in my history class and she's been bullied several times this year. And someone said her family was living in an all-white neighborhood."

"So you deny you were there as a lookout for the firebombing tonight?"

"A lookout?"

He stared at me.

"God, no. Stan and I were trying…"

"Stan?"

"Stan Bukowski."

"What were you and Mr. Bukowski doing hiding in the bushes at the Franklin home?"

"We were waiting…"

"How did you know something would happen tonight?"

"Like I said, a classmate told me…"

"What, exactly, did your classmate tell you?"

"That there would be a cross burning."

"What is that classmate's name?"

Which made me take a deep breath. What if I gave him Donna's name? What then? Would they question her too? And if they did… jeez, I didn't want to think about that.

"Who tipped you about a cross burning?"

"Well, I promised not to tell anyone."

"Miss Finley, may I remind you that you agreed to answer my questions truthfully? This was not a school prank."

I cleared my throat, wishing I could have a sip of water. I didn't want to give them Donna's name. On the other hand, I didn't want the FBI escorting me to a jail cell.

"Donna Jenkins," I said. "But all she said was – she heard some guys talking about a cross burning. She didn't do anything wrong."

"Did she say who would carry out the cross burning?"

"No, but…"

I closed my eyes for a moment, suddenly feeling drained.

"But what?"

"But there are two boys I suspect of harassing Valerie at school."

"Do you have proof? Witnesses?"

Thinking about it, I realized I had nothing concrete to prove it was Billy and Jack. Except their racist obnoxiousness and their suspicious behavior. There was no doubt in my mind they threw water in her face the first day of school, that's for sure. And that they engineered her fall with the baby oil. But I didn't actually see them do anything.

"No."

The secretary scribbled her shorthand on her pad so quickly, she had to pause to wait for Agent Armstrong to continue.

"So you were sitting in the bushes with your boyfriend..."

"He's not my boyfriend."

"...waiting for a cross burning?"

"Yes."

"And how, exactly, was sitting in the bushes supposed to help your friend, Valerie Franklin?"

"Well..."

He stared at me as I struggled.

"I brought my camera with me," I said, pulling it from my pocket. "I had this idea that I could take photos as proof of who did it."

"May I see it?"

I handed it to him.

"Did you take any?" he asked.

"Yes, right after we heard glass breaking, I ran toward the street and snapped several pictures. Of course, it was so dark, I don't know if they'll turn out."

He passed the camera to the woman in brown standing stiffly beside him. "We need the film developed and photos printed right away."

She nodded and dutifully walked from the room, closing the door quietly behind her.

"If Mr. Bukowski isn't your boyfriend, what's your relationship with him?"

"He's a friend, a classmate."

"Did he drive you to the Franklin home tonight?"

"Yes."

"Did your parents know what you were doing?"

"No, I…"

"You lied to your parents about your whereabouts?"

"I told my mother we were going to the Sadie Hawkins dance."

"Who is your mother?"

"Barbara Finley."

"And your father?"

"Ray Finley. Master Sergeant Raymond Finley."

"He's in the Army?"

"Yes."

"His unit?"

"He's in Vietnam right now. Please don't tell him. He's got enough to worry about."

"Do you know his unit?"

"82nd Airborne. First Air Cav Division."

He nodded like that meant something to him.

"Where did you learn to make a Molotov cocktail?"

My mouth dropped open.

"I don't even know what a Molotov cocktail is," I finally replied.

I tried to swallow but my throat was so dry, it hurt.

"Have you ever broken the law?" he continued.

"No. And I didn't break the law tonight."

At least, I didn't think I'd broken any laws.

The interrogation continued with Agent Armstrong asking some questions twice or even three times. I was exhausted when he walked out with his secretary in tow, leaving me alone in that dreary room. Scared out of my wits pretty much sums up my state of mind at that point. I ached for a glass of water but I sat quietly and waited. And waited.

Finally, he returned and led me to an office where, to my great surprise, Dr. Kelley sat talking with yet another man in a wrinkled white shirt and black tie. He was slender with short brown hair and might've been nice looking, except it was hard to tell with that ominous scowl on his face. He sat at a big cluttered desk. She was in a leather chair facing him.

Then Stan appeared in the doorway, looking as shaken as I felt.

The man gestured for us to sit in a couple of brown leather chairs. Neither he nor Dr. Kelley stood. I had almost thawed out by then and suddenly felt ridiculous in my Sadie Hawkins get-up.

"Miss Finley, Mr. Bukowski, the name's Ross – Agent Ross," he said. "I'm releasing you into the custody of Anne Kelley, who promises she'll make sure you get home safely. But before I let you go I want you to know just how stupid you were tonight."

Dr. Kelley nodded.

"Do you realize you could've gotten yourselves killed?" he said.

I looked at Dr. Kelley's feet. She looked so strange in white tennis shoes and navy slacks.

"The FBI appreciates any and all tips, but we do not appreciate kids putting themselves in the middle of a potentially dangerous situation. I held off calling your parents only because Dr. Kelley assures me she'll make sure you comprehend the gravity of the situation."

That was as close as he got to thanking us.

He handed me my camera, which no longer had film in it, I noticed, and nodded his head in dismissal.

Dr. Kelley accompanied us to the parking lot where we piled into her black Volkswagen.

"Do you know if the agent who was rushed to the hospital is all right?" I asked.

"I didn't know an agent was hurt."

She cranked the engine and drove slowly to where Stan's car was parked. She didn't speak until she pulled up behind the ugly station wagon.

"I know you both meant well," she said. "But I truly hope you understand what a volatile situation you put yourselves in the middle of. I'm on the fence about telling your parents."

"Please don't, Dr. Kelley," Stan said from his spot in the back seat. "My old man would explode. Sorry, bad choice of words after what happened tonight."

Finally, I opened my door.

"Do I need to follow you home?" she asked as we climbed out.

"No," Stan said.

When we got to my house he parked on the street and walked me to the side door.

"You okay?" he said.

"Yeah."

No sense in telling him the truth, that I felt like I was about to puke. He probably felt the same way.

Without warning he wrapped his arms around me and gave me a church deacon hug and left without another word.

~24~

Not one word about the firebombing in the Sunday paper. Nothing on the TV news either.

But the real shocker came when I sat down in homeroom Monday morning and found the low-life junior Klansmen sitting in their desks as usual, cocky as ever. Dr. Kelley worked her jaw like she hoped someone would be foolish enough to cross her. And Stan and I were left wondering what happened.

Valerie once again had her nose in a book, making it as obvious as the outrage oozing from my pores that she didn't want to talk. I slipped a note to Stan asking him to speak with her after class while I tried to get some answers from Dr. Kelley. But she gave me the brush-off, telling me to come back after the last bell.

I caught up with Stan in the hallway just as Valerie slipped into her second period class.

"She says her family moved in with some friends over the weekend," he said. "But that's all she would say."

Dr. Kelley was strictly business when Stan and I stopped by after school.

"Will anything come of it?" I asked.

"We'll just have to wait and see."

"Wait and see?" My voice was shrill.

"Nothing I can do," she said, turning away to erase the blackboard, clearly dismissing us.

~

When I got home I picked up the paper in the yard and spread it on the kitchen table. I was about to give up on my search when I found a tiny story buried near the obituaries. The headline read: "Fire Damages Two Homes." The story was five sentences long. Nothing about a firebombing. Nothing about a racist attack. Nothing about any arrests. And zilch about the FBI being involved. The only detail worth noting was this sentence: "A fire department spokesman says it's possible a propane tank exploded."

The phone rang and I knew immediately it was Stan.

"You see it?" he said.

"Yeah."

"Pitiful."

"They didn't even mention the FBI agent who was taken to the hospital," I said. "I'm going to write my own news story."

"I don't know, Angie. Not sure it'll get published."

The deadline for *The Wildcat* was the next day so that didn't give me much time.

Tuesday morning I got to school early and found Valerie standing with a small group of black kids under the bare maples out front. They gave me a suspicious look as she introduced us, giving her friends an "I'll see ya later" nod as we moved toward the street for privacy. I told her what I was doing and asked for an interview.

"I've got my family to think about," she said, shaking her

head. "I definitely don't want you quoting me."

"Maybe getting this out in the open might help."

"You really don't understand."

"And neither do any of the other white kids at this school. So why don't we tell them?"

"We've already had to move. I don't want any more violence. And that's a very real possibility."

"But..."

"My little brother, he has nightmares now, wakes up crying. My mom and dad, they take turns staying awake at night, keeping watch."

Her eyes were puffy like she wasn't getting much sleep either.

"How old is your brother?" I said.

"Eight."

"Can I at least ask you why..."

"Why we moved into a white neighborhood?"

I nodded.

"I guess you might say my mother and father thought the time had come."

She shrugged, a sad look on her face. That's all she would say.

So I finished writing my article without her help. Dr. Kelley approved it. The hard part was waiting for the school paper to come out on Friday. I was a nervous wreck.

When I arrived at school that morning, the first thing I did was find a stack of *Wildcats.* I assumed my story would be on the front page but there was a big article on the basketball team's unbeaten season and full coverage of the Sadie Hawkins Dance. I finally found my story on the back page. I rolled up the paper and hit the wall with it, before grabbing five more copies and slipping into the library.

It was really weird now that it was in print.

LHS Sophomore Is Victim of Racial Intimidation
by Angie Finley

While most other high school girls worried about getting a date and deciding what to wear for the Sadie Hawkins dance, sophomore Valerie Franklin has faced far more serious challenges since starting tenth grade at Lafayette Senior High. Valerie has been the victim of a series of racist attacks, including the firebombing of her family's home February 18th. While students were having a good time dressing up like Li'l Abner and Daisy Mae, Valerie and her family were in hiding after being tipped off that their home might be targeted that night. The house was gutted by the blaze. The fire also damaged the house next door. No arrests had been announced as 'The Wildcat" went to press.

The Franklins may have been singled out because they are the only Negro family on their street.

The firebombing was the latest in a string of incidents targeting Valerie. The intimidation began on the first day of school when her book satchel was snatched by white students as the first bell rang. That same day she was splashed with water in the hallway. Another incident occurred several weeks later when someone poured what appeared to be baby oil on the floor, causing her to slip and fall. Valerie insisted at the time that both events were accidents.

Right before Homecoming, though, a small burned cross was found on Valerie's desk in history class. Cross burning is associated with the Ku Klux Klan's persecution of Negroes. LHS Principal Harold Lancaster interviewed students in Dr. Anne Kelley's history class but no police report was filed.

In January, what appeared to be a white Ku Klux Klan hood was found hanging in Valerie's locker. The Franklin family called the police.

So far, no students have been disciplined in the school incidents. The Franklins have had to move because of extensive damage to their home.

"I just hope Dr. Kelley doesn't get fired for approving this," Stan whispered when we ran into each other in the hallway.

"No way. I didn't say anything about the FBI being involved. Nothing about the injured FBI agent, nothing about us being there, nothing about Donna."

Valerie pretended to be reading again when we walked into homeroom, refusing to look up. Dr. Kelley didn't make eye contact with me at all during class, which was unsettling.

I suppose I expected a pat on the back. But as the day wore on and no one said a word about it, I wondered whether anybody even read *The Wildcat.* Finally, on my way to the cafeteria, Mitch called out to me from across the courtyard. He left the guys he was walking with and trotted over.

"Great article!" he cried.

"I'm surprised you got past the front-page story on your basketball season." Although I didn't mean to sound quite so sarcastic. "Congratulations."

"We lucked out. Listen, I was really impressed with your story."

The senior bell rang.

"I want to hear more about it," he said. "A group of us are going to Methodist College Friday night to see a film. Wanna come?"

I liked the way he looked at me – you know, like I actually had something to say. Seemed like the more average I looked, the more seriously he took me. The more seriously other people took me too. Like Mr. Big Shot *Wildcat* Editor Mike Andrews. He didn't snicker anymore when I said something.

"Meet us at Waffle House, seven o'clock," Mitch said, dashing off for his afternoon classes.

Stan found me as I approached the lunchroom.

"Guess what I did this morning," he said.

I shrugged.

"I cut class and walked downtown."

I was distracted, still basking in Mitch's admiration.

"You're supposed to ask me why," he said, waving his hand like he was in a hurry for me to respond.

"Why?"

"To visit the newspaper."

"*The Fayetteville Post?*"

"Correct. I took a copy of your article and showed it to the city editor," he said.

"My article?"

"Yeah. And I asked him why the paper isn't covering the story."

"And?"

"He treated me like a first grader. Patronizing as all get out."

When we entered the cafeteria it only took a few seconds for me to scan the crowd. Craig was sitting with Donna the

Peroxide Blonda in her usual spot. He was gazing into her eyes just like he used to gaze into mine.

"I wonder what gives," Stan said.

"Me too," I said, although we were talking about two very different things.

I couldn't help it. I was fantasizing about Craig taking me out again. About how I would melt in his arms. Surely he knew I was better than Donna.

"Burns me that the paper's not interested," Stan said, jolting me out of my daydream.

"Yeah," I said, realizing he was right to be angry. And that's when it popped into my head. "Let's skip school tomorrow and take the story to *The Raleigh Herald*."

Stan walked backwards in front of me as we got in the lunch line, a glint in his eyes.

"Great idea," he said.

Not sure what got into me.

~

I hardly recognized him when we met in the school parking lot the next morning in decent grey slacks, a navy sport coat that almost fit, and a tie. He even had on a pair of brown wingtips. I'd never seen him in leather shoes and he looked surprisingly conventional. Except for the shaggy hair.

"My, my, my," I said, shivering in the cold. "Did you go shopping?"

"Borrowed some stuff from the old man," he said, opening the car door for me. "You should talk."

I guess you could say we were both trying our best to be taken seriously. My blue tweed suit, stockings and black pumps meant my legs and feet were like ice. But with my professional outfit, my brown hair and glasses, I figured I might pass for a reporter.

We made it to Raleigh in less than two hours and found the newspaper office. A middle-aged editor named Harry Abrams, wearing a rumpled white shirt and ratty brown tie, met with us in a bustling newsroom filled with clacking typewriters, people yammering on telephones and shrieking police scanners. Pretty much like I'd pictured, but a lot smokier and messier.

"Hope you don't mind if I eat my lunch while we talk," he said.

He didn't wait for us to reply before heading into the first of two baloney sandwiches on white bread, each one carefully wrapped in wax paper.

Stan and I told him everything we knew while he devoured his food, telling him how the Franklins' house exploded that night, how they were warned ahead of time so they weren't home when it happened, and how we thought it would just be a cross burning. We handed him a copy of *The Wildcat* and he skimmed the story as Stan and I exchanged nervous glances.

"Good job, Miss Finley," Mr. Abrams said. "I'm impressed you both care enough to try to get some news coverage."

Then he took our names and phone numbers and showed us out. He didn't make any promises, but at least he didn't give us the brush-off like we were a couple of kids. He actually handed each of us his business card as he said good-bye.

I think it helped that I didn't look like a cheerleader or a contestant in a beauty pageant. Brown hair and glasses made a big difference with a lot of guys. G.I.'s didn't yell "hey, baby!"

at stoplights anymore. Which was a real plus.

"Well, we tried," Stan said, pausing for a moment on the sidewalk. "Let's get some lunch."

It was cold and threatening rain so we looked for a place close by to get some cheap food. We sat on stools, eating grilled cheese sandwiches at the Kress's lunch counter where the buttery aroma of popcorn mingled with the greasy smells of the snack bar.

"I'll bet Mr. Abrams has already tossed our stuff in the trash," I said.

"Never know. Something might come of it."

Stan was really in his element. I could picture him going off to college and being a leader of SDS or some other group.

"We've gotta keep the pressure on to find the culprit," he said. "If the newspapers don't ask questions, chances are, there won't be a real investigation."

As I listened to him rattle on about bringing the villains to justice, I realized I admired the activist in him.

But activism had so many pitfalls. Take Susan B. Anthony, for instance. She fought her whole life for women's rights but didn't live to see the 19th Amendment passed. Of course, her work was her life and, in the end, she actually did help bring about change. Still, was she ever kissed? Did anyone ever touch her bare skin? All work and no play makes Jack a dull boy, or Jill a dull girl, as the case may be. Whoever said that knew what he was talking about. But as I watched Stan wolf down his sandwich, I found myself wondering – did it have to be all or nothing?

I thought of Valerie. Of her family's sacrifice for a cause. Of her own work with that Negro newspaper she mentioned.

Which flipped a little light on in my brain.

"Hey!" I said, "maybe we could take the story to *The Fayetteville Message*."

A huge smile spread over his face and his eyes widened.

"Hot damn. Brilliant idea!"

And he reached across the table to shake my hand, causing me to chuckle self-consciously.

On the drive back, he told me he'd been reading a book I might be interested in. A book recommended by Dr. Kelley.

"Oh?"

"Yeah. *The Feminine Mystique* by Betty Friedan."

"You're kidding."

"Nope. I decided I needed to educate myself about women's issues," he said, shrugging. "Have you read it?"

"No."

"Oh, so you're just a natural born feminist?"

"You would be too if you were a girl."

"*Touché.*"

Then he told me more about the book than I really wanted to know, about how educated women were dissatisfied being homemakers. It all seemed kind of self-evident to me. It was obvious he was trying to impress me. And I had to admit it worked. How many boys would read something like that?

The old brick building that housed *The Fayetteville Message* was nothing like the *Raleigh Herald*. Located on a dicey street on the far side of downtown, the building sagged from age and neglect. The interior was just as unimpressive. I only saw three typewriters in the tiny newsroom, which was empty except for me, Stan and a skinny young black man named Ronald Jackson. He was an assistant editor in a starched white shirt and tie. He gave us his undivided attention, asked follow-up questions and acted as though what we had to say was important. He took a copy of *The Wildcat* and said he'd follow up with the Franklins and the FBI.

Stan and I were flying high as he drove me home.

"Once the story comes out in *The Message,* the other papers will be forced to do something," he said.

"I hope you're right."

~

Just when I'd started not to pine for Craig with every waking breath, I ran into him on the way out of school the next day. It was a weak "hi" that escaped my lips. He nodded. But when I was almost to the bus stop he called after me.

"Let me give you a ride home."

A little voice in my head told me to say no thanks.

"My car's right over here," he said.

Thank goodness my London Fog hid the way I quivered when he touched my sleeve. I went with him despite my better judgment, because when he was around, my brain basically turned into Jell-O.

He opened the door for me like he did on our first date. I could tell we weren't going to my house right away, though. He took me instead to the Tastee-Freez. We got ice cream cones and sat in a booth with our coats on.

He stared at me as he licked his vanilla ice cream. My eyes were drawn to his. It was like he was reeling me in with some kind of telepathic transmission. He was even better looking than Richard Chamberlain. And that's saying a lot. Every girl in the country was praying *Dr. Kildare* would come back on TV.

"Why was it we broke up?" he said. "I can't seem to remember exactly."

"I think maybe it was because you weren't keen on brown hair and glasses," I said, pushing my glasses up.

He gave me a sheepish grin.

I was suddenly very hot and had to take off my coat.

"What would you say if I asked you out?" he said, reaching over and caressing my hand. By the look in his eyes I guessed he was imagining us together in the fullest sense of the word.

Then he leaned over to kiss me, closing his eyes as his lips touched mine. It was the same sweet, irresistible kiss I remembered. I closed my eyes too, picturing us on the bed in that beachfront apartment.

"Give me another chance," he whispered.

The flutter in my stomach traveled right up through my chest and got stuck in my throat.

"What about Donna?" I said.

"She's not you." His voice was so soft I could hardly hear him. "I was hoping you'd get jealous and want me back."

Did he have a scent I wasn't consciously aware of that made me completely stupid in his presence?

"I know a great seafood restaurant," he said. "I'll pick you up Saturday at six."

Taking another bite of my melting ice cream, I felt like a moth drawn to the headlights of an oncoming car.

~25~

I found a letter from my father on the kitchen table when I got home and a note from Deedee saying she'd gone shopping – for the millionth time. I waited till I was in my room to open Dad's letter, only to discover it had already been opened. Which meant I'd have to give my sister a piece of my mind when she got home.

This is how the conversation would play out. She'd complain Dad only wrote letters to *me*. I would explain that if she wrote a letter to Dad, he would send *her* one. That's how letter writing works. I knew, for a fact, that he'd sent at least two or three letters to Deedee, but I'm about ninety-nine percent certain she never replied.

As usual, it was a challenge making out Dad's hard-to-read chicken scratch on a sheet of paper torn from a long yellow legal pad.

Dear Angie,

Your friend Stan sounds like an interesting young man. I suppose there are more and more people like him, upset about the Vietnam war. I just hope they aren't confused about who to be angry with. The soldiers here are just doing their best. We didn't decide to fight the Viet Cong. We were sent here by our leaders who want to keep Vietnam out of Communist hands. I have to admit I have my doubts about some of the decisions made in Washington. But I'm a soldier, and just like all the other soldiers in the US Army, I follow orders. Still, I respect the right of Americans to oppose the war. Free speech, after all, is one of the most important rights Americans have – one of the rights we fight for.

As for the antiwar rally – you never know what's going to happen when you get a really big crowd together, especially in New York City! I hope you don't have your heart set on going because I feel strongly that you should not participate. I'm sending a letter to your mother telling her how I feel.

I hope you had a good time at the Sadie Hawkins dance. You'll have to tell me who you invited, (Craig?) and maybe you could even send me a picture.

God, the mail was slow.

I was thankful he nixed the big protest. Now I could tell Stan my dad said no. I'd have to think about what to say in my next letter. Maybe a little about Valerie. I could send him a copy of *The Wildcat* article on her house being blown to smithereens. No need to tell him I was there when it happened.

~

Friday night I decided at the last minute to go with Mitch and his friends. I guess you could say I was curious. I had my mom drop me at the Waffle House. He was sitting in a booth by himself, a cup of coffee in front of him. Let's see, did I misunderstand?

He waved me over, a cigarette in his hand.

"How many more are coming?" I asked, tossing my coat on

the seat beside me, trying to look calm, cool and collected.

He shrugged and motioned for the waitress to bring me coffee. I doctored it to a light brown.

"Tell me about Valerie Franklin," he said.

About eighty-five percent of me wanted to pour out the entire story. It might feel good to tell him everything. But the other fifteen percent of me worried about what would happen if I mentioned the FBI. So I kept it vague, never mentioning it was Donna who tipped me off or that Stan and I were at the Franklins' house when it happened or anything about the FBI. But I did tell him I suspected Billy Wyler and Jack Thompson. He sipped his coffee and hung on my every word.

Finally, just before 7:30 some other kids came in – Pocahontas's boyfriend John Smith, a guy named Sid and a girl named Paula. All seniors. We piled into Mitch's beat-up '59 Impala, me riding shotgun, the others in the back seat.

"Smith, what's this I hear about you taking dance lessons?" Sid said, dripping with sarcasm.

John laughed like it was a funny joke.

"I'm auditioning for musical theater programs at a couple of colleges," he said, his voice not quite as self-assured as usual. "And they say you've gotta show some footwork. So, yeah, I'm taking a dance class."

"You aiming to be the next Rudolf Nureyev?" Sid teased.

John snorted like that was the most ridiculous thing he'd ever heard.

"Nah, more like Gene Kelly," he said.

Although I couldn't see their faces behind me, the conversation made me a trifle uneasy, since Nureyev was the most famous male ballet dancer in the world and Kelly was a tap dancer.

"You should see him on the dance floor with the ladies," Mitch said, glancing at them in the rearview mirror.

We made it to the college just in time to hear some professor wind up an introduction to the film. I was having serious second thoughts about watching an old black and white movie but it turned out I really loved *Casablanca*.

Afterwards, we skipped the group discussion at the college and went back to the Waffle House where we had apple pie and more coffee.

"So you didn't think Ilsa would go with Rick?" John asked me.

"I thought she'd be loyal to Victor and the cause."

"But she loved Rick," he said. "Like I love Pocahontas."

And he slapped Mitch on the shoulder like it was an inside joke.

"Yeah, right," Sid said in a mocking tone.

"She loved Victor too," I said.

"But she loved Rick more," said Mitch.

"Yeah, but sometimes it's all about doing the right thing," I said.

"Sacrifice for the greater good?" he said, raising his eyebrows.

"But then she gave in to her heart."

"It's always that way," John said, staring at the table.

"Not always," I said, thinking of Susan B. Anthony. "Some women don't need a man."

Everyone laughed.

After the others left, Mitch volunteered to drive me home and when we pulled up in front of my house I felt invigorated.

Like I'd just gone snorkeling for the first time and seen all kinds of beautiful fish I'd never dreamed existed. He said he was getting a group together to see a Japanese film. Up until that moment, I wouldn't have been enthusiastic about reading subtitles, but suddenly it seemed an adventurous thing to do. So I said "sure."

When I walked into the house, my mom asked how my date was. I explained it wasn't a date, just going to a movie with friends.

And it wasn't anything like a date. No petting. No kissing. No struggling to keep my clothes on. And I didn't have that romantic feeling about Mitch. He was a friend. A friend who actually wanted to talk. Who actually wanted to hear what I *thought*. A friend I felt relaxed with. Which was nice for a change.

~

At precisely six o'clock on Saturday the doorbell rang. I had spent a ridiculous amount of time choosing my outfit – a black and white Houndstooth mini-skirt, black turtleneck sweater and lacy white tights. And, of course, my white glasses.

I had high hopes that Craig came back to me because he realized I wanted more from him than surging hormones. That I was interested in a relationship that included a lot more than hands and lips and certain other body parts.

"See ya later, Mom!" I called and stepped outside, intent on making a quick get-away.

"You look like a model," he said, his Hollywood smile as dazzling as ever.

"Likewise, I'm sure."

He rolled his eyes, but it was true. He could've been modeling for Belk & Hensdale instead of heading to a seafood joint. Grey slacks, cordovan Weejuns with tassels, burgundy striped shirt and a burgundy cardigan with his initials monogrammed in white.

We drove north through town, and kept driving way past Spring Lake to this really out-of-the-way seafood restaurant. Pop's Fish Shack didn't look like much but it was packed. Lots of old people and families. Not what you'd call a date destination. The walls were covered with fish nets, fake lobsters, a couple of fake swordfish, framed dime store prints of the beach and phony life preservers.

A heavy middle-aged hostess led us to a table for two covered with a red-checked tablecloth.

Craig held my chair as I sat down.

"Their hush puppies are the best," he said, opening his menu.

I could feel people staring at us. It was like we'd traveled out into the country where city folks weren't exactly welcome. Our clothes and hair didn't quite fit in. That little voice in my brain was at it again, suggesting the reason we'd come so far for dinner was to make sure nobody saw us. Especially Donna. Which made me feel shabby. He wanted to take me out but he didn't want anyone to know.

A skinny waitress with brassy hair, dark roots and too much eyeliner arrived.

"Ya'll ready?"

"Sure," said Craig. "How about two large shrimp platters?"

She scribbled on her pad.

"Craig, I can't eat that much," I complained.

"Oh, don't worry. I've got two stomachs in here." And he patted his belly and grinned.

When she was gone I thought he might compliment me on my article about Valerie but he made more small talk about the food and his other favorite hard-to-find restaurants. There was the barbecue joint in Harnett County, another seafood joint on Highway 211 and a little Chinese restaurant on 301 near Lumberton. He waxed poetic about his favorite dishes, how he liked spicy food, but not too spicy, about waiting in line to get into the barbecue place. Which made me wonder if he'd taken other girls to some of those restaurants while he and I were going out together.

Our platters arrived quickly, piled high with shrimp, hush puppies and French fries, with a bowl of coleslaw on the side. We drank very sweet iced tea from jelly jars. The food was greasy and loaded with salt.

Besides restaurants, he talked about his favorite TV shows – *Mission: Impossible, Batman* and *The Man from U.N.C.L.E.* How he liked Illya Kuryakin better than Napoleon Solo because Solo was kind of a sissy. He talked more than I'd ever heard him talk. Like he was trying to fill up the space between us as he ate every last bite on his plate and finished what I couldn't eat on mine, which was a lot.

As it turned out, if Craig wanted to make sure no one saw us together he didn't drive far enough. After he paid the cashier we stepped through the front door and ran into Dr. Kelley. She was with the FBI agent who chewed Stan and me out the night of the firebombing. Only now I could see he wasn't just nice looking, he was extremely nice looking. Movie star nice looking. And she was the picture of femininity, with dangly earrings, a silky black shawl and his arm wrapped around her like they were on their honeymoon.

The usually unflappable Dr. Kelley was obviously flapped.

"Angie Finley and Craig Anderson, fancy meeting you here," she said, her voice coming out a notch higher than normal.

"The food's great," Craig said, pulling me along. "Enjoy your dinner!"

He gave them a bogus smile, which disappeared as soon as we were in the car.

"What the hell are they doing here?" he said.

Good question. I don't know if Craig realized it or not but she hadn't introduced her date. Agent Ross. If that was really his name. So that was her "in" with the FBI.

And now we'd been caught. Everyone knew Craig and Donna were going together. Even Dr. Kelley. Donna made a big enough deal of it, showing off his class ring every chance she got, always saying "Craig this" and "Craig that." So there was no way Dr. Kelley didn't know I was going out with a guy who was cheating on his girlfriend. It bothered me that she might think less of me.

After he cranked the engine, he returned to his upbeat mood, reaching in the glove box and bringing out two home-made brownies wrapped in wax paper.

"Dessert!" he said, handing me one. "I made 'em myself."

"You cook?"

"Every once in a blue moon," he said, laughing.

"Gosh, Craig, I already feel like a stuffed sausage."

He let out a big guffaw.

"Come on, you gotta try it and tell me what you think."

So I reluctantly took a bite.

"Mmm," I said, although I'd had much better.

He devoured his and motioned for me to finish mine. How could anyone eat that much, I wondered. Trying my best not to hurt his feelings, I slowly consumed the unappetizing brownie as we drove.

We listened to the radio on the way back. He sang along with *Secret Agent Man*. He sang along with a lot of songs.

I recognized his friend Dave's house when we pulled into the driveway.

"Are we picking Dave and Sylvia up?" I asked.

He raised his eyebrows.

"Craig?" I said.

"It's a little party."

"But there aren't any cars."

"We're the first ones here."

He pulled me playfully from the car and led me to the front door. There was a lamp on in the living room but nobody answered when he knocked. I started back down the steps but he turned the knob and opened the door.

"Dave said to go on in if we got here first," he said, glancing at his watch. "The others will be here in a few minutes."

He took my hand and led me inside. I couldn't help but remember his wandering hands the last time we were here.

~26~

Uneasy. That's how I felt standing on the cream carpeting beside an expensive cherry wood book case. I was also a little fuzzy around the edges.

"Anyone home?" Craig called, looking at his watch again, then giving me a playful wink.

Only a fool couldn't see that Craig had "romance on his mind." Of course, I'd been dreaming of something similar ever since we split up. So why was I nervous?

"Guess we're a little early," he said. "Dave said to go ahead and make ourselves at home. Want a Coke?"

"Craig…"

"I love it when you say my name," he said, disappearing into the kitchen.

I heard the clinking of ice and the sound of the refrigerator opening and closing. I looked out the window, hoping to see another car pull up as I laid my coat on a chair. Then he returned and handed me a large tumbler.

"Here's to you," he said.

We clinked glasses and I took a sip. It was Coke with a generous shot of whiskey.

"And, here's to all the great times we've had together," he said, tapping my glass again.

I sipped and he gulped. Then he put a record on – the Righteous Brothers – and pulled me close. He took my glass and held it to my mouth.

"Drink up," he said.

I drained it, shivered, and coughed a little as he set it on the mantle. I couldn't help but giggle – I don't know why – which caused him to smile and wag his head.

We slow danced, his hands on my waist. Mine rested on his shoulders, partly to steady myself because I was feeling a bit woozy, but partly because I wanted to touch him.

"Did you miss me?" he whispered.

If he only knew how I'd dreamed about him, how I'd wished I could have him back. Just having his arms around me now made me so lightheaded and... I don't know. The uneasiness drained away as he breathed on my neck.

He sang along to *Unchained Melody,* his lips tickling my ear as he whispered about hungering for my touch. Then he kissed me, a soft, dreamy kiss that made me want more.

"You missed me," he said. "I can tell."

"Yeah."

He kissed me again, deeper this time, and rubbed his hands over my back.

As we swayed to the music, I realized I was dizzy and my legs felt weak, although our feet weren't really moving anymore. My hands had slipped from his shoulders to his chest.

"Oh, Angie."

His voice was husky. I sighed and closed my eyes. And that was all he needed. He picked me up and carried me down the hallway.

"What're you doing?" I cried.

He carried me into a bedroom at the end of the hall, kicked the door closed with his foot, and heaved us both onto a double bed covered with a white bedspread.

"Craig?"

He pulled my glasses off and set them on the nightstand, then wrapped me in his arms and French kissed me in the most passionate way, fondling me through my sweater. I knew he was intent on penetrating my defensive line, which was growing weaker by the minute.

"I don't want to..." I whispered when he finally pulled his lips from mine.

"Okay," he whispered back.

But he kept kissing me and touching me, putting his hands under my sweater. He smelled so good and his kisses were so addictive... and my head was swimming... and my body had turned to... pudding.

This is what I'd wanted ever since... ever since the night of the beauty pageant. I wanted to know he loved me... no matter what I looked like.

Then he reached behind me and unhooked my bra. And from there it was step by hurried step until we were both undressed and I was kissing him as much as he was kissing me and I was caressing his skin as much as he was caressing mine. He finally pulled my panties off.

"Craig!"

"It's okay. I've got a rubber."

He paused for a few seconds while I closed my eyes, and then... we did the deed. At least I think we did the deed. Although that makes me sound like I've had a lobotomy. All I know for sure is that it was fast and furious, it hurt, and when he was through panting and groaning, he flopped on top of me like a fish that couldn't thrash anymore after being pulled from the water.

I'd always thought when you made love it would be so romantic. You'd feel... well... like you were totally and rapturously in love. You'd feel this overwhelming passion and sweet affection. Like you'd been transported to a romantic paradise. Instead, I felt sweaty and dirty, like I needed to take a long shower and wash every inch of my body fourteen times.

I pushed him off of me, gathered my things and left him spread-eagled on the bed. In the bathroom my hands shook as I pulled my clothes on and fixed my face and hair. When I returned to the living room, he was holding a can of beer and smiling. I tried to act cool but I couldn't look him in the eye.

"I told you we were perfect together," he said. "All you needed was a little loosening up."

He stepped close and held me with his beer arm and used his free hand to squeeze my butt, like it was now his property.

"Loosening up?" I mumbled.

"A magic brownie and a little Southern Comfort."

"Pot was in...?"

"Like I said, I made 'em myself."

He smiled like Janet used to when she shoplifted a plaid hair bow from old man Swanson's store when we were in seventh grade, all puffed up like she'd won a gold medal at the Olympics or something.

"Listen, I wanna buy you a new pair of contacts," he said. "I heard your mom won't buy you another pair. Hell, I'll pay for you to get your hair blonded – or whatever you call it – while it grows long again."

I forced myself not to cry.

"I'll get my ring back from Donna on Monday," he added.

~

My shower lasted until all the hot water was gone. But I still didn't feel clean.

~

I called Craig's house Sunday afternoon to tell him not to ask Donna for his class ring. I didn't want it. It was like a sign of ownership. And, besides, if he took his ring back, she'd know what was going on. And I didn't care to think about what would happen if he told her he was giving me the ring instead. It would be proof I'd reneged on our deal.

And there was this other little problem: my burning desire for Craig had been squashed like a bug on the grill of his GTO as he raced down Highway 401. I didn't want a guy who would push me and push me to go to bed with him, and when pushing didn't work, drug me to get his way.

Maybe I'd proven a point. I could get him back, even with my glasses. Big deal.

No one answered the phone.

~27~

I was so uncomfortable in my skin Monday morning, it took me a few minutes to notice something was up.

Dr. Kelley sat silently at her desk, which was very unlike her. When the bell rang, she waited a moment and then stood slowly, almost as if she were in a trance.

"I have some heartbreaking news this morning," she said.

For once, no one made a sound, her voice was that melancholy.

"Donna's brother has been killed in Vietnam."

Someone in the back of the room said "Oh my God" as I turned and stared at Donna's empty desk.

"Private First Class William Jenkins died four days ago. He just graduated from Lafayette Senior High last year."

She stopped talking and stared out the window as Monday morning announcements crackled through the intercom above the blackboard. A girl with an unbearably chirpy voice said "Good Monday morning, LHS!" No one listened as she and a boy with an equally peppy tone babbled on for several minutes about totally irrelevant stuff.

My mind raced back to Saturday night. I felt like I'd stolen a blind man's cane. Worse, actually.

~

I couldn't bring myself to go to the funeral, opting to read about it instead. The newspaper didn't just run an obituary. It covered the service for a local boy killed in action as a news story. There was a picture of Donna dressed in black beside her father and mother as a military honor guard carried the coffin. I could just make Craig out wearing a dark suit in a group of people behind them.

As soon as I finished reading the article, I sat down to write my dad a long letter. I told him about Donna's brother and asked him if *he* was safe. I guess I'd always known there was a chance he might get killed, but it seemed an abstract idea. I knew lots of other kids whose dads went to Vietnam and came home without a scratch. It seemed like just another tour of duty – like when he went to the Dominican Republic – until now.

So when Stan came bounding out the front door at school the next day to catch me before I got on the bus, I was what you might call receptive. He said he had his mom's car and wanted to drive me home so we could talk about organizing an antiwar rally at the entrance to Fort Bragg.

"Not there," I said. "People will think we're against the G.I.'s. If we're going to have a demonstration it ought to be somewhere else. Like in front of our congressman's office."

"You have a point."

"Of course I have a point! My dad didn't ask to be sent to Vietnam!" I threw my hands up in frustration.

"You're right," he said, giving a small shrug.

"I know I'm right! Those guys getting killed over there are just following orders!"

"We'll find out where the nearest congressman's office is."

"Okay!"

I finally realized he wasn't arguing with me.

"When's the rally?" I asked.

"A week from Saturday."

We agreed to get together to make signs and flyers. I felt like I had to atone for doing it with Craig. Do penance, you know. And what better way than to protest the war that killed Donna's brother?

~

Stan's house was a red brick home that looked like it was built in the forties, with two rounded arches above a big front porch. The kitchen was what my mother would call quaint. Aqua dinette, knotty pine cabinets, an old rounded white refrigerator and a linoleum floor worn through in front of the stove and sink. It made my mom's kitchen look modern in comparison.

"Mom?" Stan called out.

But when we set our supplies on the table, we found a note saying his parents had gone to the commissary. Suspicion must've been written all over my face because Stan apologized immediately.

"I didn't know they'd be gone. I swear."

Was it obvious to other people when a girl had gone all the way? Did my eyes look different? Did I give off a different scent?

"Maybe we should go to your house," he said.

"No one's home there either." I paused a moment to decide whether I trusted Stan, staring at the colorful fruit wall plaque above the stove. He may have started out with a backward attitude about girls, but he had never once tried to take advantage of me. "No big deal," I finally said.

So we covered the table with newspapers and got to work, cranking out flyers and posters as fast as we could, setting the flyers on the counters and standing the signs up around the kitchen to dry, careful not to get any paint on the floor. Some of the posters said "Make peace, not war!" Some said "Bring our soldiers home!" And we painted some that said "Stop the bombing!"

"I hope we get a decent turnout," I said.

"I hope we don't get arrested."

"We might get more news coverage that way."

He laughed out loud.

I was far from calm about the possibility, but when Stan and I were together I had more courage for some reason.

"I can picture you behind bars," he said, chuckling.

"You'd bail me out, wouldn't you?"

I stole a sideways glimpse, watching as he pursed his lips and squinted like he was considering whether I was worth the trouble.

"Only if you agree to type up my term paper," he said.

The cocky expression on his face only lasted a second because I lunged with my paint brush and smeared his nose with green.

"Agh!" he cried, preparing to retaliate.

That's when his mom appeared in the doorway, two brown sacks filled with groceries in her arms. Right behind her was his stepdad, also carrying groceries, with a look of extreme displeasure on his face.

Stan's smile disappeared instantly.

"Mom, Bill, this is Angie Finley," he said in a formal voice. "Angie, these are my parents, Gloria and Bill Stutts."

"Nice to meet you, Angie," Mrs. Stutts said, looking around for somewhere to set her bags.

She was short and round with a woman's version of Stan's unruly brown hair. His stepdad was her opposite – tall and wiry, with a greying flat top above a humorless, leathery face.

I was about to answer when Mr. Stutts spoke.

"I thought you were having a friend over," he said, raising an eyebrow at Stan.

"Angie *is* a friend."

"Yes, and I see the two of you have been working very hard," Mrs. Stutts said, obviously trying to lighten the mood and head her husband off at the pass.

"We were just finishing up the posters," I said, aiming for a cheery tone. "Thanks for letting us use your kitchen."

"See how fast you can get this mess out of here. We need to put the food away," Mr. Stutts said, clearing his throat. "I've gotta start packing."

~

The car reeked of paint as we drove to my house. I opened the vent to get some air. We agreed to store the signs in my carport so they'd be safe, as Stan put it. Safe from his stepdad, I suppose. I could tell he was embarrassed.

"Where's your dad going?" I said.

"Stepdad."

"Right."

He kept his eyes on the road, grinding his teeth. So I dropped the subject and gazed at the bare trees along the side of the road. Finally, he broke the silence as we turned into my neighborhood.

"He's headed back to Vietnam."

"But he just got home, what, a few months ago?"

"He's in Special Forces. He's already done two tours of duty."

"Dang."

"Bill's determined to make my mom a widow," he said, shaking his head. "Again."

"But why?"

"It's a guilt trip. His best pal was blown to bits right in front of him by a land mine his first time over in '63. His friend was walking point, even though it was Bill's turn. He had a hangover, so it was his buddy leading the A-team through the jungle that day. And it was his friend who paid the price."

There was something odd about the way he said "friend." I couldn't put my finger on it, but thought again of the cold expression on Mr. Stutts' face.

Stan gripped the steering wheel tightly.

"His friend – the guy who got killed," he explained, "was my father."

"Your real father?" I whispered.

He nodded, keeping his eyes on the road. His jaw tightened and he blinked several times.

My mind raced, puzzling over how his stepdad came to marry his mother after his father was killed, wondering about the terrible remorse Mr. Stutts carried around with him, about the distant relationship between Stan and his stepfather, and how his mother could forgive – and then marry – the man who held himself responsible for her first husband's death. God, it was hard to imagine.

"The longer the war goes on," Stan said, "the better his chances of finding another land mine with his name on it."

Maybe that was the real reason Stan was so passionate about ending the war.

Later, in my bedroom, *The Ballad of the Green Berets* came on the radio. I listened to the whole song, knowing tears would well up in my eyes. They always did. But after what Stan told me about his father and his step-dad, the song really pulled at my heartstrings. Regardless of my feelings about the war, I really sympathized with the soldiers and their families.

~

We handed out some of our homemade flyers at school. And each day after school, we targeted one local college, passing out leaflets at Fayetteville State, Methodist College, FTI, Pembroke State and St. Andrews College.

Stan called the Fayetteville paper and the Raleigh paper, hoping they might send reporters. I called the local radio stations and the TV stations in Raleigh and Durham. No one sounded the least bit interested.

Although there was a congressman's office in Fayetteville, we decided to hold our protest in front of the post office since it was part of the federal government. It was also on the main drag, whereas the congressman's office was on the third floor of an office building off the beaten track.

When Stan and I arrived at noon on that blustery Saturday in early March there was one person waiting for us – Valerie, wearing earmuffs and gloves, and bundled up in the heavy tan coat she got for Christmas.

We must've had stunned looks on our faces because she gave a small lift of the shoulders and smiled.

"Broad daylight," she explained. "In a group. My parents couldn't really object."

"Wow," said Stan.

Three black guys showed up about fifteen minutes later from Fayetteville State, the Negro college. A white couple who went to Methodist College came too. We shared our signs with them and marched quietly up and down the sidewalk, walking single file to stay out of people's way. We walked quickly though, because, despite the cloudless blue sky and bright sunshine, the wind made forty degrees feel like twenty-five.

It took all my nerve to hold my sign up for everyone to see: "Bring our soldiers home." I gripped it firmly on both sides so the wind wouldn't snatch it. I could feel myself blushing as people stared like we were freaks, shaking their heads in disapproval.

"Shame on you!" an elderly woman said as she passed by, wagging her finger in our direction.

Stan snapped some shots with an old Brownie camera he borrowed from his mother. He was going to write an article for *The Wildcat* about the demonstration. He could finally do his story about student activists.

Two guys who said they attended Fayetteville Tech joined us a few minutes later. We were happy to have more marchers, but the good vibes faded as soon as they began chanting: "Hey, hey, LBJ, how many kids have you killed today?" I was mortified. Stan asked them to stop but they ignored him. The three Fayetteville State guys chanted "Make peace, not war," trying to drown them out. The rest of us joined in.

It was at that moment I spotted Donna, her blonde hair billowing in the wind, walking down the granite steps of the post office with her father. She saw us right away, a grim expression spreading over her face. Her father saw us too and quickened his pace, leaving Donna behind as he charged toward the guys doing the LBJ chant.

"Shut the hell up!" he yelled. "My son never killed any children! You're a disgrace to our country! You wouldn't have the courage to put on a uniform and go to Vietnam!"

The two young guys tried to walk away but he got right in their faces. To make matters worse, a photographer showed up then and started snapping pictures, which made Mr. Jenkins even more furious.

"My son was a hero! But you wouldn't know anything about being a hero! You're probably goddam draft dodgers! Going to some liberal college to avoid doing your duty!"

He was so red-faced, he looked like he might fly apart at the seams.

"Get away from me!" he shouted, shoving the photographer.

Stan tried to talk to him.

"We don't mean any disrespect, Mr. Jenkins," he said. "We're very..."

"My son died over there fighting the gooks! Protecting sissy punks like you!"

The photographer continued shooting with his big Nikon camera as a reporter arrived and started taking notes.

Donna touched her father's arm.

"Let's go, Daddy."

"You're not real Americans!" he yelled at all of us. "You're Communists! Goddam Communists!"

He grabbed Stan's sign and ripped it in half, flinging the torn pieces to the sidewalk. The wind instantly seized them, hurling them into the street where they were flattened under the tires of passing cars.

"Hey, man!" one of the LBJ chanters shouted, going toe to toe with Mr. Jenkins. "This is a free country!"

Stan tried to intervene but Donna's father shoved the skinny college kid so hard, he landed on the hood of a parked car, his antiwar sign flying into the air. He pulled himself up and lunged at Mr. Jenkins but Stan jumped between them just in time to take a punch to the jaw, sending him sprawling on the concrete. Then Valerie stepped into the fray, positioning herself between Donna's dad and the FTI student.

"Don't you get uppity with me!" Mr. Jenkins seethed at Valerie, reaching out to grab her.

"Mr. Jenkins!" I cried, leaping in front of Valerie. "We're not questioning your son's patriotism. There's no doubt he was a brave soldier. What we're questioning is the war that took his life."

Donna rushed over, tugging his arm as she glared at me.

"Come on, Daddy," she said. "Don't trouble yourself with these yellow-bellied scum."

The photographer and reporter followed as she steered her reluctant father to their car, Mr. Jenkins yelling "none of your goddam business!" as they pressed him for his name. Donna talked to them briefly once her dad was behind the wheel. Then he cranked the engine and backed into the street so fast, he nearly ran into a passing car before tearing down Hay Street, taking all the steam out of our protest.

Funny how things worked out. I'd told myself I was doing this for Donna. My sign drooped to the sidewalk and I was ready to call it quits.

"Are you all right?" Valerie asked Stan.

He nodded, rubbing his jaw.

The FTI students stalked away, calling Mr. Jenkins an asshole and some other choice names. The rest of us were taken aback by the confrontation but Stan begged us to continue marching.

"His son should never have been sent to Vietnam," he said. "He died for nothing. What we're doing is important. It might save other lives."

The three black Fayetteville State guys left anyway, politely handing their signs to Valerie and explaining they didn't want to be involved in any kind of violence.

The newspaper photographer wrote their names in a little notebook and then came up to each of us and got our names as well.

Stan talked with the reporter for a few minutes. Then the Methodist College couple joined Stan, Valerie and me, marching for a while longer to make sure the reporter knew we were serious before a police officer showed up, asking if we had a permit. Which, of course, we didn't. I didn't know anything about a permit. He told us to clear out but didn't stay to make sure we left. We weren't even worthy of being arrested for disturbing the peace.

"Isn't it great the newspaper sent a reporter *and* a photographer," Stan said as we carried the signs back to his car.

"We may come across looking like the bad guys after that run-in with Mr. Jenkins," Valerie said, sounding wise beyond her years.

As we loaded the signs into the back of the station wagon he pressed me about the New York protest.

"You've gotta come, Angie. It's gonna be a huge rally. Dr. King will be there."

"Dr. King?" Valerie said.

"Yeah, and a whole slew of people. New York, April fifteenth. You wanna come?"

"I can't," she said. "But I've already heard Dr. King. I went with my family to Washington a few years ago and heard him. He's a wonderful speaker."

"See, Angie! Valerie's been to a big rally!" he said.

She smiled apologetically.

"Valerie is fearless," I said. "I'm not."

"I'm not fearless," she said. "But sometimes we have to take a stand to make the world a better place."

Her eyes were so earnest, so determined. Of course, she obviously knew what she was talking about.

"You're right," said Stan. "And this demonstration just might make a difference. Think of the news coverage. The networks will be there, the big newspapers, the magazines."

"Ah, Stan Bukowski's face on the cover of *Life* magazine!" I said, giving him a little smirk.

"It's the cause," he said. "Like Valerie said."

Valerie and I laughed.

"Well, I've gotta go," she said.

"How's your family?" I asked, realizing I hadn't asked yet, consumed as I was by the protest.

"We're good."

She didn't seem to want to say anything more and started toward Hay Street.

"Let me give you a lift," Stan said.

She gave us a friendly shake of the head and waved as she walked away.

"Thanks, Valerie!" Stan called after her. "You don't know how much it means to me that you came today. You're an inspiration!"

I felt like a bruised apple as we drove home. It occurred to me that if it was this hard to march in a *little* protest, I didn't want to think about what a *big* one would be like.

"We've got to change people's minds," he argued.

"Stan! My dad wrote back and said it would be too dangerous. And he wrote my mom too. Besides, I don't like marching and carrying a sign. I don't wanna go!"

~28~

"The agitator," Mitch said, grinning at me when I ran into him and John outside the cafeteria on Monday.

"What're you talking about?" John asked.

"Man, you need to start reading the paper."

A small story and a photo had made it on the front page of the B section in the Sunday paper. The photo showed Donna's dad, his face contorted with rage, shoving the FTI student onto the hood of the car. In the background, you could see Stan, Valerie and me, our eyes wide with alarm. Stan was already in motion, heading toward Mr. Jenkins. It was a dramatic photo.

The article identified Donna and Mr. Jenkins and mentioned that Donna's brother had been killed in Vietnam. The only protester identified by name was Stan as the organizer.

My mom wasn't sure how to react. I think she worried my chances of getting a well-to-do husband might be damaged. On the other hand, it was kind of exciting for her that I was in the newspaper. Fame, you know.

"You gonna write an article about it for *The Wildcat?*" Mitch said.

"Actually, Stan Bukowski is writing it."

"What happened?" John said.

Mitch gave a mocking shake of the head.

"We're taking in another flick Friday night," he said to me. "Wanna come?"

"Yeah," John chimed in. "This one's gonna be a Japanese film."

"Great," I said, rolling my eyes.

But I agreed to go. Only this time, I was surprised when it occurred to me I kind of wished it would just be me and Mitch.

~

Dottie sat with me at lunch.

"Where's Janet?" I said.

She shrugged. "She now officially hates me."

"Why?"

"Because Mom says I can get contacts this summer!"

I gave her a sympathetic look.

"She liked me as long as..."

"As long as she didn't think of you as competition."

"Bingo," she replied.

She sucked on a long spaghetti noodle, pulling it into her mouth bit by bit. I scanned the lunchroom till I saw Janet sitting with Sherry.

"You see who she's sitting with?" Dottie said. "Sherry was *my* friend! And I can't believe she's so dense. Obviously, Janet buddied up to her because Craig is her older brother. Janet invites Sherry over to spend the night and then Sherry says when she returns the favor, Janet prances around in these sheer nighties hoping Craig will see her. What a floozy!"

I watched as Janet laughed at something Sherry said.

"Janet told me once that she'd been in love with Craig since fifth grade," Dottie said. "Did you know that?"

"No."

But I remembered in fifth grade how Janet used to stare at the older boys and talk about how cute they were. I also remembered how she'd been the first girl in our fifth grade class to get a bra, even though she didn't need it, and how proud she was. She'd wear a white blouse to school so everyone could see her bra straps, making sure she strutted right by the sixth grade boys on the playground.

"She's pulling out all the stops," Dottie said. "Setting herself up to practically live at the Andersons' house this summer, hoping she can hang out at their pool. She went to Raleigh and bought not one, not two, but three new bathing suits! Can you believe it? All of them teeny-weeny bikinis. She's already working on her tan. She doesn't care how cold it is, she goes out every weekend and sunbathes. She was so envious when you drove down to the beach with him. She wants him to take *her* to the beach. And, guess what?"

"What?"

Dottie looked around to make sure no one could hear and then leaned closer, pushed her glasses up and lowered her voice.

"She's taking birth control pills."

Ah, I thought. Another victim of the severe cramps epidemic.

I looked over at Janet again as Donna sat down on the other side of Sherry. I kind of felt sorry for Janet. Donna too. For me, looking at Craig had been like seeing a mirage in the desert when you were dying of thirst. No amount of logic could keep you from rushing headlong toward the pool of refreshing water that wasn't really there.

~

After school I stopped by Dr. Kelley's class at her request. She asked if I could help her carry some things to her car. Which was odd. Teachers usually asked boys to do that kind of thing.

We each carried a cardboard box to the teachers' parking lot. She said she didn't know when Donna would be coming back to school. It was so awkward, I found it hard to meet her eyes. She'd seen me with Donna's steady boyfriend.

She unlocked the trunk on the front of her ugly black Volkswagen and we put the boxes inside. I swear it looked like a little car you'd see on TV near the Berlin Wall or something.

"Can I drive you home?" she asked.

If she'd offered earlier in the school year before we bumped into each other at the Fish House for Sneaky People, I'd have jumped at the chance. But now, I really just wanted to keep my distance.

She opened the passenger door and gestured for me to get in. I was trapped.

As we pulled out of the parking lot, I asked her about the FBI agent who was rushed to the hospital the night of the firebombing.

She paused for a moment before answering. "I understand he was blinded in his right eye. He's recovering, but he won't be able to return to the same job."

I was relieved and sad at the same time.

First thing you know we were pulling up at the Dairy Queen on Bragg Boulevard.

She bought us both milkshakes and then drove a short distance to a tasteful bungalow in an older neighborhood. The pink blossoms of a large tulip tree made it look like a spread in *House Beautiful.*

When she unlocked the front door, we were met by two pretty cats – one a tabby, the other a calico – both meowing eagerly and rubbing up against Dr. Kelley's legs as she headed for the kitchen. She opened a can of cat food first thing, the kitties hardly able to contain themselves until the food was scooped into their bowl.

I braced myself as we sat down in a cute booth in her plant-filled kitchen. The table was sunshine yellow, contrasting sharply with my mood.

"I'm sure you're wondering why I hijacked you," she said.

A nervous smile was all I could muster.

"I just wanted to talk a bit in private," she said.

I sipped my strawberry shake.

"I wanted to apologize for not making proper introductions when I saw you at the restaurant," she said. "You recognized my date, I'm sure."

I nodded.

"Well, I didn't want to put Tom in a bad spot," she said. "And I'm hoping you'll do me a very big favor and not mention that you saw us together."

"Let me get this straight. I was worried about you seeing me with Craig and you were worried about me seeing you with the FBI man?"

She looked at the ceiling for a moment.

"You see, he's about to file for divorce. But he really needs a squeaky clean record, even in his personal life."

Trying to conceal my surprise, I popped the straw back in my mouth.

"Tom and I were college sweethearts, but he married another woman and..." She shrugged, a frown appearing on her face.

Now that we were sitting here drinking milkshakes together, she looked younger somehow.

"I thought it was ironic we both seemed to be in similar situations," she said.

I made a loud sucking noise as I drained my cup, causing the calico cat to lift her head and give me a quizzical look.

"Sorry," I mumbled.

Funny, I'd built up this image of Dr. Kelley as a strong, idealistic woman who chose to teach high school so she could open the eyes of teenagers before they got to college. Turns out she just came to Fayetteville to chase a married man. I couldn't help feeling she wasn't very different from my sister. But at least Deedee wasn't stealing her husband from another woman.

~

Despite Craig's claim that he used a condom – and that's all it was really, a claim – the fear that I might be pregnant had been hanging over me like a dark nimbus cloud ever since the night of the magic brownie. So it was a huge relief, for once, to feel my cramps coming on after supper. And then, around ten, the phone rang and it was Lover Boy, himself – the first time I'd heard from him since we'd gotten to know each other in the Biblical sense.

"Angie, I'm in a tough spot."

"Craig..."

"I just can't give her the brush-off right now. Know what I mean?"

"I..."

"But you know I love you, right?"

"Craig, could you listen for a minute? I think you should stick with Donna for the long haul because..."

"The long haul?"

"I don't think..."

"You know what I can do? I mean, once all this intense grieving has eased off... I can make her want to dump me, you know? Of course, you'd know all about that. You could probably give me some pointers."

"Craig, I just think you and I..."

"Are perfect together."

"No, Craig, we're not perfect together."

"Yeah, we are. And I want to see you real bad. I'm gonna drive over there right now."

"No, you're not."

"Yes, I am."

"Craig, don't..."

"Watch for my car."

"No!"

There was a click and a buzz.

"Craig? Craig?"

Fifteen minutes later the doorbell rang and Mom let him in. He barged right into my room – she didn't seem the least bit concerned, busy as she was helping Deedee plan every last detail of her wedding. Besides, she *wanted* me to become Mrs. Craig Anderson one day. She didn't care that I was in a flimsy nightgown and my blue robe.

"Your mom is cool."

"My mom's lost her mind and you need to get out of my bedroom!"

He closed my door and locked it, then rushed over to my record player and placed the LP he was carrying on the turntable. Beach Boys music filled the room.

"I got this album for my birthday," he said. "Did you know yesterday was my birthday?"

A twinge of guilt caused me to let my guard down.

He wrapped me in his arms and kissed me like a sex-starved madman. He held me tight against him like I'd seen married couples do when the husband came home from Vietnam and his wife picked him up at the airport and it was obvious the soldier was about as horny as a guy could get after a year overseas.

"Now, that's what I wanted for my birthday," he murmured, already in full grope mode as the Beach Boys sang *Wouldn't it Be Nice.*

"Let me go!" I tried to push him away but he gripped me tighter.

"Your mom said we could make out in here. I asked her."

"You did not!"

"Okay, I didn't, but..."

He pulled me down with him as he fell back onto the mattress.

"I want to tell you something, Craig. Do you hear me?"

He shut me up by covering my mouth with his. I started slapping him about the head as he pawed me. He thought I was playing but I took the steam out of his engine when he came up for air.

"We are *not* perfect together, Craig!"

"So we're *im*perfect. Big deal. We'll look perfect again once you get your contacts and your hair grows out and you dye it blonde again. And sex will be better next time, I promise. I was in too much of a hurry."

He let out a groan as he caressed me.

"Man, you've got the best..."

"I am *not* a pair of mammary glands!"

He finally stopped and looked at me.

"Hey, don't get mad. I'm in love with all of you. Every juicy inch of..."

"We're history!" I cried, yanking his hand off me.

"Angie, Angie, we don't have to be history. I just need to ease out of this situation with Donna. Listen, I can even see us getting married one day. You're the one I want. And I want you real bad."

"This has nothing to do with Donna!"

His mouth fell open. It was starting to sink in that I was serious.

"We made love," he whispered.

"We had sex. And it was a mistake of epic proportions."

Oh, those dreamy eyes. I had to look away. I began to understand why addicts can't come clean.

"Angie, look into my eyes and tell me you don't love me and don't want me."

I steeled myself and met his gaze.

"I don't love you and, without a doubt, I don't want you. Why would I want a guy who thinks stop means go? A guy who would get me stoned without my knowledge so he could ..." But I didn't finish my sentence.

He loosened his grip at last and I struggled to pull myself off the bed.

He lay there with his eyes closed for I don't know how long. So I sat down on my vanity stool and stared into space.

"Angie?" he said.

"Yes?"

"Are you tricking me again?"

"No."

~29~

My insides were roiling all day Tuesday. I couldn't keep my brain focused on my classes. It was as though my shoes were lined with lead so that each step took longer, each motion required more effort. I caught sight of Craig walking alone in the courtyard, head down. I did a quick U-turn and hid in the girls' bathroom. To say I was relieved when school was over is putting it mildly.

I'd just gotten off the bus at my house when Stan pulled up in his mom's Rambler. He ran across the front lawn holding a newspaper in his hand.

"Look!" he said.

There on the front page of *The Fayetteville Post* was this headline: *City Councilman Indicted in Racial Firebombing.*

"Go ahead, read it!" he said, thrusting the paper into my hands.

He peered over my shoulder as we stood in the middle of the yard.

A Fayetteville City Councilman has been indicted on federal charges in the February firebombing of a Negro family's home. Councilman Thomas Duncan is facing a number of charges, including arson and violating the civil rights of Mr. and Mrs. Clarence

Franklin and their two children.

While no family members or neighbors were injured in the explosion and fire, an FBI agent lost his right eye in the blast.

"Oh my God," I whispered, turning to stare at Stan for a moment. "He was only trying to protect Valerie and her family."

He nodded, his expression mirroring my own shock and sadness.

Then I continued reading.

The federal indictment describes Duncan as a leader of a local Ku Klux Klan chapter and alleges that he planned and carried out the attack as part of the local Klan effort to intimidate Negro families who integrate white neighborhoods. An FBI spokesman said more indictments are expected.

Duncan was released on $10,000 bond. The City Council will discuss his status in a special session Thursday.

Duncan is a lifelong Fayetteville resident and owns several local businesses, including Duncan Real Estate, Duncan Motors, Duncan Mobile Homes and Duncan's Hay Street Bar.

He is accused of throwing a homemade bomb into the Franklin home at 225 Bridge Hollow Drive. No one was in the house at the time. The family received an anonymous tip that their home would be targeted in retaliation for moving into the previously all-white neighborhood.

A juvenile may face lesser charges for allegedly participating in the attack. His name has not been released.

"Junior's dad?" I said.

"Correct."

"I don't believe it."

"I want to know who the juvenile is," Stan said.

"I can't believe Junior would do such a thing," I whispered, putting my hand over my heart.

Then Stan pulled a copy of the Negro newspaper from his back pocket.

"*The Fayetteville Message* broke the story yesterday," he said, showing me the front page story.

"Forcing *The Post*'s hand."

"And maybe the city council's hand."

"And maybe the FBI's hand."

~

And guess who wasn't at school Wednesday morning? Junior and Valerie. I couldn't stand it. After class, I asked Dr. Kelley about it. She shrugged her shoulders. But I was sure she knew who the "juvenile" was.

Even the kids who usually knew nothing about what was going on in the world knew about the indictment. That's all anybody talked about.

Walking down the hallway after class, I caught up with Linda. She looked really dejected, so I asked if she was okay.

"I thought he was a nice guy," she said, a faraway look in her eyes.

Linda and Junior had become a regular couple over the last few months. I'd even bragged a couple of times about playing cupid.

"I'm really sorry," I said.

"He talked a lot about you."

"Me?"

"The more I think about it, I'm not so sure he ever really got over you. He was always watching you."

I suddenly felt like I had creepy crawlies on my skin. But if I had the willies just thinking about Junior watching me, why had I been congratulating myself for playing matchmaker between him and one of my friends? If he gave me the heebie-jeebies, why did I think it was okay to set him up with Linda? There was a contradiction there. At the time, of course, it seemed like the perfect solution. In one fell swoop, I gave Mr. Exciting as Celery a guilt-free brush-off and Linda something she couldn't seem to manage on her own – a boyfriend.

"He said you ignored him when he warned you not to be friendly with Valerie. He said it wasn't right for a girl like you to lower yourself like that."

"Jesus."

"And he said white people who mixed with Negroes would get their comeuppance."

Which left me speechless. My comeuppance? Was it possible the firebombing of Valerie's home was my comeuppance? I felt queasy.

~

On my way out the front door that afternoon, who should come walking up the steps but Junior Formerly Boring as Field Peas Duncan and his dad, Councilman Kleagle of the Ku Klux Klan. They looked so normal. So respectable. So utterly ho-hum.

Junior kept his eyes lowered as he walked past me. Something about the way he held his head in that subservient manner as he walked behind his father made me feel a bit sorry for him. Which was kind of perverse, really. Why would I feel sorry for a guy who'd done what he'd probably done? Especially considering they threw the firebomb – maybe more than one firebomb – into the house assuming the Franklins were home. If Valerie and her family had been there, they'd be dead now, and Junior and his father would be facing murder charges.

Just as they reached the door I heard myself speak in a calm voice.

"Tell me you didn't really try to kill innocent people to give me my comeuppance."

His head drooped so low, it touched his chest. But his dad, dressed in an expensive grey suit, glowered at me over his shoulder.

"Don't flatter yourself," he said, the embodiment of hateful arrogance.

Then they disappeared inside.

I felt like the wind had been knocked out of me. Or like someone in my family had died. I'd been feeling all victorious after the indictment was announced. But if this was victory, I'd hate to know what it was like to go down in defeat.

When I turned toward the street again, there was Stan.

"Let's talk with Dr. Kelley," he said, looking as uptight as I felt.

Her classroom was dark and the door was locked. But because she'd driven me to her house that day for milkshakes and a private chat, I now knew where she lived. So we drove over uninvited.

She gave us this resigned look when she found us standing on her front porch, reluctantly inviting us in. We followed her to the kitchen, which reeked of cat food. She gestured for us to sit down as she finished feeding her insistent cats their supper. She'd only arrived moments before and was still wearing her green suit and heels, her briefcase and handbag sitting on a kitchen chair.

"I can't tell you anything," she said, pulling the handle of an ice tray and filling three glasses with ice.

"You can tell us where Valerie is," I said.

"No, I can't. And you want to know why? Because I don't know."

Stan raised his eyebrow at me as she poured ice tea from a pitcher.

"All I know is that her parents have withdrawn her from school and I'm told she won't be back," she said setting the glasses on the kitchen table and sliding into one of the chairs. "My guess is the government relocated them before the indictment was read."

She gestured for us to sit down.

"I've been told to keep my mouth shut," she continued as her tabby jumped onto her lap. "And you need to do likewise. It's not a good idea to mess with the Klan. You may not comprehend just how dangerous it could be for anyone connected with this case. And I mean anyone."

"You mean us," Stan said.

"So if either of you planned on writing about this, forget it," she said, scratching the cat's ears. "It won't be published in *The Wildcat,* that's for sure."

Our gloating balloon was officially punctured and deflated. Even the usually argumentative Stan was quiet.

~

I was thankful when Friday arrived. I was itching for

summer vacation already and it wasn't even Easter break yet. Geometry, history, English, biology, French, P.E. – they all seemed utterly irrelevant.

So while I wasn't exactly dying to see an old black and white, subtitled Japanese movie with Mitch and his friends, I figured it might be a way to take my mind off everything. Plus, I was hoping Mitch and I might get a chance to talk.

We met at the Biff Burger on Raeford Road and ate our hamburgers and French fries on the way to St. Andrews College. Mitch drove. I sat in front between him and John Smith. Sid, Paula and a guy named Bruce sat in back.

The Klan indictment was the topic of conversation for the first fifteen minutes. Mitch wanted me to tell what I knew about Valerie and the firebombing. But I was careful what I said, remembering Dr. Kelley's warning. I never mentioned that Stan and I had been there that night. Of course, I also didn't want anyone to know Junior might've targeted Valerie to teach me a lesson.

Then Sid lit a joint.

"Just one toke each," he said, taking a deep draw himself before passing it to Paula.

We talked about the film we were going to see by this famous Japanese director I'd never heard of. Sid had already seen it three times. Which boggled my mind, once I'd seen it.

Seven Samurai was made back in the fifties. There was lots of violence as these Japanese samurai helped the farmers fight some bad guys. Maybe it was because I'd skipped the weed but I just didn't get into it like they did. I didn't tell them I liked the American remake better. I'll take *The Magnificent Seven* with Steve McQueen and Yul Brynner – in Technicolor – any day of the week. If that meant I wasn't intellectual enough, tough beans.

On the drive back to town, Paula commented that she preferred *Casablanca.*

"I like *Seven Samurai*," Sid said. "Don't you, John? I mean, it's hard not to like all those manly men going at it with swords and arrows."

Although I couldn't see behind me, there was a sneering tone to his voice. I was sure he was giving Paula and Bruce a snide grin.

John chuckled, but sitting so close beside me, I could tell he was nervous.

"Both films will probably stand the test of time," he said, "but I guess I like the theme of sacrifice in *Casablanca*."

"Well, well," Sid said. "I think we got us an intellectual ballerina right here in the car with us tonight, folks. A real live faggot."

John stiffened beside me. So did Mitch.

I could feel myself recoiling from the unpleasantness, just like I did on the first day of school as that racist keep-away game played out around me. Staring into my lap, it all came together in my mind. I think I'd known about John for a while now, but I hadn't wanted to think about it. I knew that being what Deedee called "a homo" could be dangerous.

"I think you're barking up the wrong tree, man," Mitch said, eyeing Sid in the rearview mirror.

Mitch was trying but I knew it wasn't enough. And I suddenly realized I couldn't be a bystander this time. I would hate myself afterwards. I had to do something.

"I *know* you're barking up the wrong tree," I blurted, grabbing John's hand and squeezing it repeatedly, trying to send him a message that the trio in the back seat couldn't see. "I wouldn't be dating a ballerina."

There was a grunt of disbelief behind me.

I turned to John then, holding his arm tight so he couldn't pull away, and leaned into him.

"You said you'd let me decide," I said, using a coy tone, hoping like hell he'd play along. "And I've decided I want to see *Walk, Don't Run* with Cary Grant and Jim Hutton next weekend. It's showing at the Midway Drive-In. Is that okay by you?"

Dead silence. Then, after what seemed an eternity, he responded with a muffled "Sure."

"You can keep me warm," I teased.

I leaned in close and kissed him on the mouth. At first, he didn't respond, but he finally caught on, and kissed me back. I pulled away slightly and looked into his eyes, which were filled with sheer terror. I smiled, trying to send him a message and then kissed him again, pushing his arm so that he'd know he should wrap it around my shoulder. I could feel his heart pounding as he followed my lead.

Sid finally shut up. I could only hope he would spread the word about Angie Finley and John Smith making out in Mitch's car on the way back from seeing a samurai movie.

As we pulled into the Biff Burger I turned to John.

"Can you drive me home?" I said.

He nodded, probably because he didn't trust his voice.

Mitch put the car in neutral as the rest of us piled out. John could hardly get his key in the lock to open the door of his dad's Corvair, his hand shook so badly. I got in before him, only sliding over to the middle of the bench seat so I could sit close beside him. He slipped behind the steering wheel and nervously cranked the engine. Neither of us said a word until we were on Raeford Road, at which point I gave him directions to my house. He glanced in the rearview mirror several times.

When we pulled into my driveway, he exhaled like he'd been holding his breath the whole way. I could tell he was struggling mightily.

"Thank you, Angie."

He held on to the steering wheel for dear life.

"When you see me at school, put your actor hat on," I said. "Pretend you've got the hots for me. Tell Mister Bunghole and his buddies what a great kisser I am. And that you're hoping to get past first base before graduation."

He laughed self-consciously.

"Tell them what a great ass I've got," I continued. "And how sometimes I let you put your hands inside my bra."

It was obvious he was afraid to look at me.

"I'm serious, John. You're an actor. You can do it."

He finally met my gaze, swallowed hard, and nodded.

I stood in the grass as he backed out and drove away, turning slowly to walk up the driveway. Before I reached the carport, I heard a car approaching. It was Mitch.

He parked by the curb and rolled down his window.

"I know it's late," he said, "but could I interest you in a cup of coffee?"

We went to the always open Waffle House.

"What if Sid and Paula drop in too?" I said, my eyes darting around the restaurant.

"He said his parents are out of town. Which means they've got other plans."

We slid into a booth but he waited until a waitress poured our coffee before saying another word.

"You may have saved his life," he said.

I poured milk in my cup as I thought about it. "I couldn't sit by again and let something like that happen."

"Again?" he said.

So I told him what Billy and his friends did the first day of school. And how I kept waiting for someone else to put a stop to it. And how I loathed myself for being such a chicken.

"Well, I'm sure you know if word got out John's a homosexual..." But he just shook his head, not finishing his sentence.

"Did you know?"

"He never told me. But, yeah, I knew. I tried to give him some cover."

"Hm."

"I should never have let Sid come with us. He's a turd."

I realized then that I was still stirring my coffee and set the spoon on the table.

"You all right?" he said.

What was the answer to that question? I wasn't sure. Overwhelmed, maybe.

"It's just that I'm so ready for graduation," I said, pushing my bangs out of my eyes.

"Not good since you've got a long way to go."

"No joke."

"Now, me, I have to admit I'm looking forward to spending the summer in Europe."

"Europe?"

"Yeah. Hitchhiking around. Seeing whatever I want to see. Hanging out with whoever I want to hang out with. Smoking whatever I want to smoke. *On the Road*, you know."

I sighed, leaned my elbows on the table and rested my chin on my hands.

"I'll be drinking coffee at a sidewalk café with some beautiful French girl in a couple of months," he said.

"You make me sick."

"You oughta do something like that when you graduate too."

To think, I'd started believing he might be my cup of tea and his kettle wasn't even on the stove.

But then he leaned across the table, raised his eyebrows and looked into my eyes, his face only inches from mine.

"Too bad you're not graduating, too," he said, giving me a lop-sided grin.

"And if I was?"

"I might ask you to go with me."

His face was so close I could smell cigarettes and coffee on his breath.

Gazing into his brown eyes, I imagined the two of us riding in a gondola in Venice, walking the Acropolis in Greece, holding hands atop the Eiffel Tower.

"Still, I really want to French kiss a French girl," he said, leaning back and tapping his ashes. "Maybe buss a Brit, tickle an Italian."

He laughed.

"Snuggle with a Spaniard?" I said, trying to be cool, though I wasn't feeling the least bit cool.

"Good one. You should do that when you graduate."

"What? Snuggle with a Spaniard?"

He laughed again, stubbing his cigarette out and laying his hand in the center of the table.

"If you end up at UNC, we can go for coffee," he said. "And maybe I can make it with an American."

Which only transported me back to fourth grade when a boy named Chuck passed me a note in Mrs. Patterson's class. "Dear Angie," the note read. "I love you third best after Elizabeth and Cindy. Do you love me? Check yes or no." Naturally, I checked "no." What a moron. I didn't want to be loved third best. Or when there wasn't a more *intéressante* French girl around.

Just as I was getting my dander up, he put his hand on mine, an amused look on his face.

"Thought you liked to let the girl make the first move," I said.

"I do."

I thought he'd say something else but he didn't.

We were quiet all the way home. I couldn't figure out what I wanted to say. I thought about telling him how much I liked him. I thought about telling him how stimulating it was to talk about films and ideas with him. But the part about his summer in Europe stuck in my craw. It was obvious he was ready to leave high school behind and that I was about to be in his rearview mirror. Making the first move, or the second move, in this case, seemed rather pointless, especially since he'd made it clear he was going to sample the produce and I was just one apple in the bin.

When we stopped in front of my house, I didn't know what my mouth would say if I opened it. When I looked at him looking at me, a smile appeared on his ruggedly handsome face.

"I'm organizing a group to see a Swedish film in a couple of weeks. Wanna come?" he said.

About sixty percent of me wanted to lean over and kiss him. But the other forty percent didn't want to spoil our friendship.

"Love to," I said, trying to sound casual.

I reached for the door handle, but hesitated. Then, before I lost my nerve I slid across the seat and leaned in until our noses were nearly touching. He didn't make a move, just waited. When my lips touched his, it was like tasting... the future... adulthood... uncertainty. He returned my kiss in a way that said "no hurry," but he didn't touch me. It was like he was waiting for me to lead the way. But I wasn't sure how I felt. Wasn't sure my pride would let me be one of many. Then again, maybe he had the right idea – thump the melon, inspect the apple for bruises, the tomato for worms. Try the baklava, the quiche, the teriyaki to see what you like best. But what if you liked them all?

What I saw in his eyes only made me more unsure.

I smiled, not knowing what else to do.

"Later," I said.

He did a slow nod, a mischievous sparkle in his eyes.

"Hope so."

~30~

Saturday's mail brought a small package that made me sad. It was from Valerie. Inside, I found a record wrapped in white tissue paper and a letter.

There was no return address but there was an Atlanta postmark.

Dear Angie,

Dr. Kelley told me it was you who saved my family. My mother and father want you to know how grateful they are. We are all grateful.

I also want to thank you for being a real friend. You were the only white girl at school who ever talked with me like I was a human being. I'm enclosing a small gift which doesn't nearly measure up to the gift you gave me.

Stan told me one day that he gave you a Bob Dylan record – one activist to another. So I thought I'd follow his lead. I'm giving you Aretha Franklin's new record – "Respect" – one activist to another. I think you'll like it.

I'm sorry I didn't get to say good-bye. I hope we'll see each other again someday. Good luck in everything.

God bless you.
Valerie

I tore the paper off and immediately put the 45 on my record player. She was right. I loved it. What better song for a woman to sing?

But I was suddenly filled with shame. I'd treated Valerie as a cause. A cause I'd taken on so I could compete with Stan. If I'd really been her friend I would've – let's see – invited her over? Eaten lunch with her? Talked with her for more than two minutes at a time? Listened to records with her?

But her note made me feel better about the whole comeuppance thing. I'd almost begun to think she might've been better off if I'd ignored her like everyone else did. But that wasn't true. Mr. Duncan's put-down on the school steps – "don't flatter yourself" – finally sank in. The Franklins moved into a white neighborhood and the Klan wasn't going to let it slide. If anything, I should've tried harder to help her. But, as Dad put it, I'd had a lot of romance on my mind.

~

"Ray, is that you?"

That's what I heard when I woke up Sunday morning – my mom practically yelling into the phone just outside my bedroom door.

"Are you all right?" she said.

I burst from my room, finding her slumped on the telephone chair, a confused look on her sleepy face. Deedee was right behind me, both of us in nightgowns and bare feet.

"What happened?" Mom said into the receiver, holding her hand up to warn us to be quiet.

She listened intently for a moment, her eyes closed tight in concentration. Something was wrong. This was the first time Dad had ever called from Vietnam.

"Okay… yes," she said. "Hold on."

She held the phone out to Deedee.

"Your dad."

Deedee grabbed it and put it to her ear.

"Daddy, are you okay?"

I couldn't stand waiting my turn.

"He's all right," Mom whispered to me, shuffling to her room for her robe and slippers. "A minor wound."

"He's wounded?" I cried.

She shushed me. I paced in tiny circles around the hallway till Deedee finally handed me the phone.

"Daddy!" I blurted, tears spilling over and running down my cheeks.

"Don't worry, honey, It's just my leg."

"You were shot?" I said, wiping my eyes with my other hand.

He had to speak really loud so I could hear him over the crackling phone connection. He told me how his unit came under fire and had to bug out.

"As we were barreling down the road, a small mine exploded under the jeep, injuring my left leg."

"How bad is it?"

"Nothing to worry about, honey. They choppered me to a field hospital, then to an Evac hospital. I just wanted to call to make sure you didn't get upset by any news coverage."

It was such a short conversation. A phone call from Vietnam cost a small fortune. Deedee and I put robes and slippers on and we all slumped at the kitchen table, not knowing what to say. I blew my nose as Mom fixed a pot of coffee. It was scary that his camp was attacked.

"He sounded tired," I said.

"And his words were slurred," Deedee said.

"He's going to be all right," Mom said, her voice so soft, it didn't sound like her.

There were no reports over the weekend, but on Monday evening we were stunned when Walter Cronkite said two American soldiers with the 82nd Airborne's First Air Cav Division were killed when the Viet Cong shelled their camp. Eight Americans were wounded. My father had just made the evening news.

Minor wound! Dad had nearly been killed! I believed his reassurances that he wasn't near the front. But the front could be anywhere and everywhere. So naive of me to think just the young guys were getting shot at over there, not middle-aged supply sergeants. Two men in his unit were dead and he could've been as well.

Turned out he was much more seriously wounded than he let on. Mom broke the news with tears in her eyes a week after his call that Dad's leg was amputated just below the knee. That he was evacuated to a hospital on Okinawa and was headed soon for Walter Reed Army Hospital in Washington for further treatment. He wrote us a short note that we read together at the kitchen table, his chicken scratch even harder to read than usual.

I want you both to know I'm going to be okay. They're taking good care of me. Once my leg heals, I'll be fitted with a prosthesis. I've decided to retire from the Army when I'm back on my feet again. I'm thinking I might open a garden store if I can work out the finances. And since I won't be living on post anymore, I'll have to buy a house. So you two can keep your eyes peeled for a home you think I'd like on a wooded lot where I can plant some flowers, with maybe a nice sunny spot for some tomato plants.

~

Three weeks later, on a chilly, rainy Saturday in the middle of April, I carried a sign as I walked with over a hundred thousand people in New York City, a daffodil tucked behind my ear – my "flower power" symbol, and a symbol of rebirth and new beginnings. Just like Dad told me.

My feet were already tired from the long walk just to get to Sheep Meadow in Central Park where we were greeted with a slew of chants, including "I don't give a damn for Uncle Sam." And tons of signs. I was surprised when I saw a scraggly group of long-haired guys holding signs that said "Viet Nam Veterans Against the War."

Around noon, the multitude began the long trek to the United Nations to hear antiwar speeches. Dr. King, himself, was on the program. They said he was leading us through the streets but we were too far back in the pack to know for sure. I was exhilarated, still finding it hard to believe I was here. Amazed at the size of the crowd.

When Dad was wounded I knew I had to go. To her credit, Mom didn't try to stop me.

Stan was on my right. His brother, Nick, and his girlfriend, Marlene, were on my left. Nick's hair was even longer than Stan's. He carried a homemade sign that said "Bring our G.I.'s home." Marlene's sign said "Get the hell out of Vietnam." She looked the part of an antiwar protester, with bell-bottom jeans, long, straight brown hair and not a speck of makeup on her freckled face.

We moseyed along together, singing *Where Have All the Flowers Gone?* We were on the left side of the group, which put us in the line of fire about an hour later when some counter-protesters threw red paint. We all got splattered good – bright red splotches all over our faces, our hair and our clothes. It reminded me of all the blood being spilled in Vietnam. Stan started singing *Blowin' in the Wind* and some others joined in.

But gradually the crowd got quieter, flowing along the street like a river of molten lava slowly spreading out from the base of a volcano. Then there was jeering from the right side. Someone waved a homemade sign that said "Support our GI's." Like we weren't.

When we got to the UN, we heard singing. Nick said it was Pete Seeger. Finally, the speeches started.

We were so far from the stage, Dr. King looked small in the distance behind a bank of microphones. But his voice was strong. He called on the president to stop the bombing of North Vietnam. He also urged people to keep demonstrating until American troops were brought home.

Finally, the rain that had been on-again, off-again all day, turned into a downpour and the marchers began drifting away. I looked at Stan and he gave me the most satisfied smile.

He rummaged in his backpack, pulled out a slender book and opened it to reveal a record.

"I've been carrying this around, waiting for the right moment," he said, handing me the 45.

I looked at the label, expecting a protest song or some-thing, but it was the Beatles' *From Me to You.* I knew the words by heart, especially the ones about arms longing to hold you and lips longing to kiss you.

He stepped close as the rain came down harder, looking into my eyes. Which was sweet. But when he reached over and took my hand, I pulled away.

"I'm *not* going steady with you," I said, "or with anyone."

"But..."

"In fact, I'm planning on going to Europe when I graduate and swap spit with a Swede."

He busted up laughing.

"No lie," I said. "I might even neck with a Norwegian."

"I knew it. You're crazy too."

"I'm serious. I don't wanna be tied down. So don't you even think about kissing me."

He rolled his eyes and stepped even closer.

"Well, then, why don't you kiss me instead?" he said.

I studied him for a long moment, taking in the mop of wet brown hair, the hopeful hint of a smile on his lips and the intensity of his green eyes. And it dawned on me that it wasn't lust in his eyes like it was with Craig. It wasn't intellectual curiosity like it was with Mitch. I think maybe it was some kind of love. And I realized I actually did want to kiss him. But why? Because Stan was the person I felt most alive with, most passionate with. He had important things on his mind. And I wanted to have important things on my mind too. We weren't perfect together. No way. But that little voice in my head reminded me that it was 1967 – the modern era. It was okay for me to kiss him. He was, after all, the most modern guy I knew. It didn't mean we were committed to each other for eternity. It just meant, well... it meant I wanted to kiss him.

Of course, I didn't have high expectations that he would be a great kisser like Craig. But when I closed my eyes and put my lips on his, he kissed me back in the most wonderful, meaningful way. We kissed as the rain poured down and the crowd thinned out. I didn't care who saw us as I leaned into him even though my hair was stuck to my head, my glasses were wet and I was splattered with red paint. In other words, I looked like crap.

"I fell for you the first day of school," he said, "when you blew your cover by turning around and talking with Valerie. I knew then you were a born activist. Even if you did stink of perfume."

I punched his arm.

"I might also pet a Pole," I said, trying to contain a rising giggle.

He gave me a blank look.

"When I go to Europe," I said. "And I *am* going to Europe."

"*I'm* a Pole. My name's Bukowski, you know."

He had a sly expression on his face. I think I did too.

As we followed Nick and Marlene to the subway station, I pictured myself typing a newspaper article about protesting the Vietnam War in New York City. That's what Stan did for me. He fed my fervor along with my focus on something besides myself.

He was one of those brave people willing to take risks to drag our country kicking and screaming into a future where everyone has rights, regardless of race or gender or whatever.

Where people can stand up and oppose wars waged for the wrong reasons.

I thought about Susan B. Anthony who struggled her entire life to give women the right to vote. I remembered Dr. Kelley's comments the first day of school, that without activists, the United States might not exist, people could still be bought and sold as slaves, and women would still have no say in government.

Stan was the kind of person who refused to be cowed. The kind of person who made history. But what an unexpected discovery that he was sexy too. And he must've read my mind because he held my hand as we walked and sang *From Me to You*, start to finish.

Of course, who knows how long it'll last. But then again, who cares.

The End

Review it

Thank you for reading *A Daffodil for Angie*. If you enjoyed it, please help spread the word by posting a short customer review wherever you buy books. Or tell your friends. Or both! Thanks very much!

About the author

Connie Lacy writes speculative fiction, magical realism and historical fiction, all with a dollop of romance. She worked for many years in radio news as a reporter and news anchor. She and her husband live in Atlanta.

Contact/follow

Website: www.connielacy.com
Facebook: Facebook.com/ConnieLacyBooks
Twitter: @cdlacy
Goodreads: Goodreads.com/ConnieLacy
Amazon author page: Amazon.com/author/connie.lacy
Email: connielacy@connielacy.com

Sign up for occasional author updates

www.connielacy.com

Acknowledgements

Special thanks to fellow author Leah Noel Sims for her valuable feedback and suggestions. And to editor Deborah Halverson for her early advice on my manuscript. Love and appreciation to my parents for believing in me. Thank goodness my own mother and sister are nothing like Angie's, and my dad came home unharmed from his tour of duty in Vietnam.

The Time Telephone, also by Connie Lacy

What if you could save your mother's life by calling her in the past on a time telephone?

17-year-old Megan McConnell is grieving, bitter and skeptical after her mom is killed covering the war in Afghanistan. When she stumbles on an antique phone in the farmhouse where her mother grew up, she decides she has nothing to lose, and maybe everything to gain by giving it a try. She's also desperately hoping for another chance at a real mother-daughter relationship with a woman who chose her career as a foreign correspondent over motherhood.

With encouragement from a couple of unlikely friends, including a boy who's in love with her, Megan speaks with her mom in the past.

The Time Telephone is an intriguing coming of age story about a teenager dealing with feelings of rejection and abandonment.

VisionSight: a Novel

Seeing the future is a curse, not a gift for Jenna Stevens.

That's Jenna's take on the gift of VisionSight she inherits, because there's nothing she can do to stop all the heartache lying in wait.

It happens when she looks into the eyes of the people she loves. So she nips a flowering romance in the bud, gives her best friend the cold shoulder and distances herself from her family.

She throws herself instead into her acting career and the arms of a young director she's not too sure of.

Can she save anyone from The Fates? And can she ever give love a chance?

VisionSight is a heartfelt novel of Magical Realism and Contemporary Women's Fiction.

Made in the USA
Middletown, DE
18 March 2018